BRITISH PROFESSOR

LYDIA MICHAELS

BAILEY BROWN PUBLISHING

Lydia Michaels

Romance
BRITISH PROFESSOR {McCullough Mountain 4}
Copyright © 2019 Lydia Michaels
Originally Published in 2014 as FAKING IT

All characters and events in this book are fictitious. Any resemblance to actual persons living or dead is strictly coincidental.
www.LydiaMichaelsBooks.com
First E-book Publication: February 2014 as FAKING IT
Cover design by Lydia Michaels
All cover art and logo copyright © 2022 by Lydia Michaels

McCullough Mountain
Publication Order

Find more McCulloughs in Jasper Falls!

DEDICATION

This book is dedicated to my awesome editor/right hand, Elise Hepner a.k.a. conspirator in world domination, coffee on Wednesday buddy, and substitute brain when I can't find my marbles.

Thank you for recognizing my voice and helping me sing.

Hugs,
Lydia

PROLOGUE

The house is quiet without Kelly and Bray. I miss them, but they're too busy to miss me. Mum and Dad are off doing their thing and the quietness is suffocating. When it's silent, I have nowhere to hide. I'm thinking too much. I have to do something reckless, something large enough to hide behind and get them stirred up before the silence swallows me whole.

*W*hy was she doing this? Sheilagh McCullough dispassionately glanced down at her outfit. She was better than this. She had an IQ that testified she was a genius, yet here she was making another stupid decision.

The lining of her sequined bra chaffed her breasts and her ass was currently being flossed by the world's tightest thong. Her finger pulled at the collar around her throat, searching for some measure of comfort.

Bass pumped like a pulse adding to the thrum of adrenaline rushing through her veins. Why was she here?

Because no one cares. They don't see you and if you don't do something soon, you're going to die inside.

She should have earned her Bachelors by now and been on the way to her doctorate. Aside from the college level courses she'd taken in high school, she had nothing to show for an education. Five years wasted and the only thing she'd succeeded at was being Center County's biggest loser.

She was turning twenty-four and she wanted to do something reckless. That was how she'd wound up at some grungy bar on the outskirts of town about to give her first peepshow.

In their small town, McCulloughs outnumbered the population three to one. If they weren't her relatives, they were married to a relative, or had slept with a relative. After accounting for that majority, the leftovers were either old, married, or gay. The remaining handful of eligible men was simply sad. Momma issues, commitment issues, anatomy issues—no one measured up to the man she wanted and on most days she felt like ripping her hair out and screaming, because no matter how desperately she wanted him she'd never have him.

There was nothing really wrong with her. She was pretty. She had a nice body. She knew how to have fun. Why didn't men see her?

She was sick of being invisible. That was why she was determined to be seen once and for all. Afterward, the adrenaline would fade and shame would creep in, but for the briefest moment she might actually feel alive and forget her uglier parts for a minute or two.

"Shei, you about ready?"

Her palms were clammy and she had nowhere to wipe them. She glanced at Tasha, the senior dancer at Puss n' Boots and nodded. "Ready as I'll ever be."

Tasha smiled. "Just remember not to get too close to the edge of the stage. The boys get rowdy when they see fresh meat. We got a good size crowd tonight, so you should do pretty well. Take your time and don't forget to breathe."

Breathe. Yeah, she was sort of struggling with that at the moment. "Thanks, Tash."

"You're up after Candy."

Sheilagh turned toward the curtain and watched as Candy took the stage. The all-male audience cheered as she twirled around the pole and dropped into a split. Sheilagh didn't know how to do all that, but she would try. She'd been secretly practicing basic moves for several weeks.

"Jesus mother fucking Christ. I'm going to kill you."

She turned and sucked in a breath. Her brother, Kelly, stood at the door to the back entrance, a hand over his eyes, and his mouth clenched tight.

"Kelly! What the hell are you doing here?"

His fist closed and she actually heard his knuckles crack over the pulsing beat of the music. "Cover yourself."

"You have to leave!"

Her brother muttered something. His eyes were still covered. "When I heard you were here, I nearly maimed a guy for spreading rumors. Then we called around and no one knew where the hell you were. Never in my life did I think you could be this stupid. Get your shit and get in the fucking car. We're leaving."

"You're not my father, Kelly."

"Should I go get Dad? Will that make you leave?"

Her eyes widened. "You wouldn't."

"Try me, Sheilagh. I am this close to losing it. Get in the fucking car."

She was tired of being told what to do. "No. I'm next."

He growled and marched forward. His hand landed on her upper arm and squeezed. "You're not getting on a stage and jiggling your lady bits for every pervert in Center County. Now move!"

"Get off me!"

"Kelly."

They both stilled and looked to the door. Her shame bloomed and folded into something unbearable. Tristan stared into her eyes, his jaw locked, freezing her in place with that glacial stare. What the hell was he doing here?

Kelly released her. "You try talking some sense into her," Kelly snapped and marched to the door.

Sheilagh couldn't take her eyes off of Tristan. He looked furious. He looked beautiful. "You're not doing this, Shei," he growled in such a low voice she was amazed she could make out his words, words that only made her want to defy him.

She'd been in love with him since the day she first saw him. He'd moved to Center County from Texas. Her cousin, Ryan, had been his roommate at State. Tristan had fit right in with the McCulloughs and Sheilagh had never seen any man quite so devastatingly sexy.

But he would never see her as anything more than a little girl. She could do whatever she wanted. He wasn't her keeper. "You don't get a say in what I do, Tristan. My days of hero worship are over."

He marched to her in two strides. In a soft voice he said, "Don't do this, Sheilagh. We won't let you. You're better than this. Your other brother's in the car. Don't make them see you like this. Let's go."

He was tall with tanned skin and dove gray eyes. His brown hair was threaded with shades of gold from working outdoors. Most of the time he pulled it back with a torn piece of cloth, which only accentuated his strong, scruff covered jaw.

He was gorgeous, but that wasn't what attracted her to

him. No, there was something magnetic about Tristan. When he looked at her he seemed to see into her when most people accepted the bullshit façade she'd been perpetuating since puberty. Those eyes and that incredible mouth followed up with that Texan lilt could make a girl drop her panties and forget her name in seconds flat.

Her body trembled. He didn't need to clarify that the other brother was Luke. Of course he was there with Tristan. She was sick of them all. No one wanted her, but whenever someone got close enough, they all acted like a pack of protective dogs guarding a bone and scared anything with male parts away.

Gritting her teeth, she met his cold stare and said, "Tough."

She didn't have time to step back. A split second later she was lifted off her feet and thrown—not gently—over Tristan's shoulder. The door slammed behind them and the hot July air tickled her skin. "Put me down! I'm up next!"

A car door opened and she was tossed inside. She scrambled to an upright position on the leather seat and heard Luke curse. The door slammed and she jolted as the car was thrown into drive. A blanket or some article of clothing was thrown at her and someone ordered her to cover herself.

Wheels squealed out of the parking lot as Luke shouted a litany of disapproving words in her direction. Her gaze turned toward the front passenger seat and narrowed on Tristan. He was no better than the rest of them.

Tristan was a flirt. There had been numerous times when he'd plucked loose the strings of her bikini or tickled her in a borderline inappropriate place. As a teenager, she'd been certain he found her attractive, but she'd never been more wrong.

It had been years and she still wasn't over the shock. Tristan wasn't attracted to her, or *any* woman for that matter. No. He was madly in love with her brother, Luke, and the two of them had been in a secret relationship for years.

The family didn't know. They knew of her hopeless crush, because at that time in her life there was no limit to her shame. But no one knew about Luke being gay. She would have never believed it if she hadn't walked in on her brother and Tristan in an indisputably sexual moment. That was the day something inside of her broke.

She'd only been eighteen when she discovered their secret, but she never got over what she saw that day. Luke hadn't done anything wrong, but it took a long while for her to get over the sense that her brother betrayed her by loving the man she loved first.

Some of that old resentment returned as her brother continued to shout at her. Completely enraged, she sat up and shouted at Luke, "You have no right!"

"Shut up!" the three of them shouted at once.

Her eyes prickled with unshed tears as they drove.

Under the passing shadows she saw each one of them staring away from her, fury stamped into their set jaws. She kicked the seat in front of her and Tristan grunted.

After she discovered Luke and Tristan's affair, Tristan handled her with kid gloves. Sheilagh didn't want his pity. She was tougher than that. She was a McCullough, for Christ's sake. She had five crazy brothers and she could hold her own with every single one of them.

The farther they drove out of town, the more self-doubt crept in. "Where are we going?"

No one answered. The commercial storefronts faded away as Kelly turned the SUV onto the highway leading out of town. As they took the jug handle onto the interstate her concern doubled. Their anger was so thick it seemed to siphon the air right out of the car.

Her concern for herself doubled as her eyes rapidly blinked back tears, forcing those telling little spills to stay put where others couldn't see. Her entire existence focused on hiding those telltale signs of weakness from the world.

She hated that her stupid, childish heart was permanently damaged and her life derailed. Since the day she'd discovered Luke and Tristan, she'd been going at the world like a runaway train, making one poor choice after another and leaving nothing but self-destruction in her wake. It was the only way she knew to control the pain, control herself. But in truth, over the last few years she felt out of control and with every stupid transgression came another reason to hate herself.

She wasn't sure she'd ever be normal again. She wasn't breaking hearts, just breaking herself, battering pieces of *her* broken heart, little by little, with each poor decision.

Suddenly the car swerved. She slammed into Luke and he pushed her off. Gravel spewed under the tires as Kelly tore onto the shoulder and threw the SUV in park.

It was dark and no one said a word. Fear tickled her spine. Why were they there? It was completely dark and eerie and she wondered if this was their version of some kind of confessional.

The sound of their breathing sawed out of their lungs and she waited. Luke, of course, broke the silence. "Are you out of your god damn mind?"

She turned to unleash the fury inside of her. "Oh, shut up, Luke! You have no right to pass judgment on me!"

Kelly swiveled in his seat, his blue eyes boring into her through the dark. "What did you suspect people would do after you bared your titties for the town? Praise you? Christ, Sheilagh, use your fucking head!"

"Like you have any room to talk, Kelly! There isn't a woman in Center County who hasn't seen your wank!"

"And do you think I didn't pay a price for my actions, Sheilagh?" Kelly stormed.

No, she didn't. Kelly lived the high life and still managed to find his soul mate. No one in this car had a right to even pretend they understood what it felt like to be invisible.

"It's like the sheep fucker!" Kelly snarled and turned toward the windshield.

What? "What?"

"Shamus the sheep fucker!" her brother snapped. "The old Irishman in the bar that built the church and sailed the sea, but no one remembers that because he fucked *one* sheep."

"No one's fucking a sheep, you moron!"

"Well, what do you think people would say if you started stripping? You wouldn't be Sheilagh the beautiful McCullough or Sheilagh the genius. No, you'd only be Sheilagh the stripper. Do you want that kind of reputation?"

She crossed her arms over her breasts and glared out the window.

Tristan turned. "Why would you do this, Shei?"

She blinked repeatedly. *Because no one notices me anymore.* Forcing an expression of indifference, she shrugged. "Why not?"

"You're better than that. You know you are," he said in a soft voice.

She didn't know what to say back. Maybe she wasn't better than that. Maybe that's all she was meant to be, a stripper in some Podunk town.

Luke wouldn't look at her, but she still heard him growl. "This is bullshit. When are you going to grow up?"

She pivoted and turned her glare on him. "Me? How about you, *Luke*? When are you going to grow up? You have an awful lot to say about how everyone lives their life, when you don't have the balls to let the world see who you really are!"

The car grew deathly silent. Kelly said her name in warning and she snapped. "No! I'm sick of it! Just say it! Say it!"

"What do you want me to say?" Luke roared.

Tristan's stare cut to her and she felt a pinch of regret much like the lament she saw in his eyes. Why couldn't they just come out and let everyone know they were in love?

"This isn't about Luke," Tristan said quietly. "It never was. I'm sorry, Sheilagh. I know this isn't what you asked for, but sometimes life is unfair."

She fumed as she glared back at him. "I wanna go home."

No one said anything for quite some time. "You're going away," Kelly finally announced.

"What?"

"You're going to college. There's nothing for you here and you know it. It's time for you to get on with your life and make something of yourself."

"You don't get to decide for me, Kelly."

Luke turned to her. "Stop being a brat. Do you have any idea what kind of potential you have? You don't know what it's like to have such opportunities snatched away."

She knew he was referring to his own life. Luke was supposed to be recruited by the NFL until he blew out his knee in college and was sent home, scholarship revoked.

"I really don't care what any of you think. This is my life—"

"Then do something with it!" Luke snapped. "You haven't done shit since you graduated. What are you waiting for?"

I don't know! She wanted to scream.

It had been years since her self-made, carefully organized plan was shattered. Life used to be simple. She coasted through school, never really having to study for the A's she'd earned. Then she was expected to accept one of the full ride scholarships being thrown at her from several noteworthy colleges.

But that never happened. Before she left for school, she wanted to actually accomplish something that meant something to *her*. She wanted *him*—Tristan. Her failure haunted her in ways she could only stifle, but never truly cope with. All she wanted was closure. She wanted the pain of rejection to disappear once and for all, but no matter how she tried, she couldn't get over her hurt.

Kelly stared out at the road and quietly said, "Here's how this is going to roll. You're going to get dressed and we're going to take you home. Tomorrow, you're going to fill out applications and this fall you *will* be enrolling in college. You either agree to that, here and now, or we drive your ass right to Dad."

Her heart raced. They wouldn't do that. They wouldn't

shame her like that in front of her father. She wasn't the best daughter and her dad knew it, but he'd always been patient and forgiving. This would crush him. It finally struck her how stupid her plan was. Frank McCullough would have eventually heard about her stripping had she gone through with it. Center County wasn't that big and everyone knew who the McCulloughs were.

She swallowed the hard lump in her throat. There was no ignoring the pain in her chest that even her family didn't want her around anymore.

"Do we have a deal?" Kelly asked.

She didn't answer. Tristan continued to watch her. "Sheilagh, do this for yourself. You deserve better than the life you've been leading. Go be something amazing, because the rest of us don't have the gifts you have."

A tear tumbled past her lashes and she batted it away. They put so much pressure on her. High school was a breeze, but once she became an adult she only wanted one thing and when she set her mind to it she failed miserably. What if she failed at other things?

"We're all scared, Sheilagh," Luke softly said. "No one ever truly gets what they want in life. You need to do this. You need to get out of here and make something of yourself."

It wasn't that easy now. She was older. People her age didn't move into dorms. The moment had passed and she'd missed it.

Her arms were suddenly cold and she shivered.

Reaching for the material on her lap, she realized it was a shirt and fit it over her head. She wouldn't agree with them now. She was too stubborn for that, but they were right. She was losing herself here and she needed to leave. Her family was simply too overbearing and the thought of moving away, although terrifying, was suddenly more appealing than it had been in years.

She shut them out, their presence no longer registering. Knowing she could be stubborn, they eventually understood this was all they were getting from her. They made their way back to their family home in utter silence.

Luke and Tristan were cowards. She hated the way they closeted their true selves away from the world. Yes, she'd been about to bare it all and knew that wasn't right either, but thanking them for saving her was something she'd likely never do. Her humiliation was far too great, her shame too raw.

When they reached the house someone said her name, but she climbed out of the car and slammed the door on all three of them. Done. She was done.

CHAPTER 1

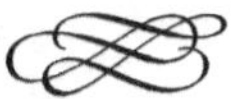

I think I've finally decided my major. I know it's only the first day of the second semester, but I love my new classes, especially Philosophy 101. The opening lecture was so profoundly moving, it was the first time I forgot I was forced here and found myself enthralled in learning. I'd love to major in philosophy, but I can't find the sense in such a career. Psychology, however, I can turn into a career. Plus, I'll be able to minor in philosophy, which I'm shockingly passionate about. This sudden burst of energy to dig in and explore is unexpected, but so very needed. Finally, I have something to distract me from the depressing thoughts I've been having.

As Sheilagh walked off the campus and down the street to her apartment, she could barely contain her excitement to tear into her syllabus and start on her reading. Dr. Alec Devereux was an awesome professor. There was just something about him.

He was older, likely nearing forty, but something about the way he lectured made him seem younger. He had a captivating presence. As his voice filled the lecture hall with that throaty, British baritone she found herself hanging on his every word as if he were reading poetry. He cursed from time to time and told the class they could call him Alec, which had Sheilagh rolling her eyes at first, but then, as he'd introduced Philosophy 101, she found herself enthralled and wanting nothing more than to be on a first name basis.

He definitely knew his shit. He proclaimed this semester would alter their way of thinking forever and he would enjoy watching them grow into mature adults. She was already older than most of the students enrolled in the class, but she looked forward to the mental challenge.

They were starting with Plato's *Allegory of the Cave*. She'd heard of it, but never read it. There was truly a geek hiding under her wild façade, because nothing gave her a rush quite like learning. On the other hand, nothing set her on a self-destructive path like boredom. When the simplicity of her existence spread wide and dull, Sheilagh often did terrible things she later regretted. Her reckless behavior was due to a need for constant stimulation she couldn't always feed. She savored those moments when her brain was challenged to accept new theories, because so long as her mind was actively engaged the sense of emptiness went away.

Mathematics was all about thoughtless equations. Long ago she'd mastered the art of impressing people with her ability to solve formulas and piece together algorithms. Math was also a very isolated field. She couldn't bear the thought of spending her life in some régime facility breaking down codes and inadvertently driving the world into the next war by unearthing some piece of detrimental information the government was after. That was too much bad karma.

She could have gone into the medical field, but blood made her queasy. When she was seven she memorized the Periodic Table and that convinced everyone she would go into a science field, but she didn't want that either.

Some days she only wanted to be normal. Normal people were never asked to perform polar tricks to demonstrate the complexity of their mind like some freak show exhibit. She liked when people forgot she was exceptional and treated her like a regular woman. Gifted or not, there really wasn't anything remotely exceptional about her. She'd simply been smart enough to disguise all her other—less appealing—sides.

Years were spent doing stupid, juvenile things, which helped people forget she was hiding an IQ that went off the charts. It was nice when her family stopped expecting her to be Sheilagh the virtuoso and accepted her as just one of them. The problem was, being the 'smart one' was her shtick. When she acted dumb, people stopped paying attention to her all together. It hurt, realizing her mind was the only remarkable thing they noticed. But she had to keep up the act in order to keep the hollow parts of herself hidden from the rest of the world.

She didn't want to be Sheilagh the savant any more than she wanted to be Sheilagh the sad and pathetic. Overtime she'd managed an entirely fabricated persona of Sheilagh the outgoing, up for anything, wild child. Amazingly, people bought it. The only drawback to keeping up the act was actually having to act on certain situations. More than once she'd left a stranger's car feeling dirty and used, but hey, no one wanted to hear about all that. No, they just wanted wild Shei-Devil, always a good time and up for anything.

She didn't know why her intelligence irritated her so much. The only excuse she had was being smart was sometimes lonely. She was always the youngest in her classes, which made her current situation new and refreshing being that she was years older than the rest of the freshmen at college. Still, being advanced made her early education incredibly isolated and it wasn't until she finished school that she thought to discover other sides of herself.

She should probably be grateful she wasn't stupid. Moments like today made her glad for her aptitude. There was no doubt she'd impress the professor when she aced her first paper and, for the first time in a long time, her IQ didn't seem like such a burden. Perhaps college was finally helping her embrace who she really was. She was gonna rock this class like a casbah.

She unlocked her apartment and dumped her bag on the ratty chair by the door. Most freshmen lived in dorms, but Sheilagh couldn't handle the thought of rooming with some kid just out of adolescence. She lived alone and having always lived with her crazy family packed into one house, she really enjoyed the solitude.

Her finger flipped on her iPod sitting in the dock and The Dropkick Murphys filled her apartment. Off went her sweater and shoes and down came her hair. She bounced to the small kitchen and turned on the burner.

As the pricking strings of *Rose Tattoo* plucked out under the scratchy voices of the Celtic punk band she danced to her bookshelf and dug out her text. The used book was worn and yellowed at the corners. She tossed the book to her couch and it landed on the afghan her grandmother, *Moira*, had made.

The kettle whistled and she pulled out a mug. Dropping a teabag in the mug, she doused it with whiskey and poured in the scolding water. It was cold in Princeton, New Jersey in January, but not nearly as cold as Center County.

Her first semester had been lonely. It was definitely an adjustment, but she was coming to love the historic town built around the university. There was something nostalgic and magical about being able to cut through Albert Einstein's front yard on her walk from the campus to her apartment. The town was charming with a scholarly air she found refreshing. Here, she could be herself and not worry about intimidating the locals.

Sipping her spiked tea, she plunked down on her sofa. Yes, it was only eleven in the morning, but she was a McCullough and it was five o'clock somewhere. The song on her iPod switched to the *Warrior's Code* as she pried open her text.

A fist pounded on her wall and her pain in the ass neighbor yelled through the plaster for her to turn down the music.

"Blow me!" she shouted back, and ignored him.

When she'd first moved there, she'd been a touch more courteous, but then she realized her neighbor, *Wesley*— which she said in her head with the snobbiest dialect— had an issue with a light sneeze. *Wesley*—who called their kid Wesley anyhow?

She only knew his name because their mail sometimes got mixed up. She'd seen him once and was pretty sure they'd never be friends. He was the kind of guy who wore scarves as accessories and probably polished his shoes. Basically, he was the poster child for every prep school in Princeton, but he was a dick, so she didn't care about being all Mr. Rogers won't you be my neighbor with him.

The not-so-phantom hand behind the wall pounded again and she reached for the remote, turning up her music to drown him out. She turned onto her stomach and settled into Plato's *The Republic,* the philosopher's greatest work.

An hour later she was completely submerged in the science of logic and psychology. Her mind stretched over theories of means and ends, causes and conditions, rational, concupiscent, and irascible elements, and truths veiled in metaphysics.

Plato's work differed from Aristotle's. She found herself recalling literary works and seeing similarities that were undoubtedly borne of great thinkers' theories. Memories of *Troy,* legends of *Arthur,* and myths of Atlantis swirled in her mind as her eyes plowed over each written word.

The essay, which wasn't due until just before spring break, took her four days to write. Her other classes, totaling her twenty-four credit class load, only served as minor distractions from her task.

The following Tuesday she waited until Alec had finished his lecture to walk her masterpiece to the front. He'd rolled up his sleeves and removed his blazer sometime in the middle of their three hour lecture. As she stood by his desk watching him drag the soft eraser over the board she noticed he had a dark dusting of hair on his forearms.

She cleared her throat and he turned. "Ms. McCullough, did you have questions about today's lecture?"

His dark hair showed flecks of silver by his temples and she swallowed, finding his hazel eyes intense, regardless of the friendly creases at the corners. "No. I wanted to give you this."

Returning the eraser to the tray running along the board, he brushed off his hands and stepped closer. She grinned and held out her essay. He took the neatly annotated paper and flipped open the clear cover.

His brows rose. "This is your midterm paper."

"Yes."

"But it's only been a week."

"I've read the entire text."

He met her gaze and she smiled, sure he'd be impressed once he read her summary. "Plato's work is indeed readable, but I find it difficult to believe you've had time to digest the fundamental meaning behind such thought provoking work."

Shrugging, she said, "I enjoyed reading it."

A slight chuckle escaped his lips. "I should hope. I'd hate to think I've been suggesting rubbish for the past fifteen years of my career."

She shifted her shoulder bag and stepped back. "I just figured I'd turn it in since it was finished."

His long fingers, stained with pen at the knuckle, flipped the cover back into place. He grinned. "I look forward to reading it."

Sheilagh nodded. "See you next Tuesday." The moment the words left her mouth she gasped, realizing she'd just said the euphemistic backronym for calling someone a *cunt—C U Next Tuesday*. Eyes wide, she quickly corrected, "I mean, see you at the next class."

The side of his mouth kicked up and shoulders twitched as he chuckled again. "I look forward to it."

Turning abruptly, she quickly left the lecture hall. She wasn't sure what was worse, the fact that she'd said that or the fact that he laughed, implying he noticed the slip. But if he laughed, he must have a sense of humor, right?

When she stepped outside she forced the embarrassing episode out of her mind. You could take a McCullough out of Center County, but putting one in a sophisticated environment was about as normal as putting a donkey in a tiara and tutu. At home they could say whatever they wanted, but she was at Princeton now and the standards of couth were dramatically higher.

As she walked home, taking in the lovely old homes she passed along the way, her mind wandered to home. Anger with her brothers for forcing her to go away still lingered, but she missed them anyway. As she entered her apartment her mind considered what she had left to do. She needed to keep busy in order to keep herself from getting homesick and sad.

Like every other time she finished a good book, she lamented. Her free time was cumbersome and her other classes only occupied a small amount of her days. Paging through her assignments, she tsked. There wasn't much left to finish and she was already ahead in her reading assignments. Maybe she should start looking for a job.

Her tuition was covered by a few grants she'd held in her account for the past five years. She didn't have the same amount of funding she would have been awarded had she attended college right out of high school, but she still was attending Princeton under a decent scholarship. A job wasn't necessary at the moment, but it would definitely ease the remainder of the loans she'd have to pay when she graduated.

Snatching the newspaper off the table, she kicked on her iPod and went about making lunch.

Wesley the Wank pounded on the wall. "Shut up!"

She growled. "Bite me, Wynona!"

"It's Wesley," came his muffled shout.

"Sorry, you sounded like a girl."

That silenced him and she went back to eating her PB and J and reading the paper. As she was walking her plate to the sink there was a sharp knock at the door. She sighed and pulled it open. Wesley stood on the other side, his brown hair sticking out on end and his mouth set with displeasure.

"For months I've tolerated your abysmal taste in music and tried to be respectful. Will you *please* turn it down?"

She scoffed. There was just something about this guy that bugged her. He walked around like he was better than everyone else, but she had as much right to be there as him.

"What's abysmal is your wardrobe. Stop banging on my wall."

His eyes narrowed. "Look, I have a heavy course load this semester and I can't afford distraction."

She ignored him and sucked a dab of jelly off her thumb. His cold stare followed the motion, his glare slightly thawing, and she scowled at him. "Then go to the library. This is my home and I'm not breaking any rules. My music isn't even that loud."

He scoffed. "Everything you do is loud. I'm asking nicely. Please, keep it down."

Rolling her eyes, she sighed. "I'll do my best." With that she slammed the door.

On her way back to her couch she turned the volume down three notches, but that was all he was getting. It wasn't that she was a bitch. She was sympathetic to his need for quiet. But she'd given him quiet—bucket loads of it—and he'd still complained. She'd keep it down and he'd complain again in a short matter of time.

THE FOLLOWING Tuesday she arrived at Philosophy anxious to see her grade and hear Alec's praise. The three-hour lecture seemed to take twice as long as usual, but that was because her anticipation had a way of slowing down seconds to hours.

When class finally ended, she slowly gathered her books and waited for the others to leave. Alec popped his briefcase on the podium and casually approached her desk. She smiled up at him and he nodded in greeting.

"Ms. McCullough."

"You can call me Sheilagh."

He nodded again. "Sheilagh."

"Is that my essay?"

"It is."

She tried to read his expression, but found he gave away nothing. "Did you like it?"

"I found it… interesting."

Interesting. That was good. She waited for him to say more.

"You certainly have a firm grasp of the English language. Your use of metaphors is impressive and I couldn't find a single grammatical error."

"Thank you." She stuffed her pen in the side pocket of her bag.

He hesitated and she wasn't sure why. Her eyes drifted over the buttons of his dress shirt and lingered on the buckle of his leather belt. Dr. Alec Devereux dressed nice.

"I want you to know, if you ever need any extra assistance with the material, my office door is always open."

She smiled tightly. That was a nice offer, but she'd never been one to require tutoring. "Thanks."

"I also want to direct your attention to the portion of the syllabus that details my rubric. I always allow students to go back and correct any mistakes. My goal is to teach them. I have only a few months to make an impression, but I want them to get their money's worth. No grade is ever final in my class."

"Okay." She frowned. Why was he telling her this?

"Okay then. Here you go." The paper landed on her desk with a gentle click. Alec stepped back and turned, his attention on packing up his briefcase.

She flipped open the cover and waded through the pages of her essay. There were no markings until the last page. She read his note and then suddenly choked. *"You gave me a D?"*

His broad shoulders tensed and he slowly turned. "Like I said, your mechanics were impeccable. They saved you from an F."

Her jaw unhinged. No one had ever given her a D. She'd only ever gotten a B once and that was in gym and mostly because she'd been going through a bratty teenage stage and didn't like running because she'd just developed boobs. This—*this*—was a bunch of bullshit!

"You've got to be kidding me!"

"I'm afraid not, Ms. McCullough. While I'm certain you read the material, your grasp on the moral is lacking. I suggest you read it again and try to take your time.

These are some of the most intricate philosophies you will likely ever find, broken down in simple form. It's not a book report, Ms. McCullough. I'm more interested in your thoughts and application of the subject matter."

"I gave you my thoughts!"

"No, you gave me a synopsis."

"That's not fair. The syllabus said to summarize *The Republic*."

"Thank you, Socrates. Perhaps you should go back to Book I if you intend on arguing the quarrels of justice. Your essay provided a source of characters and descriptions. What I want to know is how those characters relate to you."

Her lips pressed tight. Every nice thought she'd had about the professor went out the window in the face of his bullshit grading scale. She gathered up her belongings and stood.

"I suppose you're the philosopher king that wields the advantage of the stronger."

His mouth kicked up in a half-grin. "Very good, Ms. McCullough, but if you'll recall, his theory was disproved, stating that even political figures are imperfect and sometimes transact unjust laws. Justice is for the people's benefits, not the ruler's."

"Yeah, I can really see how this D benefits me," she snapped, shoving the strap of her bag over her shoulder.

"Then make it an A, Ms. McCullough. I've seen your transcripts. I know what you're capable of. Don't come into my classroom and think to give me a fraction of the effort my class deserves."

"I'm afraid I'll have to side with Socrates on this one. This is a blatant crime against wisdom meant to benefit a certain group of people, not the whole."

Alec nodded, seeming unimpressed with her response, but accepting it all the same. "And like every other free thinking individual, you hold the right to remain ignorant."

She gaped at him. What a fucking asshole. She had nothing else to say. He'd given her a D and called her ignorant. Turning on her heel, she marched out of the lecture hall and fumed the entire way home.

When she reached her apartment she threw her bag against the wall and growled. She should go to the head of his department and complain. She should talk to her advisor about withdrawing from the course and finding a professor who wasn't an idiot.

The knock on the wall drew her glare. She shouted at the place the pounding came from, "Eat shit, you ninny!"

CHAPTER 2

That cock sucking motherfucker thinks he's so smart with his oxford shirt and dapper tweed blazer. He's an idiot! How he works here is beyond me! I intend to inform the board they have a jackass on their hands and insist they find a new professor with the actual credentials to teach and grade! Stupid cockney speaking dick face! This is not over!

S heilagh didn't go to the head of the philosophy department. Nor did she visit her advisor. What she did do—after her temper faded—was open up *The Republic* and start from the beginning.

The stories read the same as they had the first time. Thank God she was actually interested in the subject matter, or rereading such a fat book would have been intolerable.

It took her three days to finish and when she was done she sat down at her laptop and started typing. Her words were impassioned this time around. She seemed to breathe a bit of fire into every sentence, slipping jibes into her phrases and grinning as she imagined Alec interpreting her essay for the slap in the face she wanted it to be.

How dare he give me a D!

She didn't wait until the following Tuesday to turn it in. She missed her Friday morning classes in order to apply the finishing touches to her essay. As she closed her freshly printed pages into a new glossy binding, she grinned. "Let's see what you have to say now, Dr. Devereux."

Bundling up, she marched her way down to the Philosophy building. Dr. Alec Devereux's office was on the fourth floor. When she reached it, the door was open and the soft keystrokes of Chopin filtered into the hall.

What a pretentious prick. She knocked.

"Enter."

Easing the door open, she waited for him to turn. His office was filled with relics from around the world. She was surprised he didn't have a bust of himself sitting front and center for him to admire. Clearing her throat, he slowly turned, removing the glasses perched on his nose in the process.

"Ms. McCullough."

By the way his brows lifted she knew he wasn't expecting her. She dropped the essay on his desk. "There. I think you'll find this one a bit more acceptable."

He eased back in his chair, steepling his fingers under his chin, and making no move to take the essay. "Tell me something, Sheilagh. Are you used to getting your way?"

Shifting, she met his challenging stare. "No. I'm used to being ignored and getting the exact opposite of what I want." That was a little TMI but she certainly wasn't spoiled.

"Yet, you've always been gifted A's in school."

"I wasn't gifted anything. I earned every grade I got."

He nodded slowly. "But I don't believe you've ever had to work hard for those grades."

"I did every bit of the work expected of everyone else in the classes I've taken."

"And with those impeccable grades I see you've also earned a sense of entitlement."

Her mouth opened in a shocked gasp, despite herself. "You don't know me, Dr. Devereux."

"No, I don't, but I've known other students. Do you know which ones impress me? The ones who have to pour their sweat and tears into earning a C. There are students here who have sacrificed everything and worked themselves to the bone trying to avoid academic expulsion. Your arrogance is an insult to them."

She could not believe she was standing there listening to this garbage. "Where do you get off insulting me? You've called me ignorant and arrogant and I've never said more than a few words to you."

"I said that you, like every other individual with free will, have the right to *choose* ignorance. The choice is yours, Sheilagh. If you're intelligent, which I believe you are, make the educated decision to enlighten yourself, otherwise you are choosing ignorance over wisdom."

She wanted to choose to give him the finger. "I am not arrogant."

"No?" He eased forward and swooped up her essay, paging through it leisurely. Without looking at her, he asked, "What did you think of Gyges' theory in Book II?"

She shrugged. That was one of the least interesting books of *The Republic.*

He raised a brow and speculated aloud, "Did you tell your peers about the asshole professor who dared to give you a D?"

"No."

"Why? I wonder."

Mostly because she didn't have peers. She lifted a shoulder with indifference. "Because I don't care what others think."

"Ah. And when Gyges suggested that to give a man a

ring granting them invisibility would only give them license to perform unjustly, did you agree with him?"

"I guess."

"We all act differently when we assume others can't see us. The issue, Ms. McCullough, is that I want to see into your mind." He held out the essay. "You can't hide behind words and ink. This isn't a simple essay. I'm going to give this back to you to save you the outrage of what is likely no better than a C. Take off the invisibility ring and show me who you are."

Was he kidding? "You aren't going to read it?"

"Do you really want me to? Is this your best work?"

Gritting her teeth, she snatched the essay out of his hand and turned to leave.

"Have a lovely weekend, Ms. McCullough."

She couldn't reply without cursing him out so she just kept walking.

IT TOOK her a full week to rewrite the essay. The second draft went into the shredder and this time she really put her heart and soul into examining the theories of Plato and paralleling his philosophies with her own experiences.

She wasn't an open person. That didn't mean that she was shy. She had a very outgoing personality, but she also kept her personal business to herself. The idea that she was expected to bare her innermost thoughts to some man who thought he was a supreme being didn't sit right. This was philosophy, not confession.

When she finished her essay she read over it several times, looking for any pitfalls Dr. Devereux might find. This was definitely an improvement from her first two attempts.

She was surprised how quickly her opinion of her first efforts had changed. Fine, he had a point. She was capable of better, but accepting her imperfections gracefully was never a strong suit. She'd work on it. College was about growing. She just didn't want to reach her freshman fifteen by filling up on humble pie.

Sheilagh refused to let him belittle her efforts again without taking a decent look at her work. He'd drawn unfair conclusions about her based on her first essay and this was by far better. She dropped the essay off that following Friday, slipping it under his door and disappearing before he could say a word.

When Tuesday's class arrived, she found her essay sitting on her desk. Alec didn't look at her as he conducted his lecture and a knot formed in the pit of her stomach.

Taking a deep breath she turned page after page, again, not finding a single note in the text. When she reached the second to the last page she held her breath. As the page turned over, she spotted his scrawled comment.

. . .

See me after class. D-

It took everything she possessed not to scream and march out of his lecture. *A fucking D-?* This had to be some sort of a sick joke!

She didn't know what he was babbling about because she couldn't hear past the ringing in her ears. As the rest of the class scribbled down lengthy pages of notes she stared daggers at Alec Devereux's arrogant head.

At one moment he caught her stare and his words seemed to falter. Good. However, he continued his statement with the same impenetrable ease he seemed to handle everything else. She really disliked this man.

When class was over she decided to leave. She wasn't sitting through another one of his bullshit theories.

"Sheilagh?"

She stilled. People were still exiting the room and when the last person left she turned. "What?"

He carefully folded his arms over his chest. "I asked you to stay."

"Yeah, well I really don't feel like listening to any more lectures at the moment."

He ignored her. "Which did you identify with, the guardians, auxiliaries, or the laborers?"

She was so sick of this book. "What?"

"Are you ruled by appetite, reason, or spirit?"

"How should I know?"

"It's a simple question. You've read the material several times at this point. I'd expect you to easily identify with one of the three. Are you driven by your biological desires? Is it honor that directs your spirit? Or are you ruled by your reason and control? I highly doubt it's the latter."

She turned and marched down the steps that separated the desks and didn't stop until she was in his face. "You know what you are? A hypocrite. You sit up there every day and teach with other men's words. How about you, doctor? Which one are you? Why don't you bare a little of your soul from behind that podium?"

"I'm all three."

"You can't be all three," she argued.

"Sure you can." His voice was low and she had to lean closer to hear him. "My passion is what motivates me most, yet I'm honor bound to sometimes make difficult choices in order to act justly, and my reasoning for this helps me maintain control."

She growled. "You're impossible! This essay is impossible. Your standards are impossible. I quit!"

She turned and he said, "The idea is not whether or not it's possible, the point is that it's simply the ideal."

Baited, she pivoted and said, "So said Socrates in Book V."

"Very good, Sheilagh."

"Yeah, too bad I don't care anymore."

His head tipped slightly to the left. "Why is that?"

"I just told you."

"Does that mean you'll be changing your minor?"

"What?" What did her focus have to do with him and his stupid essay?

"To be a philosopher means to seek the ideal forms of things. If you don't have this desire, I'm afraid you've selected the wrong field of study."

"Well, maybe I have."

She made it to the door when his words stopped her again. "Does that invisibility ring ever get cumbersome, Ms. McCullough?"

She blinked. His entire analysis of her was a little too close to home. If she kept bombing his stupid essay how did he know her so well? Maybe that was why she liked being invisible sometimes. Invisibility made the expectations go away.

Taking a deep breath, she said, "For a philosopher to be beneficial, he must first know what is good. I've given you three good papers and it's *my* opinion you're the one who's missing the mark."

As she left the classroom she dropped her copy of *The Republic* in the trash.

ON THE TUESDAY THAT FOLLOWED, Sheilagh didn't get out of her pajamas. Rather than sit through another philosophy lecture of a class that would undoubtedly obliterate her GPA, she called her mother to kill time before her meeting with her advisor later that day.

"Hello, love!" Her mother yelled into the phone. "How's school?"

"Good."

"Are you joining any clubs yet? Meetin' any handsome college lads?"

Her longing for home and the close presence of her mum had her closing her eyes. "No, Mum. I'm too old for that stuff."

"Oh, pish, you're still a baby."

Being the youngest of seven, the stigma of being the baby would likely stick with her until she was a senior citizen. "I think I'm dropping a class," she confessed as she bit into an apple.

"Why, dear?"

"The professor's an asshole."

"Ah, a terrible affliction, that. What did this asshole do? Do I need to send yer brothers over there to straighten him out?"

She laughed. Her mother was one of a kind and she loved her, even if she was a bit nuts. "No. He's making us read this stupid book. I've read it a dozen times and every time I do a paper he tears it apart."

"He's ripping up your work?"

"No, Mum, he's giving me D's."

"Well, not every class is going to be easy, love. You're in

Princeton now. I'm sure you'll pull your grades up sooner or later."

"I'm going to take the course again next semester. There's another professor who I think will be a little more reasonable."

"If you think that's for the best, I trust your judgment."

Sheilagh changed the subject, asking about her brothers. Braydon had been home from Pittsburg that past week and the idea of all her siblings hanging out without her hurt.

The humiliation of being driven out of her hometown still stung. Kelly and Luke had embarrassed her, in front of Tristan of all people. She knew she should forgive them. Part of her already had, but her pride still hurt. Sooner or later she'd miss them enough to get over what had happened, but she wasn't there yet.

Before enrolling in college, she'd never left Center County for any extended period of time. Sometimes she wondered if she was making a mistake. Although hearing her mother's voice and listening to anecdotes of her family's shenanigans brought her comfort, it did nothing to ease her mind. Reluctantly, she said goodbye to her mum and left for her meeting with the advisor.

Later that day as she waited outside her advisor's office she contemplated the possibility that she was making a mistake. Nope. She didn't want her GPA to suffer because of one bad experience. Her faith in herself was shaken and she wasn't sure she'd be able to earn anything higher than a D from Dr. Devereux. She couldn't risk it. She was better off withdrawing from the course and starting fresh in the fall.

Her advisor understood and with only a few clicks on her computer, Sheilagh's name was removed from the roster. It should have made her feel better, but it didn't. She felt like a wuss. She'd taken the coward's way out and that was something she wasn't comfortable with. She never backed down. Except in the face of Tristan, Luke and Kelly's reaction that night.

She stopped at the Student Union for a coffee on her way back to her apartment and the one person she didn't want to see was there. As she waited in line she felt Professor Devereux's gaze on her, but refused to look in his direction.

Paying for her coffee she turned and went to the sugar station. Her fingers tore open several packets of the condiment and she jumped when he spoke from right behind her.

"You missed class today."

"No, I didn't," she corrected, focusing her attention on peeling back the lid of a creamer that refused to open. "I dropped the course."

For a quiet moment she tasted victory, knowing she'd surprised him, but it felt bitter on her tongue.

When the creamer burst open and spilled over her fingers, his hand plucked the tiny carton from hers. Nudging her aside, he expertly peeled open two creamers and poured them into her cup. His long fingers dropped a straw into the dark liquid and swirled it to the perfect shade of caramel. Did he have to be such a know it all?

"Your coffee, Ms. McCullough," he said, sliding it along the counter. "I believe this is yours as well." She stared as he held out her copy of *The Republic*.

"Did you dig that out of the trash?"

"It's a crime to throw away a book."

She picked up her coffee. "Keep it. I'm done with Plato."

He placed the book on the counter. "I've added some footnotes you may find intriguing." With that he turned and walked away.

She glared at him as he gathered his briefcase and jacket from the table he'd been occupying. Her gaze snapped back to the offending book he'd left. She should have left it there, but her curiosity was piqued. Sighing, she snatched the book and tossed it in her bag then headed out the door.

It wasn't until late that night that she gave into her curiosity and opened *The Republic*. Whatever she was expecting to find written in the margins wasn't what she read.

The same irritatingly perfect penmanship that withered her essays into useless recycling was scribbled on the copyright page of the book.

· · ·

WHEN YOU'RE ready to open your eyes, call me and we'll talk.
   ~Alec

HIS PHONE NUMBER was neatly written below his name. What did that mean? She didn't want to talk to him. She'd heard enough from him. She never wanted to talk to him again.

Once more he insinuated his shortcomings as a professor were hers. He had to be a crappy teacher. Every other class she'd ever taken testified she was a great student. It galled her that, even though she never had to deal with the guy again, he thought less of her.

She tossed the book against the wall, earning a knock from Wesley through the plaster. She growled and fell onto her pillows. Maybe she'd go home that weekend and come back with a fresh perspective. At the moment, her outlook on higher education sucked. She wanted to toss the entire experience and go back to what she knew.

CHAPTER 3

Alec waited for Sheilagh to call. He was shocked she'd actually withdrawn from his course rather than accept the challenge he presented and learn something. It was arrogance, pure and simple, to come to a university like Princeton and expect to graduate only by regurgitating all the knowledge one arrived with. Students were there to learn and there was no doubt in his mind that Sheilagh McCullough was brilliant. So why hadn't she called?

The week passed with the same faces he'd come to expect in his classes. Some of his students were scholars and thriving under his direction. Others were simply hoping to get by. They'd all likely pass. He didn't believe in failing pupils unless they absolutely refused to turn in their work.

He was by no means an easy professor, but he also

wasn't a tyrant. His classes flowed with open debates and he enjoyed stimulating discussions with younger minds. Never before had he lost a student and losing such a promising one didn't sit well with him.

It had become his practice to read up on his students before each semester. He liked to know whom he would be passing his days with. When he'd read Sheilagh's file he was beyond impressed.

She had an impeccable record and he knew she'd leave his course with another A to add to her transcript. He was only mildly surprised when she'd turned in her paper that second class. Her tenacity was admirable.

As he read her original essay her aptitude was evident. She had an incredible grasp of vocabulary that allowed her to concisely encapsulate the theories of Plato in a matter of a few words. She'd summarized the entire book better than most experts could manage.

What she hadn't done was give him any real information beyond what he'd already known. He wanted his students to stretch themselves. He wanted them to bleed emotion into their words, think like true philosophers, and give him something worth stamping an A on.

Sheilagh had given him something great and she likely deserved a B. However, when it came time to rate her work, his instinct told him she was capable of so much more and his hand had formed a D.

The following week when she'd come to his office with yet another rapid attempt to diminish his lectures by turning out a paper in record time, he'd been insulted. Her actions reeked of arrogance and told him more than she realized. Sheilagh McCullough was not a woman who easily accepted being told no.

He'd noticed in her file that she was older than most of his students. She was twenty-four and he wondered why she'd hesitated to start her higher education. Her transcripts claimed she sacrificed multiple scholarships as a result and he was curious what would make a girl like her ignore a calling that was so clearly meant to be. She belonged with scholars. She had the potential to achieve great things if she'd simply apply herself.

He speculated that perhaps the obstacle Sheilagh McCullough faced was health related, but she appeared fit and healthy as ever. Perhaps she suffered from something internal, something like fear. Yet, her personality was so strong the idea she might be afraid didn't quite jive. She could easily graduate top of her class, even from a prestigious school like Princeton, but something held her back. If an objective wasn't immediate and easy she didn't seem interested and that made no sense. Might she be afraid?

She had to realize even the slightest effort on her part would be met with great praise. There were students who paid a fortune for tutors and barely avoided academic suspension when they gave it their all. Why didn't she try harder?

When he read her third essay he was appalled. Yes, she gave an even deeper synopsis of the material, but again it lacked any insight or application on her part. It was a slap in the face, a generic regurgitation of what could have been an esteemed accompanying text for his course. He knew she hadn't plagiarized her summary. That wasn't her style. They were her thoughts and her interpretations, but, again, they lacked every bit of personal reflection he'd been searching for.

The only way he could communicate to her that she'd missed the mark again and needed to scrap her approach and apply herself to a radically new one was to drop the grade lower than her original D. Never in his life had he expected her to quit. It smacked of her running from something.

He'd spoken to her advisor and explained his approach, something he wasn't used to doing. She was understanding and seemed to shrug off his concern, cataloguing Sheilagh as just another student who may or may not make the cut in four years. He knew she'd graduate. She was too smart not to.

However, that was a week ago. Now his opinion was changing. He didn't know how to interpret the girl. And he was getting a headache trying to figure out a woman he might never understand.

Wednesday night he'd had dinner with his son. It was a nice evening and they ended with a discussion over the mystery of Western religion. Alec enjoyed finally having his son close by. For years he'd lived in Wales with his mother. She'd moved back with their son after the divorce. Alec had always kept in contact with his only child, but currently he was getting to know the man who had once been his little boy.

When they had dinner and got into scholarly debates he took great pride in the way his son not only took after his mother, but also showed signs of Alec in his thinking. They'd grown closer over the last few months and Alec appreciated the honest way they dealt with each other.

When he returned home that evening his phone showed a missed call, but no message. His breath hitched at the possibility that a certain red headed prodigy might have found his note and used his number. He jotted down the number on the caller ID and dialed it back.

"Hello?"

"Sheilagh."

"How did you get my number?"

"I do believe we're in the new millennium. You called me." She was silent for a moment so he asked. "Are you ready to talk?"

"I don't know what you mean by that? Talk about what?"

"The *Allegory of the Cave*."

"I think I'll pass."

He tsked. "Don't be a coward, Ms. McCullough. It doesn't suit your fiery spirit." He frowned. Where the hell had that come from?

"I'm not a coward. I have better things to do."

"Such as?"

Silence.

"I'll tell you what. I know a nice quiet place not too far from campus. I'll give you the address and if you'd like to join me for a drink that's where I'll be. Shall we say in a half hour?"

He rambled off the address, not sure why he'd decided this couldn't wait until tomorrow. When he hung up the phone he was almost certain she wouldn't show. He laughed at himself and went to find a bottle of wine. Never before had a student intrigued him so much.

THIS WAS A MISTAKE. Sheilagh berated herself the entire time she drove through the town of Princeton looking for some place on some street that even her GPS couldn't seem to find. Why she wanted to torture herself and hear more arrogant musings from Alec Devereux was beyond her, but there she was, all the same, searching for the address he'd given her.

It was nine o'clock at night and she didn't have class the following day. She was bored and homesick and looking for a distraction. That was the only reason she decided to venture out.

"Ooh, there it is!" She yanked the wheel, turning onto the street she was looking for and frowned.

This was a residential street. Maybe the place she was looking for was on the other end. She squinted into the dark attempting to read the house numbers. She was looking for twenty-nine. The house she'd just passed proclaimed it was twenty-one. This had to be wrong.

When she located the corresponding number she pulled over. It was a house, a beautiful red Victorian, small, but lovely. "What the hell?"

She reached into her purse and dialed Alec's number.

"Hello?"

"Where are you sending me?"

"Are you coming?"

She raised her brow at the surprised tone of his voice.

"You told me to meet you."

"I invited you, but left the decision up to you. Thirty minutes has long passed."

What was this a freaking timed quiz? "Well, I'm at the address you gave me, but it's a house."

The line was silent for a moment. "I see you. Turn off the car."

"What?" She turned and there he was standing on the porch of the red Victorian. Her mouth opened and she ended the call. What was this, his home?

Frowning, she dropped her cell into her purse and turned off the car. This was weird and she didn't think she should be there. Something inside of her directed her actions. Ignoring her better judgment, she climbed out of her SUV.

When she reached the newly renovated sidewalk she asked, "Do you live here?"

"Yes."

She hesitated. "Is anyone else home?"

"No. It's just me here."

Right. Okay then. She didn't move.

"Would you like a glass of wine? I have a bottle of Chardonnay open. It's a good year."

Yes. Alcohol might help. "Sure." She slowly opened the iron gate that squeaked with time and took the path to the porch.

A small voice inside of her told her this was wrong. She shouldn't be there. She was a woman—a student—and he was a man she barely knew. However, there was that louder side of her, the one that seemed to always force her to do stupid things. That voice said, go inside. If something bad happened she'd deal with it.

Alec wasn't dressed in his usual slacks and button down he wore around campus. He was wearing a T-shirt and dark jeans and he looked much younger than he did behind his podium.

She climbed the steps and he smiled. "I'm glad you finally called."

Yeah, why had she done that? Alec opened the door and she stepped in. The first thing she noticed was the primitive furniture. The sight of his personal space gave her an unexpected sense of awareness as though she were trespassing in the faculty lounge or something worse. Although she was invited in, she didn't quite have the courage to fully look. Keeping her head down, she noted everything was made of dark wood and there was a rich scent to the house she couldn't place.

A dark burgundy oriental carpet covered teak floors and books dominated an entire wall. Maybe this was what she would have imagined, had she ever cared to imagine where Alec Devereux lived. She'd never really considered the thought. He was the scholarly sort though, so perhaps this sort of antiquated, timeless style suited him.

"Would you like a glass of Chardonnay?"

She flinched. Why was she so jumpy? Probably because it was totally weirding her out that she was in a professor's house. This had to be against some sort of rule. "I'm more of a whiskey girl. Do you have anything harder than wine?"

His mouth twitched, but he made no comment. He turned and went to a cool little set up in the corner and filled a rocks glass with ice. The bar was built in, looking like a reproduction of something off the pages of *The Great Gatsby* where nothing prevented the flow of champagne and toasts. "How do you take your whiskey?"

"Neat. Two fingers."

He raised a brow and dumped the ice into the small sink. *Fancy.* Using a decanter he poured two fingers into the stout glass sans the rocks. She carefully took the glass, taking great care not to let their fingers touch.

Alec settled onto a high back sofa and sipped his wine. She took a quick sip of her whiskey—which was rather fine—and let the burn warm her throat.

"Would you care to sit?"

She turned and eyed her options. There was a wing-back chair facing the fireplace, a wooden chair tucked into a nice leather topped desk, and the sofa. Right. She slowly lowered herself to the edge of the sofa, staying far on the opposite end from where he sat.

"Soooo," she said, taking another sip of her whiskey. "Wanna tell me what your note meant?"

He leaned back and casually draped an arm over the back of the sofa. She fidgeted under his scrutiny. "I'm disappointed you dropped the class."

"I didn't care for the professor."

He arched a brow. "Yet you're here."

"I'm curious."

"I know."

She finished her whiskey and sat the glass on the table. She quickly leaned forward again to relocate it to a coaster. "Sorry."

"Not a problem."

Her fingers drummed over the denim covering her knees. He wasn't saying anything, just watching. Finally, unable to take any more of the silence she asked, "How old are you?"

"I'm forty."

"Isn't it against the rules to have a student at your house?"

"You're not my student and we aren't doing anything untoward."

She laughed. "Only a Brit can get away with words like that."

"Does my vocabulary irritate you?"

"No."

"You seem nervous."

She flicked her hair behind her ear, disguising her anxiousness. "Wrong again."

He placed his wineglass on a coaster with a muffled click. "Why don't we discuss Plato?"

"Why don't we pass?"

He stood, the action completely graceful, and walked slowly to the bar. "I'm sure you recall your first reading assignment, *The Allegory of the Cave.* There's a reason I always assign that first. If you can't break open an egg, it's virtually useless. I find The Allegory a great starting point that opens students' minds for more intimate self-examination. Your first mistake was thinking yourself beyond this and jumping ahead."

He returned to the sofa with the decanter and poured her two more fingers of whiskey. If she drank too much she could always walk home. It was only about eight blocks from her apartment.

"I read the assignment."

"I know you did, but you also read the parts of *The Republic* I had yet to assign. The course is designed to take several weeks, because ideas take time to formulate. Tell me what you got from The Allegory."

She eyed him as she sipped her drink. "It's a slave puppet show."

"Who are the players?"

She sighed. If he thought she could read something that many times and not recall the details he'd highly underestimated her. "There are the men chained to the wall. They've been there all their lives. Then there are the men behind them, but the guys chained to the wall can't see those other guys. They're at their back and behind a fire."

"So the shadows are their reality."

"Yes. That's all they've ever seen. They don't know there's anything else."

"And what happens when a chained man discovers the world outside of the cave?" he asked.

"It hurts. The sun hurts his eyes."

"What does the sun represent, Sheilagh?" He was sitting across from her again.

She drew in an exasperated breath. "You? I imagine you'd like to pretend you're the center of the universe."

He chuckled quietly. "Close. The sun represents knowledge."

"I knew that."

"But you must apply it, Sheilagh. Socrates describes the outside world as painful and confusing to the men who have been trapped in the cave their entire lives. All they know are shadows, illusions, not even of real men, but of puppets held by men in front of a fire."

"Yeah, but the man adjusted once he got used to the real world."

Alec sipped his wine. "Yes, and eventually he wanted to share his new found knowledge with his friends still chained to the wall, but should he attempt to enlighten them, they'd only accuse him of being crazy."

She rolled her head back on the cushion, completely fed up with the story. "Right, because they're all convinced the shadows are reality. I get it."

"Do you? The men chained to the wall are the ordinary people. They mock philosophers, because ordinary people aren't able to see the world as it truly is. Their stubbornness keeps them from enlightenment. To be a true philosopher, one must first have the courage to leave the cave. My question for you, Ms. McCullough, is are you planning on staying in the cave or will you eventually brave the light?"

She frowned. "I'm not in a cave. I'm in your living room, praying my ears don't bleed from hearing the same exact story for the hundredth time."

His hazel eyes narrowed. "You may hear it, but you aren't listening. Life can be as simple as shadows on the wall, Sheilagh. It can exist in the safe environment you've always known—giving a false sense of control—or it can be real. But it will never be anything more than the same illusion you've lived for the past twenty-four years if you don't push yourself to learn what else is out there."

She dipped her head and gave him an incredulous

stare. "You think I live in a cave? That I'm not smart enough to be here, is that it?"

"On the contrary, I think you have every right to be here. I think it's a crime you aren't embracing the education being offered. I have no doubt you can move from the morons chained along the wall and be a great puppeteer by the fire. You can return home with a degree and enchant them all with your limitless knowledge, but you're only fooling the people who don't know any better and you know it. I want to know how that is enough for you. You're at one of the finest universities on the continent, yet you seem determined to leave here no more enlightened than you were when you arrived. Is it the degree you want? I can give you a piece of paper with your name on it right now, if that's the case. That paper doesn't give you knowledge. When I read your file I assumed you were the kind of student prepared to learn, but your arrogance has baffled me."

He pointed to the wall where several diplomas were framed. "I don't give a damn about those pieces of paper. They could burn for all I care. It's what's in here that counts," he said pointing to his head.

She finished her whiskey and stood. "Thanks for inviting me. I feel utterly enlightened."

Alec stood. "Why not learn what life is really about, Sheilagh? Venture out of the cave you've spent your entire life hiding in and have something real to go home and tell your family."

She turned and snapped. "Look, you don't know shit about me or my family, so why don't you quit while you're ahead?"

"I know that your town's population is small. I know you had the highest SAT scores in the history of your high school. I also know there's a reason you waited six years to attend college when you could have gotten a full ride the moment you graduated."

She spun, narrowing her eyes. "What's your deal? Find some other student to harass and stay out of my business."

"Why did you wait, Sheilagh?"

"It's none of your business!"

He stepped closer. "What if I want it to be my business?"

She frowned. "Back off, professor. I don't know what your obsession is with me, but get over it." She grabbed her purse and he caught her arm.

Electricity zipped up her spine and she caught her breath. He was standing very close and she was strangely lost in his hazel eyes. His voice was low, barely a whisper. "Did something happen to you?"

She jerked her arm away, completely unprepared for the feelings his touch stirred. "No. No one did anything to me. I was happy, that's why I stayed." Crap. "*Nothing*"—she clarified—"happened to me." She'd not meant to imply that someone might have done something to her.

"Do they believe you when you tell them that?"

"Fuck you." Her vision narrowed and blurred. She

blinked hard against the stupid tears, refusing their presence.

Suddenly he stepped back. He looked away and then back. For once there were traces of confusion in his arrogant eyes. "My apologies. I didn't mean to upset you," he said, his voice once again composed.

What the fuck was happening? She was out of breath and her palms were sweating. She suddenly saw him differently, no longer her superior. He was an incredibly handsome man and she was suffocating in his fancy living room.

"I have to go," she said and fled to the door.

He didn't follow her. When she made it to her car she locked herself inside, unsure why she was suddenly so unnerved. Glancing back at the Victorian, she saw his shadow in the window and that was enough to kick her into gear. The drive home was a blur of familiar impressions, yet as she parked outside of her apartment, she had no memory of getting there.

CHAPTER 4

I can't turn it off. Everything inside of me
feels so exceedingly dark and hollow, yet
so incredibly heavy. I'm exhausted from
lugging this sense of nothingness around.
I just want to sleep. Sleep and cry. Is this
the cave? Am I the cave? I hate that
fucking analogy. Stupid cave. I need to do
something crazy, something distracting,
something to shut off the unending
silence. But I'm so tired, tired of the
game, tired of performing, tired of all of
it. Maybe I'll just sleep and this horrible
feeling will be gone when I wake.

Sheilagh immersed herself in her studies. By that Saturday she'd managed to finish every upcoming project due over the next month. When she couldn't bear the quiet solitude of her apartment a moment longer, she decided to go out.

Dressing in jeans and a simple black sweater, she went to a microbrewery just off campus and settled in at the bar. For as much as she didn't want to be alone, she really wasn't looking for company either.

What were Finn and Kelly doing at that moment? Kelly was probably working while Finn, Luke, Tristan, Ashlynn, and Mallory all kept him company. Colin and Sammy might even be there too. This bar sucked compared to O'Malley's.

"Hi."

She turned and found a guy smiling at her. He looked about nineteen. "Keep moving, sonny."

He frowned and did as she said.

The brewery was crowded. The noise was comforting. The bartender brought her another glass of Oktoberfest and she slid a ten across the counter. Her phone buzzed and she pulled it out of her pocket.

The screen read *Captain Ass-clown.* She frowned and opened the text.

Not having whiskey tonight?

· · ·

HER SPINE STIFFENED and she couldn't breathe. Where was he?

Trying not to look like a spaz, she casually searched the bar. Her phone buzzed again.

ACROSS FROM YOU.

SHE LOOKED OVER THE BAR, past the large microbrew concoction taking up space and past the bartenders rushing to fill orders, sucking in her breath when she found sharp hazel eyes watching her. The sight of him made her unsettled in a way she wasn't used to. A strange sort of adrenaline rush provoked her fingers into motion and she lowered her head and texted him back.

STALKER.

A SECOND LATER HER phone vibrated. She opened the message.

HARDLY. I was here first. I think you're following me.

. . .

SHE SCOFFED, but her lips twitched with the desire to smile. Her thumbs rapidly flew over the keys.

CERTAINLY NOT, *cave boy. Try again.*

HIS TEXT CAME through a moment later.

YOU HAD *nothing better to do and you're halfway through your syllabuses. You're killing time.*

DAMN IT! How was he so perceptive when it came to her? She wasn't that translucent.

WRONG. *I'm three quarters through.*

SHE WATCHED as he smiled when he read her text. He had a very nice smile, good straight teeth. Her phone buzzed and with it came a sharp little twinge of excitement.

. . .

Lol. I should have known. Care to join me?

She read his text and stilled, unsure how to proceed.

Will we be discussing philosophy?

She waited, uncertain how he'd respond.

I promise, no talk of school or mention of Plato or Socrates. Just two equals having drinks together.

She hesitated and sighed. Finishing her beer, she grabbed her purse and rounded the bar. Alec was again dressed casually in jeans and a dark sweater. His shoulders filled out the soft material in a way that made her take notice.

"Hi."

He turned and his gaze traveled over her. Stiffening with indignant bravado, she played at appearing indifferent to the intent, yet somehow casual way he inspected her. "Hi. Would you like to get a table? I haven't had dinner yet. Are you hungry?"

Dinner was more than drinks, but she hadn't eaten yet either. "Okay."

He stood and she was reminded of how tall he was. He dug in his pocket and placed a few bills on the bar. She waited for him to choose a table and followed his lead. Keeping with his statement about being equals, he slowed his steps and walked by her side. She was completely unprepared for the press of his palm at her lower back as they worked their way through the Saturday night crowd.

When they reached an empty table, he pulled out a chair for her. "Quite the gentleman, Dr. Devereux."

"Please, call me Alec."

She thought about the name she gave him in her phone contacts and just managed to hide a smile. "Okay."

A waitress arrived and took their order. Before Sheilagh had a chance to order he said, "I'll take a glass of the house wine and she'll have two fingers of your top shelf whiskey, neat. We'd also like two dinner menus when you get a chance."

She raised an eyebrow, but said nothing about his highhandedness.

He settled into his seat and looked at her. "I promise I won't say anymore on the subject, but I wanted you to know I'm sorry about the other night. My behavior was uncouth and I was out of line."

She found the lilting pattern of his speech captivating. People with accents like that could read the phonebook and sound sexy. She was suddenly self-conscious of her slight redneck drawl.

"I don't like talking about myself." Yet she managed to somehow *explain* her behavior with such a response, a peculiar thing she didn't usually do. She frowned inwardly and told herself to knock it off.

He gave you a D.

He waited, his hazel eyes studying her. "What do you like to talk about, Sheilagh?"

She shrugged. "Whatever. Anything easy."

He nodded. "Easy. You seem to thrive with easy."

"Who doesn't? The worlds too messed up to waste time on difficult issues."

"Do you honestly believe that?"

"Are you being philosophical?"

"Sorry. It's difficult not to be in my line of work."

"How long have you lived in America?"

The waitress returned with their drinks and menus. Alec opened his and gave it a quick perusal then placed it on the table before he answered. "I moved to the States when I was eighteen. When I returned to Wales on a visit I discovered my girlfriend had a child, my child. I married her, we moved to the States. Several years later my wife asked for a divorce. I gave it to her. She and my son returned to Wales."

"Do you miss him?"

"I did, very much so. He's since returned to the States. We see each other often."

"How old is he now?"

"Twenty-two." Almost her age. "Do you know what you're going to order?"

She glanced at the menu. "I'll have the house salad and a side of fries."

The waitress returned and he placed their order. She sipped her drink. "How long have you worked at the university?"

"Twelve years."

"Do you miss Wales?"

"Sometimes. Do you miss your home?"

"Yes."

"Am I breaking rules if I ask about your home life?"

He'd just told her a whole bunch of his personal business. She supposed there was no harm in sharing a bit of her background. "I come from a family of nine. I have five brothers and one sister. I'm the baby."

"Do you like having a large family?"

"Yes and no, but mostly yes."

"Why sometimes no?"

"It can be suffocating. Not only is our family big, my aunts have big families too. When we get together it can be overwhelming. In our town you can't swing a dead cat without hitting a McCullough."

He smiled. "I imagine living away from so many relatives is something you're still adjusting to."

"Yes, but I like it, most of the time."

"What do you dislike?"

She sighed. He always tended to ask the difficult side of a question, forcing her to be introspective, something she usually tried to avoid. "Sometimes I miss the noise of home. My family's incredibly loud."

"Do you live in the dorms?"

"No. I have an apartment with a total prick for a neighbor."

He grinned. "Tell me how you really feel."

"He's this uppity, prep kid who complains over the littlest noise. I swear if he bangs on my wall one more time I'm going to break down his door with my baseball bat and show him what real noise is when I make him scream like a little girl."

He laughed. "You're quite animated when you speak of your neighbor. Have you told him to leave you alone?"

"I mostly tell him to go to hell. I tried being nice, but I could hiccup and he'd complain."

"Maybe he wants your attention."

She snorted. "I doubt it. He likes me about as much as I like him."

"Will you live there next year?"

She shrugged. "If I'm still here."

At that he frowned. "Do you intend to leave?"

Her gaze fell to the table. "I don't know if I'm cut out for college."

"What would you do if you weren't a student?"

She shrugged. "Probably work at my aunt's bar. My brother runs it."

When he didn't say anything, she looked up and found him frowning. Her answer seemed to bother him. The waitress returned and dropped off their food. Sheilagh distracted herself by removing the olives from her salad.

When she took a bite she realized he was still watching her. "What?"

"Do you find it boring?"

"Do I find what boring?"

"Life."

Wow, that was a loaded question. "If I didn't know better I'd say you're leading into a philosophical discussion."

"We're merely two adults sharing a meal and drinks."

She chewed her salad. "Sometimes."

He surprised her by admitting, "Me too."

They ate in comfortable silence, and then the waitress returned to clear their plates and replenish their drinks. Alec sat back in his chair and watched.

"You stare an awful lot."

He glanced away and she caught the hint of a smirk. "I find you quite interesting."

"Thanks?"

"It's a compliment, I assure you."

"I aim to please."

"You do. Most of the time." She frowned at him. "Why did you drop my class, Sheilagh?"

She sighed. He wouldn't be able to keep his word. "Where's the waitress? I'm ready for the check."

"Don't run away. Answer the question."

She glared at him. "It was too hard."

"No, it wasn't."

"I didn't want an F on my transcript."

"I've never flunked a student in my life."

"A D then."

"You wouldn't have settled for a D. You would have eventually earned an A, but you gave up without trying."

She crumpled her napkin in her fist. "I did try. I couldn't do it."

"Bullshit. You didn't want to do it. I have a feeling you've managed well at convincing the world you don't do anything you don't want to do, but I have another theory about the real person behind the mask."

"'Fraid not, professor. It's no act. I do it for me and the world can either take it or leave it." Keeping her breathing calm, she forced her heart rate to slow. He couldn't possibly see past the act, could he?

He drew in a slow breath and let it out just as slowly. "If you intend to take the course next semester under a different proctor, you're doing yourself a disservice. I'm better."

"Says the arrogant egotist."

He chuckled. "Just enlightening you."

Deciding to turn the tables, she licked her lips. "Does it work?"

He tilted his head. "Does what work?"

"Pretending you're smarter than everyone else in order

to divert the attention of others from your own short-comings?"

He tipped his head. "Touché."

"Let's just cut to the chase. You read my file, so you obviously have the upper hand. I know nothing beyond your geographical history and the fact that you have a son and were once married. What is it you see when you look at me? Maybe if you tell me I can save you some time before you hurt yourself."

He smiled. "Okay. I see a beautiful young woman who has the potential to be something great, but hesitates when it comes time to apply herself. I see a woman who has no right to be sitting alone at a bar on Saturday night and I'm shocked to see her turn down man after man when everything in her expression tells me she's lonely."

"I never said I was lonely."

He rolled his eyes. "I see stubborn green eyes and an attitude as scorching as your red hair. I see someone I probably shouldn't, because she's my student, or at least she was. But even when she isn't there, I see her anyway. I can't stop thinking about her and I find myself speculating if something terrible happened to her six years ago."

She couldn't breathe. No one had ever seen her that way before. She didn't know what possessed her to speak, but she quietly admitted, "I fell in love with someone I can never have."

"Why?"

"I don't talk about it."

"Did he pass away?"

"No."

"Married?"

"Nope. Impossible."

"I don't understand."

She glared at him. Never before had she told anyone about Tristan and why she couldn't have him. The temptation to unburden herself here, so many miles away from home and people who knew her, was quite real.

She'd probably never see him again after tonight. What would it feel like to finally say it out loud, to unburden herself? Licking her dry lips she rasped, "He's in love with and committed to my gay brother, has been for over half a decade."

Alec's head slowly drew back and it was clear her words took him by surprise. There was something strange in the way he was studying her. "You didn't know he was gay?"

"Nope. He flirted with me. Still does."

He frowned. "And you're sure he's gay?"

"Oh yeah. I don't know what was harder to believe, that he was gay or that my brother was and they'd been sleeping together for years without anyone finding out."

"Would your family object to such a thing?"

"No, my family's as liberal as they come. They're nuts and don't always say the right things, but there's nothing they would really have a problem with, especially when it comes to one of us."

He nodded and she could tell he was digesting her explanation. "When did you find out about this man and your brother?"

"When I was eighteen, just before I was about to leave for college."

"And finding this out was enough for you to postpone your goals for six years?"

She choked. "Did you love your wife?"

"Of course. I wouldn't have married her if I didn't."

"Well, maybe it's different for guys. I was destroyed when I found out. Everything I'd ever planned suddenly didn't make sense."

"Did you and this man sleep together?"

She didn't know what threw her off more, the fact that she was talking about this or the fact Alec was asking her about her sex life. "No."

He frowned. "How do you love someone if you've never been intimate with them?"

"Are you serious?"

"Very."

"My brother married a woman who never did more than kiss him. My other brother was going to be a priest up until a few months before his wedding. To assume you have to have sex to be in love is totally ignorant. Step out of the cave, professor."

"You misunderstand me. I believe two people can love each other without sleeping together. What I don't believe is a relationship that never really existed can cause an intelligent person to stop living for six years."

Her molars locked. "Who said I didn't live?"

"Did you?"

"If sex is your measuring stick, then yes. I lived quite well."

"And did that lessen the sting of his rejection?"

Jesus. Her breath seeped out of her as if he punched her. "No. It made me feel cheap and ugly. It made me not count for anything more than a quick screw at the cost of a few drinks. Is that what you wanted to hear? I fucked the last six years away, all from my sad little Podunk cave." She stood and grabbed her purse.

"Sheilagh."

"Leave me alone."

He stood and threw some money on the table as she quickly found the closest exit. When she hit the cold air outside of the bar, she stumbled into a group of college kids making their way in. Awkwardly extricating herself, she mumbled apologies through a constricted throat.

She made it around the corner when she heard him coming after her. "Sheilagh, wait a minute."

"Go away, professor. I'm not interested in being enlightened." She coughed to explain her thickened tone.

The sound of his footsteps grew nearer and he grabbed her arm, jerking her to a stop.

"What do you want from me?" she snapped.

"I want to understand you," he said, his brow creased with worry.

"Why? I'm nothing special. Stop acting like I am."

He shook his head. "You *are* something special."

"Why? Because I aced a few tests? How's this? I was drunk the morning I took my SATs. I didn't want to score that high. I purposely messed up on several questions and I still got the highest score in the history of my town."

He shook her. "That's special, Sheilagh. My son took his SATs six times and only scored half as well as you. Why are you so afraid of being smart?"

"I'm not afraid of being smart. I just want to be normal. Do you get that? I don't want to be above everyone else. I just want to be happy."

He was breathing hard. His grip loosened on her shoulders and he stepped closer. "But you're not. Acting like everyone else hasn't made you happy. It's all an illusion."

She turned away.

"If he'd said yes, if he'd left your brother and pretended to be hetero for you, would you have settled for that?"

She stilled. "I could have loved him enough for both of us."

Alec shook his head. "I said the same thing to my wife, but she was in love with a woman named Claire."

Her gaze jerked to his. "What?"

"My wife's gay. I didn't know. I loved her very much, but it wasn't enough. Not enough to change who she was."

She needed to sit down. Spotting a bench in the shadows, she headed that way. Alec followed and filled the space beside her.

For several minutes, they said nothing. "Did you ever forgive her?"

"There was nothing to forgive. She'd always been gay. She just didn't realize it until she was married to a man. We tried to make it work, for our son, but even his love wasn't enough. Life's too short to spend it trying to pretend you're someone you're not."

She shivered. "I didn't forgive my brother for a long time. I still haven't forgiven Tristan." Not because he chose Luke. She had come a long way, but finally figured out how to feel some level of happiness for them. However, she still struggled to fully forgive Tristan for misleading her.

"Forgive them, Sheilagh. They didn't do it to hurt you." When she shivered again, he said, "Would you like to come back to my place to talk?"

She didn't want to go home. They had nothing in common, yet there was something identical about their pasts. She wanted to know how he was all right with it. *She* wanted to be all right. "Okay."

They walked in silence and she wondered what made her confess so much to this man. Half the time she didn't like him. The other half of the time she couldn't figure out how she felt about him.

When they reached his house a few blocks away from

the brewery, he unlocked the door and held it for her to enter. "Can I get you a drink?"

"Sure. Whatever you have."

"Whiskey?"

"Why not?"

She sat on the sofa she'd occupied a few days ago and waited as he poured. When he sat beside her he placed her glass on the table on a coaster. "Do you drink a lot?"

For some reason the glass on the coaster distracted her, a symbol of his maturity perhaps. "Not really. I've been drinking a lot more lately."

"Is it helping?"

She shut her eyes. "No."

"What made you decide to start school this year?"

"My brothers forced me to."

He gave her a look of confusion. "Pardon?"

"They caught me in a—I was doing something I shouldn't have been doing and they threatened to tell my father. They said I was throwing my life away and blackmailed me. If I didn't apply to college and get out of town they would go right to my father and tell him what I'd been about to do."

He swallowed and the dark stubble on his throat distracted her. "What were you going to do?"

She lifted a shoulder and looked away. "I was going to strip at a local club."

His gaze zeroed in on her curves as though he could

see through her clothing. "I assume, if you're here, your father never found out."

"Not if my brothers plan on keeping their testicles."

He laughed. "I'm glad they stopped you."

"Me too. It was stupid. I'm still not sure why I agreed to do it."

"Maybe you were hoping to get caught."

"I doubt it. I think I was just giving everyone what they expected." The only person she wanted to notice her was entirely wrong for her. She yo-yoed between wanting to blend in with everyone else and wanting to be noticed. Half the time she didn't understand what motivated her to act the way she did.

"An illusion."

"Don't start."

He chuckled. "Sorry."

She hadn't touched her drink and was no longer in the mood for whiskey. "Do you mind if I get a glass of water?"

He stood. "The kitchen's this way."

She followed him through the house and into the kitchen. "Wow. Being a professor must pay really well."

"Don't get too excited. The university provides our housing."

"You don't own this home?" He handed her a glass of water. "Thanks."

"No. I've lived here for over a decade though. I consider it mine. I don't look forward to ever leaving."

She lowered herself to a kitchen chair and he took the seat across from her. "I'm sorry I lost it back there."

He shrugged. "It happens."

Cavalier she could do. Her brain needed a break from all the emotional stuff and she was grateful he wasn't dwelling on her little episode.

"Do you usually have students in your home?"

"Aside from my son, you're the only other student who's ever been here."

"You're son's a student at Princeton?"

"A Sophomore. He did some time at a community college before they accepted him."

"Does he like it here?"

"He's worked very hard to be here. A perk of teaching here is that our children get free tuition *if* they can make the grades. My son wants to graduate from Princeton and is extremely determined to do so. I'm very proud of him."

"You must think I'm a complete brat."

"No. I think you're hurting and confused and I want to help you."

"Why?"

"I like you."

"You could have helped me by not giving me a D."

"That wouldn't have helped you in the long run."

She sighed. "You're going to start talking about the cave again, aren't you?"

He laughed. "The cave is a great metaphor."

She groaned and dropped her head to the table. "I knew it."

"We can't perceive the reality of the world if we don't possess the courage to see past the illusions and try for something more, something real."

"Are you talking about Plato or my life?"

"Both. I know what it must have felt like to think what you were living was real and then have it come crashing down around you. I lived. I had a family. I had a wife. But none of it was real. It was just an illusion."

"Have you ever loved someone other than your wife?"

"No."

She smiled. "So you're not as all-knowing as you claim."

"I never claimed to be all-knowing. I know philosophy, and as such, I trust there's something more out there. When I suspect more, I want to understand it."

"I shouldn't have dropped the class."

His brow lifted and she could see she surprised him. "Can you re-enroll?"

"Probably not."

"Next semester then."

She nodded. Her gaze went to the clock on the wall. "It's late. I should be going."

"Would you like a ride home?"

Her apartment was only about eight blocks from his place, but she probably shouldn't be walking alone this late at night. "Thanks. I'd appreciate that."

She stood and he did the same. When he caught her hand, she stilled. "Are we okay?"

Her shoulders shook as she drew in a breath. "Yeah. I actually enjoyed tonight, if you can believe that."

"I enjoyed it too. You're good company, Sheilagh."

Their eyes met and that jolt of electricity tingled again. She was completely aware of being alone in this quiet house with a man who was very attractive and very interesting. He might not always tell her what she wanted to hear, but he kept her on her toes.

His lips parted and she drew in a breath. The silence became weighted with something heavy and charged. Suddenly he released her hand and stepped back. When he turned and gripped the back of his neck, she exhaled. She'd been certain he was about to kiss her. The strange thing was she was almost disappointed he hadn't.

"Let me get my coat."

Sheilagh nodded and went to the door. She needed to stop. Kissing Alec would be bad. He was sixteen years older than her. He was her professor, or used to be. Knowing all of this didn't seem to calm her heart from racing out of her chest.

"Ready?"

She jumped as he stepped behind her. "Yup."

"I left my keys in the kitchen."

He turned and she called his name. "Alec?"

His strides halted and he stilled, not turning to face

her. She waited. He had to feel it as well. She knew he did when he said, "You're a student, Sheilagh."

Although he couldn't see her, she nodded. Yes. She was a student and he was a professor. His son was closer to her age. It was good they cleared this up.

"I'll get my keys," he said quietly, disappearing into the kitchen.

When he returned, keys in hand, she hesitated. They both seemed to be avoiding each other's gaze. She followed him out the door and waited for him to lock it.

The car—a very nice BMW—was parked out back. He held her door and she slid onto the soft leather seat. The entire car smelled like him, sophisticated and delicious. Jesus, what was happening to her?

Alec climbed in behind the wheel and the engine purred to life. His hands flexed over the wheel and he hesitated. She chanced a glance in his direction. That was a mistake.

Their eyes locked under the dim shadows of the skylight and something broke inside of her. She wasn't sure who initiated it. She only knew they met somewhere in the middle, his soft lips brushing over hers, strong hands running through her hair.

She twisted in her seat and pulled closer, moaning into his mouth. Waves of excitement burst within her chest causing her to tremble. His tongue pressed over hers and she tasted him. He tasted spectacular. She sifted her fingers through his hair and he moaned into her mouth as she gave the silky strands a little tug. Holy hell, the man could kiss.

Her fingers traveled down the sharp stubble of his jaw and fit in the collar of his shirt. Hot skin pressed against her fingertips. His hands roamed down her back and pulled her tighter. And he jerked away.

She blinked into the darkness as he stared straight ahead. The car was getting warm. Her fingers went to her bruised lips and she was amazed at the desire swirling in her stomach. Where had it come from? It had been years since she felt anything close to that. She almost didn't recognize it for what it was.

"That can't happen again," he said sharply and she recoiled at his tone.

Lowering herself into the seat she quietly buckled her seatbelt. "I'm sorry."

"It's my fault. I know better than to kiss a student."

For some reason his words hurt. They felt personal even though he generalized his excuse. Maybe that was it. He usually made her feel so visible, not just a girl, but Sheilagh. Lumping her in a category with every other student was a step out of the neat, individualized box he'd once put her in, tossing her into a pile of generalizations. She shrunk into her seat.

Alec backed out of the driveway and she gave him the address to her place. He frowned.

"If you turn onto—"

"I'm familiar with it."

Realizing he didn't want to talk, she silently stared out the window as he drove her home. He pulled up to her apartment a few minutes later and she didn't know how to say goodbye.

"Thanks for giving me a ride home."

He gave but one nod, and she reached for the door. "Sheilagh?"

"Yeah?"

"Try not to take out your neighbor with a bat."

She frowned and got out of the car. He pulled away before she even made it inside. When she entered her apartment, she wasn't sure if she wanted to cry or eat a pint of ice cream.

She did neither. She showered and went to bed. When she couldn't sleep she waited for the clock to pass two. Once it did, she reached for her phone and dialed.

"O'Malley's Bar and Grill."

"Hey."

"Sheilagh?"

"Yeah."

Her brother's voice was exactly what she needed in that moment. "How's college life, love?"

"I wanna come home."

The line was silent and then Kelly's voice was grave. "What happened?"

"Nothing. I just don't fit in here."

"You need to give it a chance, Shei."

"It's been almost eight months. I've given it a chance."

"Give it a longer one."

"Kelly, you don't know what it's like. Nothing is working out the way I planned."

"Then stop planning and just go with it."

She shut her eyes. "I don't know how."

"Try, Sheilagh. You have to try to make it work. You need this."

A tear slipped past her lashes. She missed everything, her home, her family, the predictability of her life. "Will you guys come visit?"

"It isn't that easy with the baby."

"How is Nate?" Her newest nephew was a miracle baby. Kelly and his wife had faced some complications and once Nathanial was on his way he'd decided to pop in early. He was almost a year old, but because he was premature, he still required a lot more care than a typical child.

"He's great. He's climbing his percentiles and blowing our minds every day."

"I miss him."

"Speaking of babies—"

"Who's pregnant?"

"Kate!"

"Shut up!" Her cheeks squeezed with a smile. Kate was her eldest sibling. She already had Frankie, Skylar, Hannah, and Michael but she'd said she wanted at least one more before she hung up her maternity bras for good.

"Due in September."

"Oh, I'm going to miss the birth. See, this is why I should come home. I could just as easily commute to a college near us."

"No. Kate will have another C-section. It's probably already scheduled. You can make arrangements to come home for it. It isn't a reason to transfer. Now, tell me what happened."

She pursed her lips. "I kissed my professor."

"What?"

"Well, he isn't really my professor anymore."

"Did he lose his job for fucking around with students? Because he should."

"No. I dropped his class a couple weeks ago."

"Why? Did he push you into—"

"No, Kelly, Jesus. I told you, I kissed him. I dropped his class because it was too hard."

"Bullshit. This guy better not be playing games with you." She could hear Kelly cleaning in the background, putting chairs up throughout the bar, something she'd done a number of times.

"He's not." She didn't know how she knew that, but she was certain. "He's a nice guy."

The line was quiet. The sound of chairs being stacked was interrupted by her brother's huff and she imagined him dropping into a seat. "Isn't that frowned upon?"

"I'm not exactly sure what the rules are, but I think it isn't something the university welcomes."

"Aren't there other people you could kiss? If this is some attempt to get thrown out—"

She rolled her eyes. "Kelly, if I don't want a D on my transcript, do you think I'd be okay with expulsion? I'm not stupid."

"True."

"Besides, I don't think it's going to happen again."

"Why?"

"He seemed pretty upset with himself afterward."

"He should be."

"Oh, will you stop it! Since when are you such a prude?"

"Since the professor's trying to diddle Ginger."

"I should have never told you."

"Is this part of the reason you want to come home?"

Maybe. "No."

He sighed. "Shei, you can do this college thing. I know you can. Just give it a while longer. Enroll for the fall and if you still don't want to go back in August we'll talk about it then."

That was easy for him to say. Kelly never left Center County. She should have called Braydon. He'd left home to go to college. He'd probably be more sympathetic to what she was going through, but it was too late to call him now.

She asked Kelly about her nieces and nephews and he caught her up on who was walking, who was getting potty trained and who was talking. They were all getting so big.

Spring break was only a few weeks away and she'd be seeing them soon.

When she got off the phone she was tired. She turned on the television and settled into bed. As she flipped through the channels there was a knock on her wall. "Keep it down. It's two-thirty in the morning!"

She elbowed the wall—hard—and winced. "Blow me, Poindexter!"

"It's *Wesley*!"

CHAPTER 5

$\mathcal{A}$lec left campus and drove directly home. He was late, but he couldn't help it. A few of his students stayed after class and their debate had turned into an impromptu study session. He'd gotten caught up in answering questions and lost track of the time.

When his BMW pulled into the driveway his son's car was already there. Alec entered the house and called for him. "Wes?"

"In the kitchen."

Alec headed in that direction. "Couldn't wait for me?"

"You're late. I made you a sandwich."

Alec took the sandwich and eyed its contents. "I had ham?"

"No. You had green bread and something that might have been cheese. Don't you shop?"

Alec shrugged. "I eat out a lot."

"Well, I bought you lunchmeat and fresh bread. Most parents provide food for their kids when they're in college."

"I'm a perpetual college resident. Cooking is out of my jurisdiction. You'll have to go to your mother for that sort of tender care." He reached in his pocket and pulled out some cash, sliding the reimbursement to his son who gracefully accepted it with a nod.

"Have you talked to Mum?" Wes asked as he took a bite of his sandwich.

"Not since last week. She and Claire are talking about taking a trip to the States this March. Maybe over spring break."

"I may not be here."

"Where are you going?"

"A group of friends and I are thinking about renting a place in the mountains. Nothing fancy, but it'll be nice to get away. My neighbor makes sleeping impossible."

Alec stilled at the mention of his son's neighbor. "About your neighbor…"

"What about her? She's a pain in the ass. I hope she drops out and never comes back."

Alec swallowed the last of his sandwich. "Everyone is fighting some sort of a battle, Wesley. Try to be a little more tolerant."

His son looked at him as though he were crazy. "She's a total bitch, Dad. She has no respect for how thin our walls are. I hear everything she says. Last Saturday she was on the phone until almost three in the morning."

Last Saturday she was with him. "Whom was she speaking to?"

"Fuck if I know."

"Watch your language."

"Oh, like you can talk. I hear how Dr. Devereux curses in his lectures." He sighed, mimicking the voice of an American female. "He's so...cool."

"I say shit and damn. It's tacky to say fuck."

"I guess."

"And you shouldn't call your neighbor a bitch. She's probably a very nice woman."

He dropped his sandwich on his plate. "She's not a nice woman. She calls me a wank and constantly tells me to blow her or bite her. Nice girls don't talk like that."

He couldn't help it. He laughed.

"What's so funny?"

"Nothing. I'm sorry."

"Are you okay, Dad?"

He wiped his palms over his face and tried to curb his laughter. "Maybe you're being a bit too touchy. She can't be that loud all the time."

"She is. She's either blaring her music or talking on the phone or crying over something or another."

He stilled. "She cries?"

"Every night."

Something cold and uncomfortable settled in his stomach. "What does she cry about?"

His son balked. "Again, fuck if I know."

Alec stood and cleared the table so his son couldn't see his frown. "Did you say you had a paper you wanted me to look over?"

"Yeah. It's on the counter."

Alec picked it up and took the sheaf to the living room. He read over it slowly, his thoughts elsewhere. A while later he handed it back to Wes. "You have some typos and that second paragraph needs rewording."

Wes opened his laptop and began making the corrections immediately. Alec gave him privacy knowing his son required quiet to get his work done. Alec went upstairs and showered.

When he returned, Wes was sleeping on the couch. He often crashed at his place on Fridays. Alec covered him with the quilt and found his keys in the kitchen. He knew he shouldn't do what he was about to do, but he needed to see her. He needed to prove his son was wrong and the strong girl he knew Sheilagh possessed inside was safe and sound.

He couldn't imagine her crying, especially if she was upset due to their last encounter. That was ridiculous. She'd probably already forgotten about it. If anyone was twisted over what happened, it was Alec.

He drove to her apartment, which also happened to be in his son's building, and parked across the street. There were only two units, so it was easy to determine which was hers.

He knocked and was greeted with a shout.

"I'm not even making noise. Fuck off!"

He knocked again and the door whipped open.

"*What*—Alec. What are you doing here?"

"I missed you." He shouldn't have said that, but it was true.

She drew back and he glanced at what she was wearing. Her legs were covered in baggy sweats. Her sweatshirt was faded green and said O'Malley's. Her hair was a mess and she had two different color socks on her feet. She looked adorable.

"I wasn't expecting anyone."

"I'm sorry. I should go." He shouldn't have come there.

"No. It's fine. Did you want to come in? I just made some popcorn. I was going to watch a movie."

"Sure."

"Sorry for yelling. I thought you were my neighbor."

He followed her inside and was amazed at how different her apartment appeared from his son's. She had stuff everywhere.

He stood awkwardly in the living area. "Do you sleep out here?"

"Yeah. I need organization when I study, but I'm sort of messy. I made the bedroom my office and made this my bedroom."

There was a couch, but it was covered with books. Her

bed was against the far wall across from the television. He swallowed as he realized that was where they'd be watching a movie.

His eyes darted to a scrap of hot pink lace on the floor. *Shit.*

The smell of fresh popcorn met his nose. She placed the bowl on the coffee table and snatched up the pink panties he was staring at. "Just give me a second to clean up."

He watched her make her way around the apartment. She had it cleaned up in a matter of two minutes. The books were returned to a shelf. Her clothing found its way into a basket. And she flattened out the blanket on her bed.

Something fell out of her covers and he bent to pick it up. As he scooped up the book his mouth opened. It was *The Republic.* She snatched it out of his hands and her cheeks darkened. "Sorry. I don't know how that got there. Sit down."

She scooped up the bowl of popcorn and sat crossed legged on the mattress. He lowered himself to the edge. "What movie were you going to watch?"

"It's a toss-up between *Boondock Saints* or *Braveheart.*"

"Embracing your Celtic roots?"

She shrugged. "They're both great movies."

They were, but they were also violent. He wasn't used to women like Sheilagh. *She's not a woman. She's a twenty-four year old student.*

"Do you have a preference?"

He frowned. "Of?"

"Which movie?"

"*Braveheart*," he answered without giving it much thought. He only knew that was longer and he wanted a reason to be with her for a while. He couldn't shake the memory of Wes saying she cried a lot.

"How have you been?" he asked.

"Fine. Do you want some popcorn?"

He took the bowl and she hit play. The quiet humming flutes and strings started and the lights, all except the dim lamp in the kitchen, went out.

"I love this movie."

"Does your family share any connection to the McCullough clan?"

"No. We're Irish not Scottish."

She reached into the bowl of popcorn and grabbed a handful. Jesus, he felt like he was a teenager, sitting in the dark with her and aware of her every breath.

"The first scene's always so brutal to watch," she commented, stretching out her legs. She had little feet. And why didn't her socks match?

"Most of Scottish history is dramatized with folklore," he said in order to distract himself from the scent of her hair. Her entire place smelled like her, sweet and intoxicating.

"I know. William Wallace is supposedly real, but he wasn't the actual Braveheart. Robert the Bruce was." She was correct. He liked the fact that Sheilagh was full of useful knowledge.

She took the popcorn from him and placed the bowl on the table. "Why don't you take off your coat? Stay a while."

He slipped off his coat and set it over the foot of the bed. Spotting something black hanging in the shadows, he stilled. *Damn it.* It was her bra.

There was no way he was getting comfortable. He should go, but he couldn't seem to make himself move.

The movie carried on and soon Wallace was running off to marry his bride in secret. Alec's throat tightened as the couple stood naked on the screen.

Sheilagh sighed. "I love how much he loved her. The fact she was the last thing he saw before he died."

He turned and looked at Sheilagh. She was lying on her side, her cheek balanced on her palm as her eyes following the love scene on the television. Jesus, she was beautiful.

Her hair was the most unique shade of red, copper with strands of gold. Her eyes were a vibrant hue of green. And her skin was ivory, flawless. Her lips held a natural shade of burgundy he'd never seen before without makeup. He was suddenly jealous of every man that ever laid a hand on her.

She shifted and a piece of her long hair touched his hand. He couldn't stop himself from touching it. She turned and looked up at him. Caught.

"Sorry."

"It's okay."

No. It wasn't. He shouldn't be there and he certainly shouldn't be touching her hair. "I should go." He stood and she scrambled to sit up.

"Please don't, Alec."

He turned and faced her. What were they doing? This entire friendship had crossed a line and it was indecent. He could lose his job. "Sheilagh…"

"I don't want to be by myself," she said quickly and his heart broke, knowing what it took for her to make such an admission.

He sighed. "It isn't right for me to be here."

"Why? We aren't doing anything wrong."

"You know why."

"Because you work for the school? So? Before we kissed you had no problem inviting me to your house."

"I shouldn't have done that either."

Her face tightened and she looked down. Damn it. He didn't mean to upset her. "Sheilagh, we can't do this. It's wrong." He didn't know if he was speaking for himself. She probably wasn't even thinking along the same lines as him.

"I'm not a child."

"You're sixteen years my junior and a student."

Her green eyes bore into him, her small body the most tempting, mismatched clothed display of beauty he'd ever seen. "What if I don't care?"

"You should."

"Who would know, Alec?"

"What are you saying?" *Stop entertaining this topic. It can't happen!*

Slowly, she scooted off the bed and stood. She was about a foot shorter than him and everything about her was petite. When she glanced up at him, he knew he was done.

Her soft fingers went to his jaw and he sucked in a jagged breath. "Sheilagh…"

"Just…bear with me for a minute."

She slowly lifted and pressed her lips to the corner of his mouth. His palms balled into fists at his side, fighting not to touch her. When her tongue traced over his lower lip, he gave in.

Drawing in a deep breath, he caught the back of her neck and sealed his mouth over hers. She moaned and wrapped her arms around his shoulders. Leaning down, he lowered her with him to the bed.

His body fell over hers and she coiled her legs around him. It had been so long since a woman kissed him like this. Her mouth tasted spectacular, lips still salty with the flavor of popcorn. He braced his weight on his knees.

She arched into him and he felt the press of her soft breasts against his chest. His hand went to the waist of her sweatshirt and lifted the baggy material. Satin skin met his fingertips as he traveled upward. She wasn't wearing a bra.

He cupped her breast, dragging his thumb over the tight tip. "Alec," she moaned and he deepened the kiss.

His other hand went to her face, brushing her hair out of the way. Jesus, her lips were soft. Her fingers pulled at his hair and chills raced up his spine. His hand moved to her other breast and she arched into his touch.

"Take this off," he said against her lips.

She broke the kiss and a moment later she was topless beneath him. The dim flashes of the television played over her ivory skin and he was grateful for the light coming from the kitchen. She was breathtaking. Her breasts lifted as she breathed. The tips were the same burgundy tone as her lips. He swallowed hard.

"Kiss me, Alec. Here." Her narrow finger traveled slowly to her breasts.

He lowered his head and kissed the soft flesh. She arched and he found her nipple. Her knees tightened on his hips as he pulled one tight bud into his mouth. He nibbled the sensitive point and she cried out.

His palms cupped her curves and he moved to the other nipple. How far could he go? He wanted all of her. He released her breasts and slipped a hand down her loose fitting pants. She was soaked through her panties.

He rubbed her there and she cried out, "Yes, please, Alec."

He grabbed hold of her sweats and jerked them down. Soft lily-white thighs stretched before him. Her pale blue panties showed a patch of wetness. He could smell her sweet arousal and growled, he plucked the fabric away and replaced it with his mouth.

She nearly came off the bed as he slid his tongue into her. She tasted incredible, clean, spicy. His mouth opened over her as he pierced her slit with sharp jabbing motions of his tongue. His thumb found her clit and he strummed her.

Her voice filled the room as her nails scratched at his head, her fingers pulling at his hair, pressing him against her. He slipped a long finger into her and she moaned. His mouth moved to her little bud, lips closing over the sensitive tip as he plunged his finger deep.

He added another finger. She was small and he stretched her. Her breaths came quickly as he fingered her hard. Her body clamped down on his digits and she cried out, her climax tightening her sheath around his fingers. He plunged them in and out, fucking her hard with his hand.

Her clit pulsed under his lips. "One more, Sheilagh, give me one more."

He sucked her clit, pressing his fingers quickly in and out as she arched, her spine bowing and pressing her sex into his mouth. He drank her up and licked her clean, until she lay boneless beneath him.

Sitting up he undid his pants, glanced at her, and froze. Her hair was a copper cloud beneath her pale face. She smiled softly at him, lashes lowered in an expression of complete satisfaction. It should have made him feel like a king, but it made him feel like a wretch.

Fuck! None of this was supposed to happen. He stood abruptly and she gasped. "Where are you going?"

He zipped up his pants. "I have to go."

"What? You're leaving? Now?"

He wiped his palm over his face and growled. "Shit. Sheilagh, this isn't why I came here."

She scowled at him. He had to turn away. She was completely naked aside from her mismatched socks and apparently not fazed by her nudity. "You're really fucking leaving?"

"I have to!" he practically snarled. "This is insane. We can't do this."

Her lips thinned and her chin quivered. He wanted to go to her, but knew if he got too close he'd never leave. She was too reckless, too alluring. Never before had he wanted a woman with the intensity he wanted her. "I'm sorry."

Her chin lifted, a show of pride belied by the glassiness of her eyes. He was such a prick.

"Bye," she said snidely.

"Sheilagh, don't be like that. I'm doing the right thing."

"Which is what, getting me naked and abandoning me two minutes after the most incredible orgasm I've ever had in my life?"

His head shot up. "In your life?"

She groaned and threw a sock at him. "God, get out!"

"Please try to understand, Sheilagh. I want you. I want you more than I've ever wanted a woman. I don't know what it is about you, but I lose all control in your presence. I have to leave. If we cross that line we're only inviting trouble we don't need into our lives. I can't do that to you."

She looked away and he needed to make sure she'd be okay.

"Please don't be upset."

Her hand reached for the blanket and she pulled it over her chest. He shut his eyes.

"Don't come back, Alec. I can't deal with you anymore. You send me all sorts of mixed signals, but—no matter what—every time I leave you, I feel the sting of rejection all over again. And I feel a little more dirty."

"Jesus, Sheilagh, that's not what I want."

"Well, whatever you want, I'm once again, inadequate at providing it."

"Sweetheart…"

She rolled to her side and pulled the blanket to her shoulders, her eyes closed and face turned to the wall. He stepped close and collected his coat. Leaning over, he pressed a kiss into her silky hair. "I'm sorry," he whispered. And he was. Truly and utterly sorry.

CHAPTER 6

Sometimes there's so much frustration and disgust built up inside of me, I'm amazed I don't explode. It's there, seething like an active volcano and somehow I manage to keep the illusion of a tranquil foothill on the outside. I'm not strong. I'm afraid of my own shadow and anything else having to do with myself. Every ounce of disgust festering inside of me is for the person I've become. I hate her. She's dirty and no one wants her. Not even Alec and he's the first person that actually made me feel anything real since…

The day before spring break should have been exciting, but it was mostly annoying. Cars appeared from everywhere. People were hyper and rude and racing around shouting to friends, trying to start their holiday as fast as possible.

Sheilagh wasn't leaving until Saturday morning. Her apartment was clean—for once—and she had a suitcase sitting by the door. She needed to drop off a few returns at the library and then the week belonged to her.

By Friday at four, she sensed the emptiness of the campus. Parking lots were vacant and buildings were barren. As she walked to the library she was surprised she didn't see tumbleweeds rolling by.

She carried her bag of books to the counter. "Hi. I need to return these. Two are overdue."

The girl behind the counter scanned the books and Sheilagh put her ID on the counter to clear up the balance. Once that was handled, she walked over to the literature section to find something new to read.

As she perused the selection—steering clear of romance—she pulled out a copy of an old favorite and skimmed the last chapter.

"That's cheating."

She stilled and shut the book. Why did he always show up at the most inopportune moments? She returned the book to the shelf and took a deep breath. "I've read it over a dozen times. I like the end."

He glanced at the binding. "He dies at the end."

"And so he should. He broke her heart."

He was wearing his teaching clothes, a white button down, rolled at the sleeves, black dress slacks. "How have you been?"

Awful. "Fine."

"Are you going home for break?"

She nodded. "Saturday."

"That should be nice."

It should be, but she was strangely hesitant to return home after months of homesickness. "Are you doing anything special?"

"Just enjoying the peace and quiet."

"Will you see your son?"

"He's gone on holiday with some friends."

"Oh."

"Sheilagh, I…"

She stepped back. They couldn't keep doing this. When he left her weeks ago she wasn't sure what to make of their predicament. She'd been hurt, angry, and ashamed —none of those emotions were pleasant. She hadn't been the same since.

She kept her voice at a low whisper, aware others were still in the library. "It was nice seeing you, Dr. Devereux."

He caught her arm gently. "Are you okay? I feel terrible about what happened."

More shame. "I'll be fine."

He stood close and his rich scent invaded every breath

she took. His eyes searched hers and, finally, he stepped back. "I was hoping to see you, but I wasn't sure how to find you."

"You know where I live and have my number."

"Right."

She shifted her feet. It was painful to see him. He was yet another person she wanted and couldn't have. "I have to go."

"Have dinner with me tonight."

She stilled. Her lips parted in surprise. "Alec…"

"Please. Everyone's gone. You can come to my place. I'll cook."

"What about everything you said?"

"It still stands. Have dinner with me as a friend."

"You know we aren't friends."

"Aren't we?" His hazel eyes studied her.

"No."

His gaze dropped. What did he expect? Turning on her heel, she left him there in the literature section and walked home.

When she reached her apartment, she carried her suitcase to her SUV and wondered why she didn't leave then. She didn't want to make the drive in the dark. She'd leave the next morning as planned and that was that.

She watched some television and was ready to crawl out of her skin by eight. Finally, going against her better judgment, she grabbed her keys and left.

She pulled into his driveway and parked beside his

BMW. As she climbed out of her car, the back door of the house opened. His expression showed complete surprise. They both stilled, separated by twenty feet and a decision that would change everything.

He'd changed into lounge pants and a faded T-shirt. He didn't look like a professor. He looked like Alec. Handsome, patient, everything she suddenly wanted.

"You came."

"I was hungry," she answered plainly.

His mouth curved upward, but the expression failed. He glanced at the ground. "I would have gone to the market if I knew you were coming."

Silly man. "Not that kind of hunger."

His chest lifted as he drew in a slow breath. Was he going to invite her in or what? His gaze met hers and she trembled. Or perhaps he'd only recite all the reasons she wasn't right for him. This was a mistake. Yes, she definitely wanted him—stupid or not—but she wasn't sure she could handle more rejection.

It didn't make sense. She wasn't supposed to want him like that. She'd spent years wanting only one man while all the rest came up short. When Alec touched her the other night, she actually felt something. It felt...right.

It was scary, because she had no other experiences to compare it too. Part of her clung too easily and didn't want to face whatever this thing Alec presented was. But another part of her wanted to say fuck it and face the light, no matter how badly it burned.

Her feet slowly carried her forward, each step weighted with consequence. Perhaps it would just be tonight. Another night lost like a raindrop in a puddle, but she couldn't resist the fall.

Her legs trembled as she stepped onto the small porch. Something about him drew her in. Was it that he challenged her? Saw her? There was no explanation justifying the way he made her feel.

He exposed her, pushed her, sometimes he cracked her open so wide it hurt to see the mess inside.

Nothing had ever felt so complicated and so simple. It was him. Her past read like a blurred oil painting, nothing but smudged lines and wavy truths. He was concise, sharp edges of black on white, no gray.

Circumstances made him unattainable, and perhaps that was the draw. He was her own little form of torture, another thing she wanted, but couldn't have. Why did she do this to herself?

If he could just touch her tonight, hold her so she could fight back the tears, perhaps it would be enough to get her through the next few lonely years. Just tonight.

Stilling as she closed the last foot of distance between them, she shut her eyes and waited. She was tired of looking in from the outside. His scent closed around her and as he softly took her into his arms, everything that was missing seemed to reappear.

Her cheek pressed to his chest, warm and strong. All her rough edges and jagged pieces slipped into place and peace filled her mind. He did that to her. It took her a while to understand he could do such a thing, but he forced her to be real with him and never balked at the Sheilagh he got.

The black faded away to soft amber tones. He was autumn. The winter would return, but for now, she breathed in the radiant burst of color his presence made her feel.

His lips found hers in a slow dance and his kiss was so convincing that she could breathe again. Her arms circled him and he lifted her. She was weightless. She was beautiful. He made her so. He let the color back in, chased out the darkness.

The door shut as his mouth awakened her. His hand brushed over her hair, the presence of its gentle pull reached her soul. Only he did this to her. Only he brought her to life again.

Their bodies wrapped in each other as their kiss erased all others. There were no firsts. There were no terrible seconds. It was only them in that moment in time trapped for as long as they could hold it. They were a bubble floating in the air that would eventually pop and become just another drop falling in the puddle.

He carried her up the narrow stairs and she lay in the soft cushion of his bed. His chest lifted as he breathed looking down at her. "Are you sure?" he asked.

She hadn't been sure of anything in so long. She'd been sleeping through life, walking and making the motions like a shell flits over the sand as the waves of time beat on.

Alec wasn't safe. He wasn't easy. He was the tidal wave that could wash away the last fleck of reality she held. But if he washed her away, away would go all the sadness trapped inside.

Her fingers went to her blouse and slowly released the buttons. His eyes followed each button and his expression remained tense, yet unreadable. Slowly she eased onto her knees and held out a hand to him.

His palm weighed in hers and she drew it close, pressing it between the lapels of her shirt and holding it to her chest. "You make me real. You make me feel, Alec. Please help me."

His weight eased onto the bed, his eyes sad. The hand on her heart slowly traveled over the curve of her shoulder, tickling the tiny hairs at the back of her neck as he brushed the wisps away from her ear.

His breath was a welcome chill over the shell of her ear. He whispered, "I don't have all the answers, Sheilagh, but since meeting you, for the first time, I want to try again."

Her head turned and his mouth caught hers. Easing her back, he crawled on top. Their lips twisted over each other's. His hands found places on her no one had ever touched. No man had ever taken the time he took to learn her in such a way.

Her eyes shut and it wasn't scary, because he was there.

His fingertips kept her in the now, anchored her to what was real. It hurt, feeling the bleak emptiness slip away, because she first had to admit it existed in order to let it go.

His mouth teased over her pulse and her chest tightened at the weight crushing down on her mind, the realization she wasn't normal, that she was broken for reasons and by things she couldn't understand.

A tear trickled past her lashes and wet the soft hairs by her temple. He eased up and looked into her eyes. She knew he saw her, saw all the ugly parts she'd been running from for years.

"Do you always cry when you make love?" he whispered, stroking away her tears and combing them through her hair.

She met his gaze, determined to give him honesty. "No. I usually don't feel. You make me feel, Alec. I want to feel it with you."

He nodded. Did he know? Did he know how sick she really was inside where no one else saw?

"No more illusions, Sheilagh. Show me who you are and I promise I won't run scared."

"I'm glass waiting to fall," she whispered.

"I won't let you break."

His lips found hers and she gave over to the press of his lips, the weight of his body.

He removed her bra and she stretched beneath him. He could have been the first. No one had ever touched her with such tenderness. As his mouth closed over her nipple she held him to her, knowing he likely heard the rapid beating of her heart.

She pulled at his shirt and he sat up, lifting it over his head. He was beautiful. Regardless of his age, Alec was in impeccable shape. His chest was dusted with dark hair and his skin was dark in contrast to hers. Her fingertips dragged over his tapered abdomen. She'd never seen a man quite like him.

He slowly stood and reached for the buttons of her jeans. She kicked off her shoes and toed off her socks as he lowered her pants. As the denim peeled off her legs she waited, waited for the emptiness to seep in, waited for the darkness to return and blank her mind, but it didn't and all she saw was him.

He bent and when he stood he was naked. Her breath sucked tight, filling her lungs. He was different, older, handsome in a distinguished sense she'd never seen before.

The mattress dipped as he crawled beside her. He didn't just get to it. He held her, touched her. It was sexual, but on so many levels it wasn't. His hand traced over her ribs, her hips, her jaw. She was there, ready, but he was in no rush.

"You take my breath away, Sheilagh."

Her lashes lowered as he pressed his lips to hers. His warm hands danced over her flesh and she was amazed she remained in the moment, feeling, experiencing every breath and beat of his heart.

When he eased on top of her she could only see him, his hazel eyes, his dark hair, his broad shoulders. She parted her thighs and he fit himself to her sex. "Look at me."

She'd been looking, but now she saw, saw that this was more than just an encounter to him, saw how much he wanted her. He pressed into her and she inhaled deeply.

He was large and filled her completely. His hands lifted her back off the bed as he began to move. She stretched and preened with each slow thrust, feeling every bit of his presence inside of her, around her, creeping into her soul.

His mouth kissed her shoulders. This was different. He held her in a way no one ever had before. She broke every time in the past, but now she was held in the safety of his arms, protected by the strength that emanated from him. It was as though he was healing all the tiny fractures.

As they rocked slowly her body tightened. He breathed into her shoulder and she cried out as her climax took her to a place where sound silenced and color was born.

His fingertips dragged over her spine. Her feet pressed into the mattress as he thrust with long, deep strokes. It went on and on, and she'd never experienced such a unique sense of unity.

He thrust deep and held her. His dark lashes lowered and his face transformed as bliss took hold of him. Heat bathed her sex and she quivered.

As he lowered her to the bed, his lips pressed a kiss to her temple. Without separating their bodies, he turned them to their sides. She blinked at him, so close she could see every fleck of gold and dark splash of green in his irises.

Slow fingers toyed with the hair behind her ear. "Do you want to sleep?" he asked quietly.

"For a little."

They slept just as they were, bodies connected, face to face. She slept peacefully, knowing he held her and tonight she wouldn't break.

ALEC AWOKE with his arms wrapped in pure heaven. He breathed in her scent and committed it to memory. Tonight he realized something about Sheilagh he was surprised he'd missed until now. Sheilagh was severely depressed.

It all made sense, the whiskey, her procrastination over the past six years, her isolated existence, her fear of introspection. He ached for her and wanted to protect her, because he sensed her preparing to run again. Not from him, but from the life she couldn't escape.

She shifted and he tightened his arms as her copper lashes lifted and soft jade eyes stared into his. "Hi."

Her full burgundy lips curved. It was a genuine smile, a gift for him. His body hardened. While they slept their legs had separated them, but he found her warmth and pressed back inside.

She sighed. "What time is it?"

"I don't know."

She curled her knee over his hip and he rolled slowly to his back. Lowering herself to take all of him, she lifted and slowly began to ride him. Everything she did was sensual.

Her fingers pressed into the hair at his chest and her vibrant hair fell over her shoulders as she glided up and down. It had never felt so right to be inside of a woman.

He brushed the strands over her shoulders and she flexed her hips, rotating slightly and causing them both to moan. Her head tipped back, and he was engulfed by pleasure.

Her beautiful breasts hung full, tipped with perfect peaks. His thumb traced down her velvet skin and she moaned as he teased her nipples. Dropping his other hand to her hip, he lifted and thrust into her.

She cried out as his fingers found her clit and teased her to climax. Watching her quiver over him, jaw slack, throat working, pulse fluttering, he didn't know if there had ever been such a pure display of beauty.

When her climax finished she tumbled onto his chest. He rolled her to her back and thrust hard, filling her. Her legs wrapped around him, ankles knotting at the base of his spine. He pressed into her, going as deep as he could and soon he was shuddering as his own release took hold.

He collapsed beside her and they caught their breath. "We didn't use a condom," she whispered, dousing the soft moment with reality.

He swallowed hard. "I haven't been with anyone in two years. I'm healthy."

"Pregnancy, Alec."

He cleared his throat. "I can't get a woman pregnant. I had a vasectomy after my divorce."

She was quiet. They were only living in a moment, although he wanted more than that, but the fact that he couldn't have children shouldn't affect her. She should be relieved since they'd slipped up.

"What are you thinking about," he finally asked.

"My nieces and nephews."

Was she contemplating children because he couldn't have any? That would mean she was thinking into the future, a place he wanted to visit with her but wouldn't yet mention because he didn't want to push too hard.

"Do you want children?"

She shrugged, but he sensed she was trying to appear indifferent. If they became a couple and actually managed to make this work, there were ways around his situation. It was considered permanent, but he'd known men who had the procedure reversed.

"I come from a big family. That's all I know."

He let that be the last comment on the subject. "Are you hungry?"

"I could eat."

"I can order a pizza. Plain?"

"Okay."

He reached for his phone and dialed the pizza parlor in town. Once the order was placed he stood and used the bathroom. As he emerged from the bathroom he asked, "Do you want to shower?"

She nodded and followed him into the bathroom. Her body was incredible. She had a perfect hourglass figure.

He reached into the stall and turned on the water. She gave him a sheepish look. "What?"

"I need a minute to myself first."

Oh. Right. He nodded and backed out of the bathroom and shut the door. A few seconds later she called, "You can come back in now."

When he entered she was already in the shower. He climbed in behind her and she faced him. Her hair was already wet and darker from the water. Her eyes were large and she smiled at him. Unable to resist, he kissed her.

Their wet bodies wrapped around each other. Everywhere she touched burned. He wanted her again, but the pizza would be there soon.

Reaching for a washcloth, he soaped it up and dragged it over her lily-white flesh. When he reached between her legs she looked away and blushed. He kissed her shoulder then turned and made quick work of washing himself.

She rinsed and stepped out and he followed suit. "I

have a robe hanging on the back of the door. You're welcome to use it," he said as he dried himself off.

The robe swallowed her as she slipped it on. "Do you have a comb I could use?"

He reached in the drawer and handed her his brush. Something inside him tightened at the sight of her using his things and wearing his robe. He liked it.

Tossing his towel in the hamper, he left to find pants. Sheilagh followed him, as quiet as a shadow, and his heart skipped a beat every time their eyes met. "We should go downstairs and wait for the pizza."

Once downstairs she settled onto the sofa. There was a knock at the door and he grabbed his wallet as he let the delivery guy in.

"Hey, Dr. Devereux. How's it hanging?"

"Hey, Steve. I'm good. You not going home for holiday?" he handed over a twenty.

"Nope. Gotta work."

"Well, keep the change."

When Steve looked up to thank him, his eyes caught on Sheilagh. He smiled and nodded. "Thanks. Enjoy your night."

Alec shut the door and turned, box in hand. "Did you want to eat in the living room? I could make a fire."

She had a peculiar expression on her face. He liked that smile. It was mischievous.

"What's so funny?"

"He's in my Astronomy class."

Alec's breath stilled and then he relaxed and shrugged. "Steve's a good kid. I had him last semester. He won't say anything."

He placed the box on the table and went to get plates and napkins. When he returned she said, "You call us kids."

"No, I don't. Well, maybe I do, but I don't think of you as a kid."

"You better not."

She slid two slices onto two plates and he thought for a moment. He didn't think of her as a kid. He thought of her as a woman, so much so, he couldn't stop thinking about her.

"Does our age difference bother you?"

She shrugged and bit into her slice. "No. You don't look forty. And I haven't been a kid in years. When we talk, you make me forget we aren't the same age."

"You don't act like my other students."

She snorted. "I should hope not. If that were the case we'd have a serious problem." She stilled. "Have you ever had an affair with another student?"

The term affair struck him as tawdry and wrong. "No. I was with my wife for a long time. It took years for me to date again. I never met anyone I really wanted to pursue things with. I've been with a few women since the divorce, but never anyone associated with the college."

He pulled off another slice. "Have you ever been with someone my age?"

She placed her plate on the table. "Maybe. I don't usually check their ID."

He blinked at her cavalier reply. "How many were there, Sheilagh?"

She looked away and he regretted asking. "Enough. Every time I wanted it to be different, but every time it was the same. We'd do it. I'd enjoy it for a split second. When it was over we'd ignore the awkward feelings and say goodbye. I never sleep with the same person twice."

"You slept with me twice."

"You're different."

Her words leveled him. He tossed his pizza on the box and pressed her back into the couch as he kissed her. When they pulled apart, he whispered, "You know you're different too."

She looked away. "You didn't finish your pizza."

"I'm hungry for something else."

She smiled. "I like when you do that."

"What?"

She glanced down at her hips. "That."

"I have a confession," he whispered as he licked her neck.

She arched and he pulled open her robe. "What?"

"I *love* doing that. Especially to you."

"Really?"

He kissed down her breasts and over her tummy. "Yes."

Her thighs parted and he scooted lower. Her soft pink folds glistened and he leaned in to taste her. She moaned as he kissed her clit. His thumbs parted her and his tongue speared between her folds.

He fucked her slowly with his mouth until she was writhing beneath his touch. Slipping two fingers inside of her, he reached for her G-spot. Her spine stretched when he found it. His lips closed over her clit and he suckled, pressing into the soft tissue behind the bundle of nerves.

She came hard, her throaty voice calling his name and he licked up every taste. When he finished he rested his cheek on her hip as she panted. "I'll do that as often as you like. You taste amazing."

She sighed. "Sounds like a plan."

Eventually he stood and lit a fire. It wasn't cold, but a fire was nice. He rarely found cause to have one, living by himself. He spread the quilt onto the floor and tossed some pillows over it.

Grabbing a bottle of wine and two glasses, he met her on the floor. "This is nice," she said as he passed her a glass of merlot.

"I haven't done anything like this in years," he admitted. "My romantic side is badly out of practice."

She smirked. "Well, I haven't done this ever, so you're scoring pretty high right now."

They lounged with their backs against the foot of the sofa and stared at the fire. "Are you still going home tomorrow?"

"I have to. My family's expecting me."

"Do you no longer want to?"

She gave a slight motion with her bare shoulder. "You'll be here all alone all week. Everyone's gone. I could hide out here and no one would know."

True. The thought of her staying the week with him, without worry of who might see, sounded spectacular. "That's an option."

"I wasn't inviting myself," she quickly said.

He turned and frowned. "Of course not. I want you to stay with me."

They were silent for a moment. "When I get back everything will go back to the way it was, won't it?"

He didn't know how to answer that. "I need to find out exactly what the policy is for dating students."

"I thought it was against the rules."

"I'm not really sure. It's definitely thought of as inappropriate by the majority, but I haven't found anything in writing yet."

"You looked?"

"Guilty. After the other night I was curious. It took everything I had to leave you like that. I'm sorry."

She wiggled her toes and looked away. "I don't understand why it's taboo. We're adults. I'm not in your class anymore…"

He wished she were. He missed reading her essays and seeing her every few days. "It's a moral issue. If you were still in my class our relationship would be seen as inherently exploitative. It's also a matter of professional conduct. Some might view the relationship between student and teacher as that shared between a therapist and patient. The lines are blurred, as every situation is different, but there is definitely a line there. It's an issue of power and trust."

"I don't see why it's anyone's business but ours."

He twirled a piece of her hair around his fingers. It was still damp from their shower. "It isn't. If we keep our business private we shouldn't have a problem."

After a few minutes she asked, "Are we just sleeping together? Is that what this is?"

He turned and faced her. She was so tough yet so fragile. "If it's just sex, Sheilagh, I'm not interested. I want you, all of you."

She smiled ruefully, as if afraid to believe his words. "Nobody's ever said that to me before."

His heart raced. He didn't want to push too hard. "I'd like to show you a lot of the things I think you've missed along the way. I know I'm not always easy, but I would never intentionally hurt you. I…I want to know that what we have is something I can count on, something we can both count on."

Her smile grew. "Are you asking me to be your girlfriend, Dr. Devereux?"

That was exactly what he was trying to do. "Yes."

Her lips pressed tight, but the smile was there, impossible to hide. "I've never really had a *boyfriend*. I mean, I've dated and had sex, but…"

Mind-boggling. "How would you like one?"

"I think it would be nice."

He kissed her, tired of seeing that cheeky smirk. She was taunting him. Against her lips, he asked, "Does that mean yes?"

She giggled. "Yes."

An hour later she sat across from him and made the call.

"Mum?"

The voice on the other line was loud and he could make out the words almost perfectly.

"Sheilagh, love! I'm cooking up a storm, getting' ready for your return home. The boys have a surprise for you."

"What?" He saw she was happy when she spoke to her family.

"I'm not supposed to say a word, but you know me. My loose lips have been sinking ships since I learned to talk. They've fussed with your room."

She stiffened. "What do you mean?" Then she growled. "What did they do?"

"It's nothin' too terrible. They've painted it pink."

"*What?* Those cocksuckers!"

"That they are, love, but they did it because they're missin' you. You know how they rag on you out of love."

"I'm going to kill them."

Alec wasn't sure why this was such a big deal. It sounded to him like her brothers cared for her very much.

"So what time will we be seein' you tomorrow?"

Her scowl faded. "About that... I don't think I'm leaving until Wednesday now."

"Oh?"

"I sort of volunteered to help out one of the professors at the school."

Gaping at her, Alec silently laughed and nibbled her knee. She kicked him.

"Oh, that's nice of you. I can't say your brothers will be happy. They still have paint left."

"You tell them the next person who screws with my stuff is losing a kidney."

"Will do, love. Call me Tuesday so I know when to expect you."

"Okay, Mum. I love you."

"I love you too, dear."

She lowered the phone and sighed. "I'm going to need a sharp knife."

He raised a brow. "I take it you don't like pink?"

"I don't like people messing with my stuff. I'll castrate every one of them."

Breathing in a slow breath, he tried for a lighter subject. "Do you think your mum's upset you're not coming until Wednesday?"

"Maybe. She understands."

"So...helping a professor?"

She laughed. "What was I supposed to say?"

"No, that works. As a matter of fact I have something you could help me with right now."

She tossed the phone on the couch and crawled toward him. "Is that so?"

"Yes. Big problem."

"Mmm, how big?"

"Huge."

She climbed on top of him and pressed him to his back. "I'm intrigued."

He found her nipple and pinched the tip. She gasped and her eyes softened. "I love how responsive you are to my touch. I could spend days naked with you and never once get bored."

"Well, we have days now."

"Thank God." He kissed her.

THERE WAS NO MORNING. Every minute blended together in passionate touches, secret smiles, and stolen caresses. Their time together seemed a gift and neither of them was anxious to leave their safe little haven.

Clothes were useless. If she covered herself, he stripped her. They couldn't go more than an hour or two without finding themselves tangled into one. He made love to her in every room of the house and each time it amazed him how perfectly they fit.

By Monday, they were exhausted. They slept wherever their bodies fell and when they woke they ate, snuggled, and made love some more. Nothing existed aside from them.

He knew the world was going on around them, but for the first time in his life he didn't care about the news or friends or even his work. Everything stopped so that he could hide away with her.

He'd tried to pull her into the light and she somehow managed to tempt him into her cave. It wouldn't always be like this. Once classes started up again they'd be forced to keep their distance until they managed to find stolen moments to be as they wanted. What they had now was an illusion of the real thing, but he desperately wanted to believe it could always be this great.

He sat up in bed as Sheilagh sauntered in carrying a bowl of cherries. "You have no food."

"You sound like my son."

"I found a jar of cherries."

She placed them on his stomach and the cool glass made him jump. She straddled his hips and fed him one. His lips closed over her fingers as he sucked down the berry and all its juice.

Reaching into the bowl, he fished out a cherry and held it to her lips. As she bit at it he pulled it away. She laughed and he teased her again, her soft mouth chasing after the offering. His fingers dragged the cherry over the slope of her breast, leaving a trail of pink in its path. Leaning forward, he licked over the juice and pulled the tight tip of her nipple into his mouth.

Cherries pushed aside, he flipped her to her back and tasted skin. Her hair formed a cloud over the rumpled bedding as her arms stretched into the pillows. His mouth worked down her belly and she moaned.

He licked at her slit, loving her taste, and pressed her thighs wide. She was such a good girl, opening for him. His body shivered at the unique dynamic they seemed to share. His pride reveled in the way she surrendered to his touch. He ate at her until she was crying out. Every climax she had was stunning.

"I want to do that to you," she breathed.

He glanced at her and smiled. Moving to his back he folded his arms behind his head. She crawled over his knees and licked his cock. Breath sucked into his lungs as she took him deep to the back of her throat.

His fingers gathered her hair as she pumped her mouth over his engorged flesh. His hips lifted, meeting each motion with a thrust. His body tightened and she cupped his sack. He groaned at her gentle touch.

"Sheilagh." He needed more of her. He released her hair and nudged her round bottom over his chest. "Come here." Her mouth never left his cock as he rotated her body. His hands guided her thighs over his shoulders, her breath still teasing his cock.

Leaning up, he licked her sex some more. She moaned over his cock. It was glorious. His fingers dug into the soft flesh of her ass as he ate her. She sucked him harder the more excited she got. His thumb teased at the small rosette of her ass and he pressed the tip inside.

She made a high-pitched sound in the back of her throat that vibrated up his spine. "You like that?" he asked, kissing her swollen folds.

She moaned and he continued to probe her with his thumb. His free hand reached for her breasts dangling over his stomach. He cupped and plucked at her there.

The scruff of his chin scraped over her clit and she seemed to like that, too. Releasing her breast, he spread her cheeks and licked her from front to back. He eased a finger deep in her sex and began fingering her hard, relentlessly. Adding another, and finally fitting three into her tight sheath, he drove his wrist forward with quick, hard thrusts.

She cried out and doubled the speed at which she sucked him. He leaned in and tongued her little rosette. She deep throated him and shocked him by pressing into the sensitive span of muscle just beneath his sack. His climax rushed out of him, filling her mouth and she never stopped.

His body locked and he shouted her name. When he collapsed back to the pillows, she softly licked over his length. Never before in his life had he shared such an intense sexual experience with another.

Her swollen mouth kissed up his stomach, causing his muscles to jolt and twitch. She shifted off of him and settled into the curve of his arm, sighing. He kissed her hair and reached for the blankets.

They had two days left like this. Two days and then she'd leave for four and when she came back everything would be different.

CHAPTER 7

I could watch him sleep for hours. He's so
beautiful, he should have been a statue
carved by some artist. I haven't slept in
well over twenty-four hours, which is
odd. I'm afraid if I sleep I'll wake up and
discover it's all been a dream. I know it
will eventually end, but right now it's real
and I'm in it with no desire to be
anywhere else.

Wednesday was nerve wracking. She didn't
want to go home, yet she did. Over the
past five days she'd discovered something about herself.
She could actually be herself and let down her guard and

when she did…it was okay. Everything was fine. Alec accepted her for who she was and that satisfied her needs in a way she'd never experienced before.

Luckily, she had her suitcase with her when she'd arrived on Friday. She'd been living out of it ever since. Currently, she was in Alec's basement waiting for the washer to finish while he slept upstairs in bed.

"Sheilagh?"

Okay, maybe he wasn't sleeping. "I'm down here."

He came down the stairs and wrapped his arms around her. "I love that you traipse around my house without a stitch of clothing on." He kissed her shoulder. "If you've been naked all this time, what are you washing?"

"My delicates."

His hand cupped her breast as his lips dragged over her shoulder. Tipping her head back, she leaned into him. "Can I have you like this?" he whispered, trailing his hand down her belly to her sex.

"You can have me however you want."

He eased her shoulders forward. "I want you like this."

The width of his cock slid over her sex. The cool press of the washer on her breasts and belly made her shiver. She widened her stance and he thrust into her, hard and fast.

His strong hands gripped her hips, pulling her into him as he plunged deep. He possessed her. Her body was no longer solely hers. Alec never demanded too much. He always had a polite way of asking, but the more time they spent together the more she liked when he simply took as if he needed to have her in order to take his next breath.

His hips smacked into hers and she keened with each thrust. He didn't fuck her like other men had. Every time he touched her he removed another sad memory. He fucked her like a man taking possession of a woman. He adored her body and laughed at her jokes. He understood her and that was a first—a scary first. Being so understood left little room to hide.

His fingers fit between her thighs where their bodies connected. Her clit was pinched tight as he pounded into her. He rubbed the little bud and she felt her pleasure climb. "Yes, yes, yes, yes, yes! Oh, Alec!"

His hand gripped her breast and cupped her forcefully. He moaned and she felt him come inside of her. The warm weight of his cheek, damp with perspiration, pressed into the blade of her shoulder as his hand fell away.

"Don't go."

His whisper was so low she might have imagined it. She shifted and he withdrew from her sex. The wash cycle had finished and the room was quiet. She twisted to see his face.

He looked so sad.

"I'm coming back in a couple days." She cupped his jaw and he kissed her palm.

Looking down, he whispered, "I'll miss you."

"You could come with me."

He stilled, his eyes searching her face. "What about—"

"Nobody knows who you are there. You're just Alec. We won't have to hide. You could…you could meet my family. If you want to."

"How long do I have to pack?"

She smiled. Something light and wonderful filled her chest. "I'll help you."

ALEC INSISTED they take his car. It was warm and the roads wouldn't be a problem so Sheilagh agreed.

She hadn't told the others she was bringing him with her. No one, aside from Kelly, knew he existed. They'd been on the road for almost two hours and his nifty GPS system was making her job as co-pilot easy.

"How often do you cry?"

She faced him, totally taken off guard by the random question. "What?"

"How often do you cry?"

"I don't cry. Not really."

"Don't lie to me, Sheilagh. It's transparent."

She recalled the other night when they'd first made love. She cried then and she probably shouldn't have let herself be so open. "I don't know. I cry when I watch sad movies."

His lips tightened. He switched lanes and they drove in

silence for a mile. "Will you talk to me about it eventually?"

She frowned. "Talk to you about what, Alec?"

"Everything you keep inside."

"Why are you asking me this?"

"Because."

"Because? That's your explanation? Come on, Alec, level with me."

"If we can ask ourselves questions we can better understand who we are. If we aren't happy with our life's course, we can choose to think differently and change it."

"What makes you think I'm not happy?"

"Because when I watch you I see sadness. It isn't always there. I'm sure you have most of the world fooled. But I've seen it. I've seen you at your most vulnerable and you've said things that tell me I'm right."

She couldn't deny it. Unless the world was moving a million miles an hour and she was laughing along with the ride, she wasn't okay. When life lulled and time settled as if catching its breath, she sometimes became anxious or scared. Sometimes that anxiety turned over and rolled away until there was nothing left. The nothingness was the worst.

She liked adrenaline. She liked booze. So long as her heart was racing the nothingness stayed away. Then there were days she couldn't keep it out and she felt dead inside, but forced to live through the lifelessness.

That was how she'd started doing stupid things. If she

was occupied with a man, she wasn't thinking. Her mind was alert and moving, but when that man left, everything crashed back to nothing again. But with the absence of her self-respect it was twice as lonely.

Sometimes she wondered how long the hurt would last. She worried she'd become addicted to sadness, yet she hated it all the same. For reasons she still couldn't decipher, losing the first love of her life to her brother seemed to cement her into a place she desperately wanted to leave. It didn't seem enough to change her so dramatically, yet she was quite different from the girl she once was. That was why she acted as if she didn't have a care in the world. If she didn't like the woman she'd become, surely no one else would.

However, Alec saw glimpses of the real her and seemed to like her. She didn't have that crash back to nothingness with him. Of course, he hadn't left her yet. If he eventually left…she didn't want to think about what that would feel like.

She turned her palm up and he, seeing the unspoken invitation, settled his hand in hers. "Thank you."

"For?"

"You make me happy."

"I want to talk about the philosophy."

She groaned. "Oh, come on!"

"Please."

Huffing and pulling her hand back to cross over her chest, she sighed. "What?"

"Epictetus, a Greek philosopher, believed trying to govern things we have no control over was the cause of emotional turmoil. What we *can* control is the way we think. If we stop worrying about things we can't control, like other's opinions of us, we can find peace."

"Do you think I care what others think of me?"

"Yes."

She jerked her gaze to his and gave him a look of disbelief. "Well, I don't."

"Why are you here?"

"In the car?"

"No, at Princeton."

"Because I chose to be."

"Chose? Or because you didn't want your father to think less of you when he found out you were going to take your clothes off on a stage?"

"You're being an asshole."

"That's not my intention. I'm only asking you a question."

"Fine. But that's my dad. Most girls don't want their dad to be ashamed of them."

"I understand. I also know you're quite stoic. You can endure a certain amount of hardship without showing your feelings. But I worry what years of holding all the pain in is doing to you."

She didn't want to talk about this anymore. "I'm done talking about this."

"I want to teach you Stoic Philosophy. I think you'd benefit from it."

They were silent for a while. Perhaps he realized she'd reached her limit of psychobabble bullshit. She didn't like being put under a microscope. Suddenly claustrophobic, she wanted to get out of the car.

"Can we stop? I need to stretch my legs."

"Sure. There's a rest stop in about ten miles—"

"Can you just pull over?"

He turned on his signal and eased off the road. "Are you okay?"

"No. I need to get out of this car." Her hand pulled at the handle, but it wouldn't open. She tried to unlock it, but that was the window button. "How do you open the fucking door?"

The locks disengaged and she opened the door, yanking off her seat belt. She paced along the shoulder of the road.

ALEC CURSED as the door slammed in his face. He waited for the upcoming traffic to pass and then climbed out of the car. Sheilagh paced along the side of the road, her face tight with tension and her mouth whispering words he couldn't hear.

"Sheilagh?"

She ignored him.

"Sheilagh."

She continued to pace. He stepped closer. "Sheilagh."

"I don't want to talk anymore!"

He caught her in his arms and she burst into tears. Wrapping his arms around her tight, he held her and she cried and pounded weakly on his chest. "I'm sorry," he said, kissing her hair. "I'm sorry."

"Why do you get to see things in me no one else does? You're the one person I don't want to see that stuff." She sniffled.

He couldn't let her go. "Because I want to know the real you. I don't care what you give the rest of the world. I want the real you."

"Why though? It isn't pretty."

"It's you."

She seemed to sag against him. His hand ran up and down her back, soothing her the only way he knew how in that moment.

They stood that way for several minutes and she slowly started to calm. "Do you want to keep going or do you want to stay here a while longer?"

"I don't know what I want."

He sighed and held her. Cars passed and they simply stood there for the better part of twenty minutes. When she seemed ready, she stepped away and got back in the car.

Alec returned to the driver's side and hesitated. "If

you've changed your mind, I can drop you off at your parents' and go to a hotel."

Her eyes, still wet from tears, turned on him. "Why?"

"I didn't mean to upset you. We're more than halfway there. If you'd rather I not be with you—"

"I want you with me."

"Are you sure?"

She nodded and twisted in her seat. "All of this, the ugly stuff, it's me, Alec, not you."

"It's not ugly, Sheilagh. It's human. I just want to help you get it out, whatever it is."

She kissed his knuckles. "Thank you for being so patient with me."

His fingers traced her jaw. "Sadness hurts. You aren't the only person struggling with it."

"If I can ignore it, I don't struggle."

"Is that what you want? To go on pretending it doesn't exist, that this is as good as it gets?"

"Isn't it?"

He smiled sadly. "No, sweetheart. There is so much more to life once we stop fearing the things we can't control."

"I don't know why I'm like this. I'm generally a happy person."

"We'll figure it out when you're ready. The fact that you want to be happy is a good place to start."

"Please don't mention any of this to my family."

"Of course not." He kissed her hand. "This is just between us."

THEY REACHED Center County just before dusk. The GPS kept losing its signal as Sheilagh predicted, so she provided directions the rest of the way.

Alec steered the car onto a dirt road lined with trees and as they traveled further up the windy path, a log cabin crept into view. "That's it," she said, practically bouncing in her seat.

"It's lovely."

She sighed. "My dad built it."

His brows shot up. "Really?"

"Yup. Right after my grandfather shot him."

"Your grandfather shot your father?"

She waved the comment away. "It's a long story. Park over there, next to the truck."

He pulled beside an old battered Chevy and shut off the car. "Ready?"

"The question is are *you* ready? When I said my family was nuts I don't think you really grasped the veracity of my assertion."

He was sure they were a completely normal family, thus a little quirky in their own way. He smiled reassuringly then stilled. "Um, there's a woman on the porch aiming a shotgun at my Beemer."

She turned and laughed. "That's my mum. She doesn't know your car." Her finger pressed the button and the tinted glass lowered. "Ma! It's me! Put the gun back!"

"Sheilagh? Oh! I thought it was some lost drug lord in that fancy car." She lowered the weapon. "Who's with you?"

Sheilagh opened the door and gave him a nod. "Showtime."

He followed her out of the car and waved. Her mother, a robust woman with faded red hair, frowned at him. He dropped his hand.

He followed Sheilagh up the steps and she announced, "Mum, this is Alec. He's a friend of mine from Princeton."

"He's a wee bit old to be in college, love." Lowering her voice—not by much—she whispered, "Is he slow?"

"Ma!"

Alec had seen and heard enough. He approached the woman and held out a hand. "It's a pleasure to meet you, Mrs. McCullough."

"He's a Brit!"

Sheilagh lowered her face into her hands and groaned. "Alec, meet my mother."

Sheilagh's mother attempted a smile, but it seemed more like a nervous twitch. "Well, come in, come in."

Dropping his hand again, he followed the two women inside. The house was incredible. Exposed wooden walls, rustic furniture, it was definitely lived-in.

The large kitchen had a long farm-style table. "Your

father should be back from the lumberyard soon. Dinner's almost done."

Sheilagh went to the stove and lifted the lid off a steaming pot. She breathed in the aroma, which he couldn't place, and sighed happily. "I've missed your food, Mum."

Her mother smiled and smacked her hand off the lid. "Not until your father gets here. Go wash those grubby paws. I tell you, we've grown used to having the house to ourselves. It'll be interesting having company again. I'll have to remind your father to keep it down at night. Turns out an empty nest brings out the wild beast in him."

Sheilagh stilled at the sink. "Eeew."

"You should be grateful, dearie. With divorce the way it is nowadays, you're lucky to have parents who still enjoy each other's touch."

"Please stop," Sheilagh said in a monotone voice. "Before I have to find a carving knife and gouge out my mind's eye." She dried her hands and came to retrieve him from where he stood by the entrance to the kitchen. "Do you want something to drink? Sometimes being drunk around the family helps."

"Oh! Do you want some whisky, Alex? I have some right here." Sheilagh's mother opened the cabinet under the sink. He spotted blue window cleaner and several bottles of Tullamore Dew.

"It's actually Alec," he corrected.

"What's that, Alex? Shei, get your friend a cup."

Yeah. Maybe whiskey would help.

He watched as the woman poured a mug full of whiskey and slid it to him. He didn't usually partake in whiskey, but he sipped it anyway.

"So, how is it you know my daughter, Alex? Are you in classes together?"

"*Alec*, Mum, not Alex."

"Ah, we had one class together, but Sheilagh's roster changed."

"So you're a student? You must be taking some of those postgraduate classes, being that you're so much older. How old are you, if you don't mind me askin'?"

"Mum, why didn't you tell me Kate was pregnant?" Sheilagh interrupted, giving him a surreptitious wink.

"Did I forget to mention that? You know me. I've got so many grandbabies now it's hard to keep track." She turned and smiled at him. "This will be my tenth."

"Eleventh, Mum," Sheilagh corrected.

Her mother stilled and glanced at the ceiling. "Eleven? Is that right?"

Sheilagh quickly ticked off names on her fingers. "Skylar, Hannah, Frankie, Michaels, Tallulah, Liam, Declan, Lachlan, Gianna, Nate, and now this one. Eleven."

"Goodness! No wonder I'm tired."

"Maureen? Whose fancy car's in the driveway?"

Alec looked to Sheilagh at the sound of a man's deep voice. Her face split with a grin and she whispered, "Daddy." Her body bolted out of her chair and ran to the door. "Daddy!"

"Hey! My little Shei-Devil!" When they returned to the kitchen, the man had his arm around Sheilagh's shoulder as she leaned into him. He was a large man with thick arms covered in worn, red plaid flannel.

He approached his wife and slapped her right on the ass. Sheilagh's mother hiccuped a gasp and giggled.

Sheilagh scrunched up her face. "You guys are gross."

Her father turned. "So tell me all about Jersey—" His smile fell as his eyes locked with Alec's. "Who are you?"

Alec stood and held out his hand. "I'm Alec Devereux. I'm a friend of your daughter's."

The man scowled at his hand and crossed his thick arms over her barrel chest. "Define friend."

Once more, Alec dropped his hand and swallowed. Maybe this hadn't been the best idea.

Sheilagh smacked her father in the arm and got his attention. "Dad, Alec's a good guy. Be nice."

"I have guns," Mr. McCullough said.

"Yes, your wife showed me," Alec said, his laugh falling away as Sheilagh's father's eyes narrowed.

He did quick math in his head. Sheilagh said her eldest sister was thirty-five. That made her parents approximately in their mid-fifties, early sixties. Alec was somewhere in the middle, sixteen years older than Sheilagh and roughly sixteen years younger than her parents. Glancing at her father, who was still glaring at him, he assumed the man was doing the same sort of math in his head.

"Maureen, do the boys know Sheilagh's home—and that she brought a friend?" her father asked.

"I told the lot of them she was coming, but we weren't sure when she'd be getting here. Her friend was a surprise, so they won't be expectin' him."

How many brothers? Five? It might have been a very bad decision to come here. "I'm going to get our bags out of the car," he announced, quietly slipping away.

She glanced up at him with questioning eyes. She had to understand this was a bit overwhelming. She'd warned him, yet he hadn't been prepared for shotguns and interrogations.

He avoided placing a kiss on her head and glanced over to her father who seemed to be typing a text into his phone. Right. Likely alerting the natives.

Alec excused himself and went to the car. As he unloaded his and Sheilagh's bags, there was the crunch of gravel to his left. He turned, expecting to see a bear or another crazy person aiming a gun at him. It was neither.

A man with hair to his shoulders approached. Arms crossed at his chest, tattoo showing past his sleeve, and a barely contained wild glint in his light eyes. "You here with Sheilagh?"

Where the hell did this guy come from? There were no new cars aside from her father's truck. They were in the middle of nowhere. There was a barn in the distance, but that was it. Had this guy come out of the wilderness? He looked as if he could have. There was something rugged and unrefined about him.

"Are you one of Sheilagh's brothers?"

The man's stare zeroed in on Alec. He chewed his lower lip, seeming completely at ease with intimidating the company. He was young, perhaps thirty.

"She ain't my sister." There was a twang to his speech that didn't match the McCullough's clipped, slightly Irish, dialect.

Then who are you? Again, he attempted manners. Placing the bag on the ground, he extended his hand. "I'm Alec Devereux, a friend of Sheilagh's from Princeton."

The man eyed his hand with disinterest. What the hell did these people have against shaking hands? They were quite uncivilized when it came to common courtesy and etiquette. His English upbringing couldn't quite fathom their welcome.

"What kind'a friend?" the man asked.

Enough of this. "A good friend. Who are you?"

"Just another keeper. You'll want to watch yourself."

He frowned. "Pardon?"

The man twisted his head slowly, cracking various vertebrae in the process. "Shei ain't ever brought a man home. You look a bit…old…to be her *friend.*"

Was this someone she had a past with? The door to the barn in the distance opened and another man stepped out. This one without a shirt, his body incredibly cut with muscle and covered in various tattoos. His eyes were hidden under the shadow of his Jeff cap.

"Who's this?" the newcomer asked the man who'd been staring him down.

The first man tipped his chin. "Sheilagh's friend."

"Sheilagh doesn't have friends we don't know."

Alec arched a brow. She'd been living in a different state for eight months. Of course she had other friends. He didn't offer to shake the newcomers hand, tired of having the offer ignored. "I'm Alec."

"Alec," the man said, as if testing the word. "Shei brought you here?"

He nodded.

Suddenly the man shouted, "Sheilagh! Get your ass out here before we string up your 'friend'!"

The door on the porch whipped open and suddenly his little redhead turned ill-mannered and slightly redneck. "Don't you come up here trying to intimidate my company! Take your sorry asses on home and come back when you've found some manners. Alec, come inside. You don't need to bother with them."

Both men slowly smirked. "Take a McCullough out of Center County, but you'll never get the McCullough out of her. I can see that prep school of yours still has its work cut out, Shei-Devil."

She smiled, the expression slow and full of hidden affection. "No fancy neighborhood's gonna change me,

Luke. You should have known better if you were hoping to send me away and get some debutante back."

Ah, so this was Luke. That meant the other man was likely Tristan. He didn't know how he felt, seeing such a young—obviously handsome—man and knowing Sheilagh had been in love with him. Whatever label he put on the emotion, it wasn't pretty. It helped knowing the man was gay and not a threat to his relationship.

Luke laughed. "Pretty brazen, bringing a friend back with you, Shei-Devil."

"Well, you know me. I like to shake things up."

She didn't look at Tristan. As a matter of fact she remained on the porch, keeping her distance. He glanced at the other man who was watching her, a shrewd set to his mouth.

Alec frowned. Perhaps gay wasn't the proper term. Perhaps this man was bi. When he looked at Sheilagh there was something there. It was more than platonic affection. Alec interpreted it as territorial.

"How come you didn't come home on Saturday?" Tristan finally said, accusation in his tone.

Sheilagh shrugged. "I had things I wanted to do."

His gaze cut to Alec's who met it, mano-a-mano, and cut away again, back to her. "I'll bet. Tomorrow night we're hitting O'Malley's. You like whiskey, *friend?*"

What was it with these people and their whiskey? Alec sensed this was some sort of test. "When it suits."

Tristan nodded. "Good. I'll have your shots ready."

The door to the house opened and Mrs. McCullough came out. She smiled the moment she saw Tristan and Luke. "Oh, I didn't know you boys were here. Well, come and eat. The food's gettin' cold and I didn't cook for nothin.'"

The men grinned slowly. As they stepped toward the house Tristan made a point to walk directly in Alec's path, playing a sort of chicken until Alec stepped aside.

He frowned and watched them go in the house.

"Ignore them," Sheilagh said.

He climbed the steps slowly and stepped close to her. "Is this what I should expect from all your relatives?"

"No, Colin's nice."

Great. One out of nine. He placed a soft kiss on her lips and a throat cleared from the door.

"Mind taking your lips off my baby?"

Alec stepped back. He met the eyes of her father and simply stared, unsure what to say. The man gave him a hard look and walked away. This should be an interesting four days.

SHEILAGH'S MOTHER talked like she was propelled to do so by a small motor. There was no filter to her words and he soon realized when Sheilagh said her family was liberal, she'd extended the label as far as it would stretch.

"Sammy wants another baby, but Colin's been busy at

the school. I hear they've been going at it so hard the church bells are rockin' in their wake. I think he's making up for lost time, he is. Kate's been sick with this pregnancy. She's older now and her body isn't much caring for the stress of another babe. Ashlynn's been busy with the farm so I've been going there a few times a week to sit with Nathanial, angel that he is. Gianna's starting to walk and the twins are devilishly handsome, of course. Poor Finnegan has his hands full. Your brother, Braydon, is working on some big deal in Pittsburg and hardly has time to remember he has family elsewhere, but we'll forgive him. I do think Kelly has finally grown up some. Wouldn't you agree, Frank?"

Frank, Sheilagh's father, grunted and continued cutting his meat. Alec kept his head down, weary of looking up and finding threatening glances pinned on him.

"How long are you staying, Shei?" Tristan asked.

Unease had Alec twitching at the way the man shortened her name, never mind the inflection in his tone.

"We have to go back early Sunday morning."

"What are you majoring in, Alec?" Tristan asked.

He cleared his throat. "My concentration is philosophy."

Sheilagh drew in a breath. "Actually, Alec's a—"

"Pass the salt, sweetheart."

Everyone stilled. He'd meant to cut her off from announcing he was a professor, but slipped with the endearment. Frank stood and cleared his plate. The man lingered at the sink, presenting them his back. Tristan and Luke eyed him challengingly. Maureen, who was still chatting around them, slipped in a quick prompt for Sheilagh to slide over the salt, but then went back to her abridgment of the current McCullough events and doings.

Sheilagh swallowed and reached for the salt. She slowly slid it to him and looked down. Clearing her throat she said, "So…is Sue still working at the bar? Have they hired anyone new?"

"Oh, Sue's still there. She's been wonderful. Kelly's also hired a young woman named—Tabby is it?—Luke knows her. Sweet girl. Sort of dumb, but in a nice way. The boys seem to like her."

"Mum, it isn't nice to call a woman dumb," Sheilagh said.

"Oh, well, I didn't mean anything by it. It's just that she can't be too smart if she's lettin' every man in Center County access her knickers. A smart woman only shows her knickers to the good ones. Luke, have you seen Tabby's knickers?"

He watched as Sheilagh bent her head and laughed silently as her brother sighed.

"Her name is Tanya, Mum, and no, I have no idea what her knickers look like."

"What about you, Tristan?"

"I'm afraid I have not, Maureen."

"See," Sheilagh's mother continued. "Dumb. She isn't showing them to any of the nice bachelors in town."

Sheilagh put down her fork and muttered. "God save me from this woman."

Dinner carried on much the same. Frank left the kitchen and soon Tristan and Luke said goodnight, reminding him once more that they'd be seeing him tomorrow. Maureen went off to bed and Sheilagh carried her bag upstairs, saying she was going to take a shower.

Alec waited a few minutes, finishing his whiskey, which he was growing accustomed to, and slowly made his way to the stairs.

"Alec."

He stilled and found Frank sitting in the den watching him. He placed his bag by the stairs and entered the room.

"Have a seat, son."

No one had called him son in years, but he stepped into the room and sat on the chair across from Sheilagh's father.

"Are you sleeping with my daughter?"

Wow. If anything, this family was direct. "The relationship your daughter and I share is our own business. Out of respect for her, I'm not going to answer that."

"I'll take that as a yes. How old are you?"

"I'm forty."

"My daughter's twenty-four."

"I'm aware."

"What exactly does a forty year old do at a college?"

"I teach."

Frank nodded slowly. "That makes a bit more sense. Is Sheilagh a student of yours?"

"She was, but she withdrew from my class."

His eyes narrowed. "Why?"

Alec shifted. "I'm sure you're aware your daughter is brilliant."

"She can be."

"Yes, well, she's also very stubborn. She hasn't quite come to terms with her circumstances yet. Princeton is among one of the best schools in the country and we, the instructors, intend to challenge every mind that walks our halls. I challenged your daughter to give me her best. She didn't and she knows it. When I gave her a grade she couldn't abide, she dropped the course."

"Did this grade have anything to do with your intentions for my daughter?"

"My only intentions, at that time, were to teach her. I can't teach someone set on not learning."

"Sheilagh has a lot to learn. She's book smart, always has been, but she lets her heart get in the way of common-sense from time to time."

"I agree."

Frank scraped his fingers slowly along the stubble covering his jaw. "I'm not sure how I feel about your relationship."

Alec nodded. He couldn't dictate others' emotions. Others also couldn't dictate his actions. He didn't want to cause trouble between Sheilagh and her family, but he wasn't planning on letting her go simply because others didn't approve.

"I have a son. It isn't always easy watching strangers enter our children's lives. Innately, we want to protect them."

"How old is your son?"

"Twenty-two."

Frank's brows lifted. "Some would say he'd be more suited to call on my daughter."

"Some, but not anyone that knows her. Sheilagh's wise beyond her years. She needs someone who can challenge her, mentally and emotionally. We have a good relationship and share a mutual respect for each other. I'd never intentionally hurt your daughter, sir."

He nodded. "I appreciate hearing you say so. Saves me bullets."

Alec hesitated and then decided to push ahead. "She's contemplating leaving school after this semester. I feel this would be a mistake. Sheilagh seems to need time to find herself and come to terms with who she is."

The man's expression was unreadable. "So long as you're not the one deciding for her, I'll trust her to come to that realization on her own."

"I care for your daughter very much."

"Good. I'll remember that after my sons get ahold of you. If you're sincere, you'll feel the same when you leave here. If you have a change of heart, you'll leave her alone and I'll never see you again."

"What are you guys doing?"

They both turned and saw Sheilagh standing in the doorway, her hair wet, pajama pants patterned with frogs, a luck of the Irish shirt covering her small frame, and two extremely juvenile cow slippers on her feet. Alec smiled.

"We were just having a chat," he said.

She nervously looked at her father. The man stood and kissed his daughter's head. "I'm off to bed. Sleep tight, Devil. I'll see you in the morning."

"Goodnight, Dad."

She stared at him after her father disappeared up the stairs. "Everything okay?"

Alec nodded and held out his hand. She came to him and snuggled onto his lap. "If your family has a gun safe, maybe we should hide the key."

She laughed. "They're just messing with you. They aren't used to me bringing home men. I'm sure they treated my sister's boyfriends the same."

He nuzzled her shoulder and kissed her neck. "Where are we sleeping?"

She sighed. "In the pink nightmare that is now my room."

"Are you ready for bed?"

"Yes."

He followed her up to her room. Pink was a lovely color, often shown on the belly of a blushing cloud or on the cheeks of a shy woman. Sheilagh's room was not that sort of pink. It was hideous, the sort of putrid color medicine came in. Her brothers had painted every wall and every piece of furniture, finishing off their prank with a ruffled nightmare on her bed.

Alec placed his bag on the chair and laughed. "Why would they do this?"

"Because they love me. Of course now I'll have to retaliate. Did you bring any black clothes with you? At some point we're going out ninja style and getting even. I'm not sure what I'll do yet, but they'll be sorry."

He unzipped his luggage and removed his shirt. "I have a feeling, after tomorrow night, I'll enjoy getting a little retribution where your brothers are concerned."

She grinned and kissed him. "Those bitches are going down."

*A*lec saw a different side of Sheilagh the longer they stayed in Center County. Here she seemed freer, more comfortable to be herself. However, her behavior sometimes shrieked *performance*.

She took him for a tour of their property on the ATVs. He'd spent a good hour after the tour was finished trying to unclench. He didn't mind the speed, but the ramp jumping, close encounters with sharp mountain edges, and spiraling through muddy puddles he could do without. Still, he was fascinated by her uninhibitedness.

Sheilagh was wild and untamed. It was a side to her that was sexy as hell and he'd barely been able to keep his hands off of her when they returned to the house. But where there was one McCullough, there were many, he soon learned. And getting her alone seemed impossible.

That morning he'd woken up in her bed, made love to

her, and then went to find the bathroom. There was no other incident in his life that came remotely close to stirring the guilty confusion he felt when he stepped out of her room and came face to face with Frank.

The man gave him a cold look and kept walking. Alec had no intention of being disrespectful. He was forty years old, God damn it. Yet he suddenly felt eighteen again.

When they returned to the house after riding the quads, Maureen made them supper and chatted away. His jeans were covered with splashes of dried mud and his skin smelled of sweat and pine. He decided to shower after dinner and left Sheilagh for some private time with her family.

As he was buttoning up his shirt, she entered the bedroom. She smiled and shut the door. "Hello, Dr. Devereux."

He rolled his eyes. "You look like you're up to something."

She sashayed over to him and ran a finger down the buttons of his shirt, not stopping until she reached the zipper of his pants. "When you wear shirts like this you remind me of Alec the teacher."

He didn't know what kind of bar O'Malley's was, but he knew he'd be up against several protective brothers that night. He thought if he dressed respectable they might be respectful. He was probably wrong. "Is that a bad thing?"

"Not at all." She fit her hands into his back pockets and pulled him closer. Her breasts pressed against his chest.

She hadn't showered yet and her hair smelled of the outdoors. She wore muddy jeans and a tight T-shirt that had a vintage silkscreen for the cereal Lucky Charms. He reached up and plucked out the clip holding her hair in a twist. Copper strands coiled over her shoulder and she smiled.

The look in her green eyes was full of intent and his body hardened. "Did you lock the door?"

"Yes."

"And is there something I can do for you?"

She grinned, a full show of teeth pulling in her plump lower lip. "I was actually thinking I could do something for *you*."

He raised a brow. "What did you have in mind?"

"Me, on the floor, deep throating your cock."

He coughed. Yes, that sounded like a wonderful idea. He reached between them and lowered his zipper. Her smiling eyes glittered through her lashes, never taking her gaze off of him as she sank to her knees.

His cock was fully aroused. Her fingers curled around his thick flesh and she slowly blinked up at him, lips parted in anticipation as she kissed the tip. He brushed her hair out of her face and gathered it in his hand. A moment later he was engulfed by the tight, suctioning heat of her mouth.

He sucked in a breath and flexed his hips, softening his

knees. She moaned around him, her fingernails digging through his slacks and into his thigh. Her mouth worked over him rapidly and his toes flexed in his shoes. "Jesus, Sheilagh…"

He couldn't remember ever being so attracted to someone. Even his ex-wife, before he'd known of their irreconcilable differences, never made him feel what Sheilagh did. He really didn't care what her brothers thought about their relationship. He wasn't letting her go.

Her fingers curled around his length and she pumped her fist over him, her tongue focusing on the sensitive tip. As he felt his climax drawing near, he urged her on, holding her hair a little tighter and thrusting himself to the back of her mouth.

A lot of Sheilagh's inner turmoil came from a need for control, yet when they were intimate, she thrived under his command. Her surrender was stunning, a sight of beauty no other woman had ever offered him.

Emotion swirled inside of him as he shut his eyes and savored the pleasure. They were moving fast, yet he didn't have the slightest inclination to slow down. He should probably examine those feelings a bit closer, but when it came to Sheilagh, he wanted to gorge himself on every bit of her, submerge himself in her presence, and stop rationalizing for a change.

She did something fascinating with her mouth and his knees nearly buckled. His hand coasted over her hair as words pressed into his tongue, begging to come out. As a man who didn't easily confront change, he became aware of all the ways she was altering him. Oddly, he wasn't afraid of the differences in himself she was slowly bringing to light.

Excitement for the unknown propelled his release. His fingers tightened and he whispered, "Now, sweetheart." She hummed in satisfaction and his spine tingled with pleasure.

NEVER HAD someone handled her so aggressively and not frightened her. She relished the sting at her scalp, the sawed out pacing of his breath. Alec was so gentle and patient, yet incredibly dominant when it came to sex. His forcefulness fueled her passion and she took him deeper.

He moaned and whispered, "Now, sweetheart."

Her heart fluttered at the endearing term and she sucked harder. His hips thrust and heat coated her throat. The novelty of finishing a man in such a fashion shocked her. His hold gentled and as she licked up from the base of his length, swirling her tongue at the tip, his hand coasted over her jaw.

Strong yet gentle fingers tipped her chin, drawing her gaze to his. Bashfully, she blinked at him. His thumb traced over her lower lip. "Was that all right?" she asked, suddenly feeling exposed and shy.

Smiling, he shook his head slowly. "Everything about you is right."

Unsure how to process the effect of his praise, she lowered her eyes and hid her smile.

The tug at her hair took her by surprise. "On the bed. Your turn," he announced, infusing the emotionally laden moment with something lighter.

"I need to shower."

"Tough. I need you more."

She gave a wicked grin and backed to the hideous pink bed. He ripped off her shoes and tossed them on the floor, shucking her jeans in one fluid motion. Her panties gave him pause, probably because they were blue with white stars and had the Wonder Woman logo on the crotch. He laughed and pulled them off of her.

He wrenched her thighs apart. Growling, he dove at her sex and devoured her. She gasped and dragged a fluffy pink pillow over her face. His tongue pierced between her folds. She'd never met a man who performed oral sex so well or enjoyed it so much.

Arching her back, her thighs curled over his shoulders. His fingers bit into her tender flesh as he pulled her closer. All of her boundaries came down as she held onto the thread of knowledge that others were in the house. Her muffled cries filled the room as he teased her clit. Sweet mother of orgasms he was an oral guru.

The orgasm rushed through her, shaking her to the core. His body climbed over hers and she gasped at the press of his cock on her stomach, hard once more. He took her mouth passionately, his hands gripping the back of her neck.

Suddenly he stood and yanked her by her ankles to the edge of the bed. "I need you." Such beautiful words.

"I need you too," she rasped.

He drove into her and she twisted. He held her ankles wide, lifting her ass off the lip of the mattress and fucked her hard. The bed rocked and she hoped to God her parents weren't listening.

Her arms stretched to her side, clawing at the bubble gum pink comforter. "Come here," he said, pulling her off the mattress and into his arms.

Her hands gripped his shoulders and he lifted her off the noisy bed. Her legs wrapped around his hips and he gripped her ass, pressing her back into the wall as she bounced on his cock. His feet braced and his thighs tightened as he lifted her up and down over him.

When her gasps grew louder he kissed her. Their bodies ground together and he exploded, filling her with each thrust. They were both breathing hard as he dropped into the chair, still holding her to him.

She nestled his shoulder and sighed. Alec was potent. "You're amazing."

"So are you," he said, brushing her hair over her back and kissing her temple.

She languidly rested in his arms for several minutes, enjoying the feel of him still inside of her. Finally, she whispered, "I have to shower and change. I should be ready in about forty minutes then we can go."

"Okay. I brought some midterms to grade. I'll do that while you get ready."

She carefully climbed off of him. As she gathered her things her gaze continued to shoot shy glances over her shoulder toward him. Never had a man affected her the way he did.

SHEILAGH OPENED the door to O'Malley's, her grin wide and heart pounding with a sense of homecoming. Alec's fingers laced with hers as she led him through the crowd and to the bar. She let out a sharp whistle and everyone turned, including her brother Kelly who was tending bar. "Can I get some service?"

Kelly stilled. His face split with a wide, beautiful smile as he tossed the rag he was holding and leapt over the counter. "Well, I'll be damned. The Shei-Devil's finally home!"

His strong arms lifted her in a full body hug and she laughed as he spun her and squeezed her tight. Placing her back on her feet he said, "You're lookin' as lovely as ever, little sister. Princeton hasn't broken you yet!"

She shoved him. "Of course not! I'm tougher than the stuff they're made of out there."

He pinched her chin affectionately. "I knew you were."

He turned to Sue who met her glance with an excited wave. "Line 'em up, Sue. Sheilagh's come home to roost!" Kelly's smiling blue eyes turned and he carefully took Alec's measure. "The professor?"

"Kelly, this is Alec. Alec, this is my reprobate brother, Kelly McCullough."

Alec held out his hand and Kelly shook it, which seemed to surprise Alec, as his expression lifted. "Nice to meet you, Kelly."

"I heard you tried to give the Shei-Devil a D."

Alec's smile faltered, but he quickly recovered. "She could have had an A if she wanted it."

Her brother's smile remained in place as he lifted a sharp brow. He mumbled out the side of his mouth to her, "The guys haven't killed him yet for saying shit like that?"

"I think they're gonna try tonight."

Alec looked a bit nervous then Sue lined several shots of Tully on the bar. "Shall we wait for the others or start without them?"

"I wait for no man," Sheilagh announced, stepping close to the bar and grabbing two shots. She handed one to Alec. "Buckle up. Liquid fortitude. You'll be needing it tonight."

He and Kelly took their shots. Kelly held his high. "To you, love. I'm proud of you."

They tossed them back and Alec winced. The fiery burn made its way to Sheilagh's belly and she hollered, ready for a night of shenanigans.

They settled into their regular table and Kelly joined them. There was a loud squeal and Sheilagh turned. Her sister-in-law, Mallory, charged toward her.

Standing, she held out her arms as Mallory nearly plowed her over. "You're home!" They did a little hug dance and bounced up and down.

Sheilagh released her and faced her brother Finn. "Hey, handsome."

Finnegan smiled, his eyes taking a quick assessment. Holding out his arms he pulled her close and whispered, "How you doing, little red?"

She sighed, embracing his strong hug. "I'm good. It's good to be home."

"I'm supposed to kill a man. Is that him?"

She laughed. "Luke talked to you?"

"Tristan," he corrected.

She groaned. "Be nice." Turning, she did a quick introduction of Alec. Mallory seemed intrigued, but Finn, like her other brothers, seemed weary and guarded.

Sue brought over a few drafts and a Cosmo for Mallory. Next to arrive were Colin and Sammy. Sheilagh hugged Colin the hardest, not realizing how much she'd missed her oldest brother's stoic presence in her life.

Colin, as expected, was a complete gentleman. Sheilagh whispered to Alec that he was the brother he wanted to stick with. No one pulled any shit around Colin.

They were settling in and Sheilagh was relaxing since no one seemed to hassle Alec. When Luke arrived, she held her breath out of habit, knowing Tristan wouldn't be far behind.

Luke continued to eye Alec coldly and she wasn't sure what he was so damn broody about. She fidgeted, waiting for Tristan to show.

"You all right?" Alec whispered.

"Mmm-hm. Just having fun."

He gave her a look that said he didn't necessarily take her reply as sincere. Sometimes it was off putting that she couldn't fool him as easily as the others.

The door to the pub opened and her breath sucked tight in her lungs. Tristan strode to their table, meeting Luke's eyes and then hers. He wore rugged jeans, boots, and a thin white T-shirt stretched over his tight muscles. His hair was tied back, his chin needing a shave, and his dove gray eyes smoldered as he took her in with each stride.

Like always, Luke made no gesture of acknowledgement at his arrival. The others greeted him and he nodded. Tristan was like a surrogate brother, but not really, being that he was sleeping with Luke and she'd spent a great deal of her life wishing he was sleeping with her.

It was odd. She still got the same twinge in her belly when he looked at her, but there was something different about it now. Glancing at Alec, who was watching her carefully, she suffered a flush of guilt. She was with Alec. She shouldn't be looking at Tristan.

A round of brunette shots and one pink one for Mallory were placed on the table. They each selected a glass and she froze, just before tossing it back she heard Tristan mumble, "Drink up, old man. You're going down tonight."

Alec twitched, obviously hearing Tristan's comment, but he made no outward reply. Sheilagh blinked in confusion and slowly tipped back her shot. What the hell was that?

No one else seemed to notice Tristan's attitude toward Alec. Maybe she was imagining it, partially fantasizing that he would have some sort of possessive attitude toward her.

As the night carried on and the booze saturated their brains, Sheilagh relaxed. Everyone was laughing and shouting over each other when she stood to use the restroom. She went to the back and took the long hall.

After washing her hands she appraised her appearance. Her makeup was wearing off and she had a rosy glow to her cheeks. Smiling, because she couldn't help it, she shook off her hands and left the bathroom. She came to an abrupt halt when she found Tristan waiting outside the door.

"Having fun?"

She frowned. "As a matter of fact, yes," she said snidely.

He was being a dick, so it only seemed right to be a bitch in return.

"I see you moved from the kiddie table to the grown up section."

Her brow tightened. "What's that supposed to mean?"

"He's a little old for you, don't you think?"

"I think a lot of things, Tristan. Lately I've been thinking about what an asshole you've been acting."

His eyes narrowed. "What are you doing with this guy, Shei?"

"Wouldn't you like to know."

He took a menacing step closer. "He's old enough to be your father."

She laughed, tauntingly. "Oh, trust me, he treats me nothing like a child."

Tristan's shadowed jaw twitched. "Don't say shit like that. It makes you sound like…"

"What? A whore? Funny, when I walked right out of this bar—numerous times—with other men, right under your nose, you didn't seem to object."

His lips thinned. "Did you bring him here to piss me off?"

Her jaw unhinged. He did *not* just ask her that! "Believe it or not, Tristan, I brought him here because he makes me happy. Your reaction never crossed my mind. Now, why don't you go find my brother and get the fuck out of my way?"

She brushed past him and he caught her arm. She

winced at his tight grip. Leaning down close to her mouth he hissed, "I don't like him."

She jerked her arm away and glared up at him. "I don't really give a shit what you like. For the past six years you've made it clear you didn't like me, so as far as what or who I'm doing, you don't get a say."

He towered over her and growled, "You're not a slut. Don't act like one."

"Get away from her."

She stilled, unsure if the sharp threat belonged to Alec. Turning slowly, she found him standing in the hall, his glare nailed into Tristan. Gone was the easygoing philosopher. In its place stood a man she barely recognized.

Alec's posture was tense, his hazel eyes sharp and menacing. Tristan's intimidating stance shifted, turning on Alec. "You got a problem?"

Alec took a slow step forward and pulled her to his side, never once taking his eyes off Tristan. "I ever hear you use that word around her again and *you* will be the one with a problem. I'm not interested in some pissing match with some kid struggling with his identity. My understanding is you made your choice years ago. Whatever you think you're doing, think again. She isn't a game you get to play when you want to feel macho. I see you approach her again or manipulate her, you and I are going to have to talk."

Holy shit. Who was this man? Gone was the gentle thinker. Here was an auxiliary of the most severe guardians—swift, strong, a well-bred watchdog. The glint in his eyes was nothing short of savage. Never had she questioned Tristan's ability to defend himself, yet in that moment she knew he wouldn't stand a chance if he pushed Alec too far.

"You looking for a fight, old man?" *Oh God.*

Nothing changed in Alec's cold expression, but he slowly shook his head. "I need not raise a hand to you in order to prove you are beaten."

Tristan drew back his head in confusion. "What?"

"She's not yours," Alec stated a bit more clearly. "She's mine. Don't disrespect her again." With that he took her hand and walked her right through the bar and out the front door.

ALEC RELEASED Sheilagh's hand once they reached the pavement and paced with agitation. Never in his life had he wanted to go after another person with violent intent like he had wanted to go after Tristan.

What the hell was that guy doing? He was playing games with Sheilagh and Alec didn't understand why.

"Alec?"

"Just give me a minute," he said, dragging his hands through his hair. He needed to calm down. Her entire family was on the other side of that door and, while he'd made some headway with them over the last hour, he'd likely just set himself back quite a bit.

He turned and faced Sheilagh, who was looking unsure and a little shocked. "You said you never slept with him?"

She frowned. "I didn't."

"Then why does he treat you with such entitlement?"

"I don't know. He's always been like that with me."

"Does he always talk to you like that?"

She looked away, appearing ashamed. In a small voice, she said, "No."

He would not let her take responsibility for someone else's cruelty. Taking her face gently in his hands, he said, "Sheilagh, no one has a right to speak to you that way. What he said wasn't true and anyone who insults you like that isn't your friend."

She jerked away. "You didn't know me before. What he said isn't that far off the mark."

Anger tightened his jaw. "Why? Because you have a history? So does everyone else. Why should a woman be chastised for her past when a man's past is celebrated among peers? Do not let *anyone* make you feel ashamed of who you are."

In a small voice, she whispered, "My past is ugly."

"Components of your past seem ugly. Mine too. As with most people. That man is not content and projecting his disquiet with himself on those he sees as weaker. Be strong. Don't let his bullshit affect you. You're better than that."

She was breathing heavily and he sensed her confusion. There was nothing he despised more than nasty people who made good people question who they were.

"I never saw you act like that before," she said.

He wasn't pleased with his reaction. "I was angry."

"You stuck up for me."

"He had no right to say those things."

"You really pissed him off," she said with a timid smirk.

"Good. He really pissed me off."

Her smile was gentle and innocent. "Thank you for defending me."

His thumb grazed her cheek. How could he not come to her defense? Words better left unsaid flitted through his mind. "We should probably head back inside."

She nodded and they headed back in. When they reached the table, seven sets of eyes watched them. Tristan's expression was deadly. The girls looked curious. All of her brothers looked ready to string him up by his intestines.

Finn was the first to speak. "You're her fucking professor?" he barked.

Alec inwardly sighed, figuring Kelly had made the announcement in their absence. Luke shifted like a tiger tethered with a very thin leash. Alec looked to Colin who seemed to be the diplomat of the group, but the courteous air he'd found earlier was gone.

"Why don't you start by telling us how it is our gifted

sister nearly flunked your class and finish by explaining how you're now sharing her bed?" Luke growled.

"Hey!" Sheilagh snapped. Every man's scowl turned on her, but she didn't back down. "Get out of your glass houses and I'll give you some rocks, but unless you can claim to have never seduced the town virgin, turned your back on a commitment to God, or hid who you are out of shame, you can all shut the fuck up."

A chair slowly dragged against the floor and her brother, Finn, stood. "I didn't do any of that shit so I'll be the first to say, we don't take kindly to someone coercing our baby sister. Nor do we take kindly to some outsider coming in and starting shit with our friends."

Alec's gaze darted to Tristan. The man's eyes narrowed with premature victory and the corner of his mouth slowly curved. "I think it's time you returned to Princeton, *professor.*"

"All right, everyone just chill," Kelly said, standing from his seat and stepping between them and the group. "Sheilagh's an adult."

"Fuck that," Luke growled. "This entire situation reeks of unethical bullshit."

The girls glanced at each other nervously and the quiet one, Samantha, with the freckles said, "Why don't you guys ask Sheilagh how she feels instead of jumping to conclusions?"

"Yeah!" Mallory snapped with a little more dynamism.

Finn cut his wife a look then turned his scowl back on

his sister. "All right, Sheilagh, did this asshole threaten to flunk you if you didn't sleep with him?"

"That's it!" Alec snapped. "The entire lot of you can go to hell. Sheilagh is an adult, God damn it. She and I resisted what we—and I said *we*—felt for each other as long as we possibly could. Her grades and her personal life are none of your business. It may not seem ethical, but I assure you my intentions are nothing short of honorable. I love this woman and if you love her as well, you'll all back the hell off of her for a change without judging her or trying to decide for her. She can decide for her God damn self!"

Every eye in the motley crew widened and he played back everything he just said. Shit. He turned to Sheilagh and her expression was blank. No one said a word. "Sheilagh—"

Before he could get another syllable out, she snatched a set of keys off the table and darted for the door.

"Hey! They're my keys!" Mallory shouted.

Go after her! But he was so shocked by what he'd said he seemed to be paralyzed.

"You can't drive anyway," Finn said.

He turned to the group of McCulloughs, unsure if they were still his adversaries. "Where the hell is she going?"

They laughed, no one really looking directly at him anymore. They each seemed to find their drinks and move on to the next issue at hand, whatever that was. They were all nuts, every single one of them. He was still frozen in place, wondering where she would go and if his heated confession was truly enough to possess a person to steal a car.

When he turned back to the group Luke was scowling. Something cold settled in the pit of Alec's stomach when he saw the seat next to Luke was empty and Tristan was gone.

SHEILAGH WHIPPED Mallory's little sedan to a stop just at the turnoff to her property. She slammed her palms into the steering wheel and cursed. What the hell was she doing?

He said he loves you.

Seconds later, headlights divided the black night and a truck pulled up behind her. Glancing in the rearview she cursed again and ripped open the door.

Stomping over the gravel she shouted at the driver, "What the fuck do you want?"

Tristan climbed out of his truck and crossed his arms over his chest. "Are you all right?"

"No, I'm not all right! I just stole a car and I'm fucking upset. How the hell does that get confused with bloody all right?"

Gravel crunched as he took three lengthy strides and gathered her in his arms. "I'm sorry, baby girl. I didn't mean what I said."

Her throat tightened and her body shook with the effort of holding in her tears. When his hand brushed up her back she lost the battle. "I can't take anymore," she rasped as the force of her tears clogged her throat. Everything inside of her fought not to let him see her this way.

"Shh. It's okay."

"Nothing's okay," she argued. "Everything is wrong. Why is everything so damn hard?"

"I don't know," he quietly said, continuing to stroke her back. "Do you love him?"

"I don't know," she admitted honestly. "He makes me feel things, but I've spent the last few years convincing myself I felt something else. Nothing makes sense now."

"Shei, we have to stop. You have to stop expecting me to be something I'm not."

"But sometimes you act like..." So many times he acted like he was straight. She didn't understand.

"Maybe because it's easier to pretend. Sometimes I'm just a kid again, trying to be what my family expected. Pretending I'm not gay is something I'd always done, but I never did it well. Eventually everyone sees through me, sees that I'm hiding something. And when they do, they're angry I wasn't honest or angry I'm not straight and then they all go away. That's how I lost my family in Texas. That's how I lost my childhood best friend. And that's why I fear losing all of you.

"I love your brother, but he isn't ready to come out and

honestly, neither am I. Center County isn't the most liberal place. I'm afraid if I push him I'll lose him."

She could understand all of that, but she was tired of feeling like a rag doll. "But why do you screw with my head? I know I'm not imagining it. You say things and do things that any woman would take as suggestive."

He sighed. "I just want the best for you. I'm fucked up. You're gorgeous, sweet, and since I met you, you looked at me with those hopeful green eyes. Some days I wish I could be what you wanted. Some days it's so much easier looking in your eyes than his. Do you have any idea what it feels like to look into your lover's eyes, see utter adoration only to have it banked by swift regret, because part of him will always hate that he loves you? It fucking hurts."

"Doesn't he know none of us care if he's straight or gay? We love him. We love you."

Suddenly it seemed like she was the one hugging Tristan rather than him hugging her. "It's not a question of his family's love. That's a given. Luke has to first love himself."

She held onto him, part of her lost in complete wonderment that she was standing there in Tristan's arms. It didn't mean as much as it would have when she was just a girl in love with the Texas stranger who suddenly became a part of her family. Perhaps she was finally getting over her crush and accepting reality. But then he would say something or act like he had a right to her more than anyone else did and her emotions would set back to go and she was just a confused little girl again.

"Why are you being so nasty to Alec?"

He sighed and stepped back, taking the warmth of his arms with him. "It's hard seeing you with him. I never saw you look at someone the way you look at him. Those looks have been solely mine for so long I don't like giving them to some guy I don't know. I have no idea if he's just some piece of shit taking advantage of you. My instincts tell me to protect you, because… I feel sort of responsible for the sadness I sometimes see in your eyes. You look at him and I can tell you're really into him. He has the ability to hurt you and I want to prevent that from happening."

But no one was hurting her as much as Tristan and his twisted mind games. "But there have been others."

"None like him." Tristan walked to the front of his truck, brushed a leaf off the hood and leaned against the bumper. "He's different. You're different around him. In some selfish way I feel like he's taking you from us. You'll hate me for saying this, but knowing you were always there gave me hope that if things didn't work out—"

Her jaw clamped tight with outrage. "Don't." Her shoulders stiffened with the shred of dignity it took years to scrape together. "I'm not your fall back girl. You're gay, Tristan. *Gay.* You have a habit of making your issues mine and I can't deal with it anymore."

"But what if I'm bi?"

Her heart raced. No. She'd posed that question for

years only to have every secreted look, every passing touch, every witnessed show of affection cut right to her heart and prove otherwise. "You're in love with Luke."

He nodded and there was such sadness to his agreement. "I've never been with a woman. There have been other men, but…"

So many emotions rushed through her. So many questions. Luke was her brother. She loved him, as she loved all of her siblings. This conversation, no matter how private, was wrong. But part of her loved Tristan too. It was a love that evolved and withered and bloomed and wilted only to morph into something she no longer knew how to label.

"He's my brother," she said quietly, but it was the thought of Alec that gave her words strength. She didn't want to betray either of them.

"And I love him more than I've ever loved any man."

Then what were they talking about? Tristan stepped close and brushed a tear from her cheek. He leaned in and slowly traced his lips over hers. She sucked in a breath and his mouth tilted slowly over hers.

Shock had her incapable of pulling away, while outrage had her hands twitching. The problem was, long surrendered fantasies also had her hands twitching to pull him close.

But it was all wrong. The chemistry wasn't there. His lips weren't full like Alec's. *Oh God, Alec!*

She jerked away, her fingers covering her mouth as if she could smother her shame. "Why did you do that?"

His brow was tight. He looked away and mumbled, "I needed to see."

"See what?" she snapped.

"If it would change anything."

She pursed her lips. It changed everything. That was not the reaction she'd anticipated since she was a little girl. There were no fireworks or chills. His kiss was hollow and wrong. *Because he's gay you idiot!*

"When will you come to terms with who you are?"

"I've been asking myself that since I was a boy. It's hard. My parents hate what I am. There are vicious people in the world, Shei. It's scary being something others hate. You have no idea how easy your life is being hetero."

Hating that he was toying with her emotions, yet sympathizing with his desire to be ordinary, she gave him a pass. He was her friend. She could sacrifice her own sanity for a few seconds of experimentation. Couldn't she? God, she was fucked up.

Confused, she stared at him. "Did it change anything?" She shouldn't care, but she wanted to know, fearing she'd never have the guts to ask again.

He cleared his throat and shifted. "It felt dirty, like I was kissing my sister."

She laughed, but didn't really find it funny. "Are you going to tell Luke?" She didn't want to hurt her brother. The sense she'd betrayed him pierced her heart like a thousand little swords. *Only a whore would do what you just did.*

"No."

His agreement to keep their transgression secret should have comforted her, but it didn't. It was just another shameful secret that would be locked away with the others, choked out in tearful confessions in the dark as she cried herself to sleep during those horrible moments when she hated who she was.

She turned away. Tristan was quiet as she battled with her guilty conscience. After a while he said, "Let's go back to the bar. Your guy looked a little stunned when you took off. He's probably worried about you. God knows what they've done to him."

Oh God, Alec. She shouldn't have left him there to deal with the others. But he'd come to her defense again and this time he said he loved her. He shouldn't love her. She'd only end up letting him down eventually. She didn't have another decade to give a man that would never truly accept her.

Sure, Alec saw parts of her everyone else seemed to miss. But he would never see all of her if she had anything to say about it. He'd never know how utterly messed up she was inside. He'd expect her to be something better and she'd exhaust herself trying. Then when she couldn't try anymore, he'd get frustrated and leave her. Some masochist buried deep in her soul told her it would be best to ruin what they had now, before the rug was pulled out from beneath her, before she began counting on his love. But she wasn't ready for their time to end.

She simply had to be aloof. If she could avoid talking about his proclamation for the next three days, she could avoid confronting her feelings. When they got back to school she'd put some space between them. He'd eventually lose interest, because she wasn't that interesting to begin with, and then he'd move on. Better to face the pain now than to draw it out and make it hurt more in the long run.

"I'll follow you back," she said.

He gently caught her arm. "Are we okay, Shei? I do love you. I'm sorry for being a jerk."

Tristan. Her mind simply repeated the name, those seven letters meaning so much. What had happened to them? She used to worship this man and now she looked at him with pity. Her opinions were evolving, but nothing seemed to be correcting her state of mind. Maybe they were all broken beyond fixing.

She nodded. "We're okay."

The drive back to the pub was lost in one of those weird moments where one almost forgets one is breathing. Her mind was working overtime, yet she had no idea what she'd thought along the journey. Not a single deliberation seemed to resolve anything or clearly announce itself.

When she pulled in beside Tristan, she took a moment to clear her mind and paste on her usual careless façade.

She'd have to apologize to everyone for stealing Mallory's car and taking off. She'd also have to apologize to Alec, but she didn't want to think about that. She just hoped her brothers hadn't done anything too terrible to him.

Tristan opened her door and she climbed out. They walked to the pub and when he pulled open the door they were greeted by the loud, familiar voices of her family. Her eyes quickly sought Alec. When she found him she increased her strides. "This isn't good."

Tristan chuckled behind her and she approached the table, folding her arms over her chest and scowling at her brothers. They slowly realized she'd returned, each one stifling their laughter and doing a shit job of hiding their grins.

"Hey, Sheilagh," Kelly greeted cheekily. "We missed you."

She looked at Alec who hugged an empty bottle and sighed at her, a content grin on his face. "Isn't she lovely?"

Her brothers groaned and shoved him, not aggressively, but as if they were life-long friends.

"We might have gotten your professor a wee bit drunk, Devil," Finn slurred as he slouched into Mallory's shoulder.

"How much did you give him?"

"Just one," Colin announced innocently, his eyes mere slits, his mouth a plastered smirk.

Luke snorted and leaned forward, hiding his laughter.

Sammy, who seemed to be the only sober one, giggled. "He means *one bottle.*"

"You gave him an entire bottle of Tully?"

"Well, we had some too," Finn announced.

"I didn't," Mallory amended, ceaselessly reminding them that she found their taste in booze contemptible.

"We had a chat while you were gone, sweetheart," Alec said, his fluid accent suddenly sounding cockney.

"And?"

"We've come to agree on three inalienable truths."

She raised a brow, waiting for him to go on.

"One!" He announced, rising from his chair, none too gracefully. "Whiskey is the fruit of the devil." He rounded the table, balancing a great deal of his weight on her brothers' shoulders. "Two!" He held up a second finger, squinted at his hand as if to make sure he was counting right. "You have an incredible family." He staggered in front of her. "And three! I bloody love you and you are going to have to deal with it now that your brothers have accepted me."

Everyone at the table banged their glasses in accordance. "Here! Here!"

She rolled her eyes and looked back at Alec who gave her a lopsided grin. "Oh you poor bugger. You don't know what you're saying."

He leaned in and sniffed her hair. His mouth pressed close to her ear and he whispered, "*Doubt thou that the stars are fire. Doubt that the sun doth move. Doubt truth to be a liar. But never doubt I love."*

She turned and frowned at him. "Hamlet? Really?"

He grinned without showing teeth, his eyes slits of happiness. "You smell good."

"Oh, for Christ's sake!" She tossed Mallory's keys on the table. "Sorry I stole your car." She reached in Alec's pocket and fished out the keys to the BMW. He laughed and she shook her head. "I'm taking you home."

He tipped back the bottle he held, realizing it was empty, then proceeded to face the others and speak into the bottle as if it were a microphone. "The hour of departure has arrived, my friends. *'And we go our ways—I to die and you to live. Which is better God only knows.'"*

"Goodnight, you guys."

They laughed and begged them to stay, but she couldn't let Alec go on like this. No one, not even a McCullough, survived an entire bottle of Tully unscathed.

She shuffled him out of the bar and maneuvered him into the car.

"You recognize when I quote Hamlet but not Socrates," he slurred in an almost cockney lilt.

"That was a line from Plato's *Apology.*"

He smiled, as though truly pleased with her awareness. "You are correct. I am forever impressed by your knowledge, sweet Sheilagh."

She shut his door and rounded the car. After sliding in behind the wheel, she fiddled with the seat and mirrors.

The car started and she hesitated. Alec watched her, a look of serenity relaxing his face.

He was plastered and she knew better than to have a serious conversation with someone in that condition. Yet she also needed to unburden herself. It was for the wrong reasons and it was totally selfish, but she said the words anyway.

"Tristan kissed me."

He hadn't been talking, but the car was submerged in utter silence. She couldn't look at him. She gripped the wheel and pressed her foot into the brake as she put the car in drive. Briefly, before pulling away, she glanced at him.

He'd definitely heard her. His smile was gone and his expression was blank. But there, in his telling eyes, was the betrayal and hurt her actions had caused.

$\mathcal{A}$lec awoke in the clothes he'd worn out the night before. Sheilagh's pink blankets twisted around his hips and he turned—causing a sharp stab of pain in his head—and found her curled up on the far end of the bed.

He couldn't recall what exactly had happened last night. He knew that he said he loved her. Recalled her leaving right after he made the announcement, abandoning him with her insane relatives who'd wanted to gut him and mount him on the wall. But that wasn't what happened.

After she left, they seemed to take pity on him, claiming that loving Sheilagh would be as painful as spooning a porcupine. It wasn't that Sheilagh was unlovable. They all adored her. The issue was that Sheilagh never let herself get close enough to anyone in order to be loved. It was as if she thought herself unworthy of such high emotion.

They'd handed him a bottle and patted him on the back and the rest was a blur. He still tasted whiskey on his tongue. He'd be happy if he never tasted that again. How had he gotten home?

Memories of Sheilagh returning for him vaguely teased his mind. He supposed she drove him home. Then he remembered.

He couldn't recall exactly what was said, but he specifically remembered feeling euphoric one moment and forsaken the next. That bastard had kissed her. And she let him! The ache from the night before returned, no longer anesthetized by booze. She kissed someone else. Not just someone else. Tristan.

It took a moment for the truth to settle in. It covered him like cold snow and something bitter opened up inside of him. He knew she'd made mistakes in the past, but this was now. Never had he expected her to be disloyal. The man had called her a slut and she'd gone right ahead and kissed him rather than defending herself.

Ignoring the pain in his head, he forced himself out of the bed. She still slept soundly, curled into a tiny ball at the edge of the bed. She looked so innocent, yet she'd cut him deep.

Confused, he left the room with his bag and went to shower. When he returned she still slept. He wasn't sure what to do, so he organized his belongings and eventually she awoke.

"Are you packing?"

"It would seem," he said, not looking at her.

"Are you leaving?"

"I'm not quite sure what to do, Sheilagh. It would appear I have two choices, go home and leave you to find a ride back to school. Or tough out the next three days knowing we will never be the same."

She lowered her head and he wanted to withdraw his nasty comment, but his self-preservation refused. He did however mumble, "I find myself leaning towards the latter in fear that if I don't drag you back to Princeton you'll never return."

"And that would be bad because I have potential or because you want to see me again?"

"I know you've been thinking about dropping out."

Her shoulders slowly lifted as she took a deep breath. "I can be ready in an hour. We can leave then. That way you don't need to spend any more time than necessary with me and you can be certain I'm back where everyone wants me."

His chest tightened, knowing she was tearing herself down behind the walls she didn't let others pass. "What do *you* want, Sheilagh?" he asked quietly.

"I want to know what it is—for just one day—not to dislike myself."

He shut his eyes. "Why did you kiss him?"

"He kissed me, but I won't lie. I let him."

Alec nodded. Her honesty helped, but it didn't curb the effect of her words. "I'll be waiting downstairs." He zipped his bag and left to take it to the car.

Sheilagh felt terrible. Her mother and father didn't understand why her trip home that started late was suddenly being cut short. She made some excuses about forgetting a project that was due and said her goodbyes.

Alec had thanked them for allowing him to stay and gone to wait in the car. She was almost to the passenger door when the door to the barn suddenly flew open and Luke was barreling toward her. She faced him, knowing it was time to pay the piper.

He shoved her and she gasped, never expecting such aggression from him. The blow knocked her bag out of her hand and her eyes flooded with tears of shock. This was bad. *"What the fuck, Sheilagh?"*

Alec's door opened and he stood, frowning at Luke, but this time didn't come to her defense. She swallowed and looked at her brother. "I'm sorry. I'm a terrible person. I know."

Luke's nostrils flared. If she were his brother he'd have knocked her out by now. It was obviously taking every bit of self-control he had left not to hit her.

"When is enough ever enough with you?" he snapped.

"I'm sick and tired of feeling guilty over some bullshit childhood crush you have. He's mine. Do you fucking get that? *Mine.* We've been committed as much as society allows for five years and never has shit like this happened before. I'm your fucking brother!"

Her chest shook as she held in her tears. "I'm sorry."

He shook his head, his eyes narrowing. "Are you? Are you ever really sorry? When are you going to start thinking about someone other than yourself?"

"That's enough," Alec quietly said.

The front door opened and her father stepped out. "Luke? What's going on?"

Her brother glanced over his shoulder at their father and returned his glare to her, hissing so only she could hear, "I'm done with you."

It was as though someone punched her in the stomach. He marched back to the barn and slammed the door. Pasting on a shaky smile so her father wouldn't see she was breaking on the inside, she waved at him, picked up her bag, and climbed into the car.

A moment later Alec climbed in beside her, his expression tense as he backed out of her driveway. He didn't say one word to her the entire drive back to Princeton.

"IT WAS AN AWESOME WEEK," Wes went on. "The lakes were too cold for swimming, but we had bonfires and drank and laughed. It was a well overdue holiday."

"I'm glad you had a nice break," Alec said numbly, trying to find any form of pleasure in his son's obvious delight.

"I guess it was pretty boring here with everyone gone. What did you do all week?"

"I stayed inside most of the time, had some papers to grade."

"You should have done something with your time off. You look tired, Dad."

That's because he hadn't been sleeping. "I'm fine. Just having a difficult time shaking off the idleness of break."

His son frowned, but seemed to accept his excuse. "Promise when summer starts, you'll take some time off, maybe go home for a while."

"Perhaps."

They finished their take-out and Wes stretched, patting his belly. "I'll tell you, I feel so refreshed. Even the bitch next door hasn't been bugging me."

"Don't call her that!" Alec hissed then stilled as he tossed his leftovers in the trash. Trying not to give himself away, he asked, "She hasn't been making noise or you've learned to be a bit more tolerant?"

"Haven't heard a peep. The one day I even saw her in the hall and she might have smiled at me, I doubt it though. She sort of just mopes around. Maybe she's on drugs."

"I highly doubt that." His lungs worked as he fought to breathe normally. She was moping. It had been eight days. He'd looked for her at the Student Union, the library, and around campus, but he hadn't caught sight of her since he'd dropped her off last Friday.

It was beyond difficult to let her leave, but they each needed time to process. When he'd said goodbye, he hadn't looked at her, merely confessed he needed some time and asked her to call if she needed anything. She was obviously past a point of reaching out and he felt terrible for not handling things better.

Wes made no further mention of her and Alec thought of little else. He wondered if she'd talked to her brothers, wondered if Luke had forgiven her. Alec didn't need to forgive her. He already had. She was young and youth was the greatest cause of unconscious choices. However, he missed her.

He was concerned about her. Sheilagh had some pretty big battles going on in her head. He'd read up on depression since he'd returned home and he was certain she suffered from something called Dysthymia.

Dysthymia was a chronic condition that wasn't easily identified. It was less severe than other forms of depression, but longer lasting. One characteristic of the depression was withdrawing from stress and avoiding opportunities in order to completely avoid failure, opportunities like college perhaps.

In almost every journal article he found, there was mention of difficulty diagnosing the condition because people who suffered from such an ongoing state of mind were apt at hiding the symptoms in social settings. Sheilagh was always hiding. He'd even teased her about wearing Gyges' invisibility ring.

The further he read the more he grew concerned. What her brother had said to her was not kind. Sheilagh had a knack for beating herself up over things she couldn't control. The articles also said that when someone with Dysthymia suffered a major depressive episode on top of their already excited state of mind, they often accepted these worsening symptoms as part of their natural personality and avoided seeking help.

Alec was torn. He didn't whole-heartedly agree with the prescription craze happening in America. Yes, some people found hope and survival through medication, but others did not. It wasn't a blanket solution. He wasn't sure if Sheilagh had ever spoken to professional. He doubted she had, being she was severely closed off about anything she saw as a personal shortcoming.

When Wes left to go meet up with his friends, Alec went to bed. Sleep, again, was evasive. The following morning he chanced a trip to the psychology building in hopes of finding one of his peers. He was relieved to find Reginald Parikh in his office.

"Alec, what brings you here on a Saturday?"

"I wanted to pick your brain," he said, taking the seat across from Reggie.

The man tossed whatever he'd been reading on his desk and leaned back. "Pick away. I welcome the distraction from these term papers. Absolute shit. I wonder if anyone listens to me at all when I teach."

"Are you familiar with dysthymic depression?"

"Yes. Long lasting depression, hard to diagnose."

Alec nodded. "How would one know for sure if someone suffered from it?"

"Well, there are theories on various pathophysiological indicators, such as CT scans and the like, but none of that is universally agreed upon. I'd say, aside from the individual speaking to a professional, you could only look for obvious indicators."

"I've looked online, but I'm interested on your take."

"Well, the first clue, although not always the easiest to detect, is the length in time the person is coping. I'd say that sort of depression takes hold and doesn't let up for a *minimum* of two years, but it can span a lifetime."

She'd done nothing for six years. "Go on."

"Well, in that two year block, I'd say there are the typical symptoms, fluctuating appetite and sleep patterns, fatigue, low self-esteem, difficulty making decisions, or an ongoing sense of pessimism. Such symptoms are never absent for more than two months at a time. There doesn't have to be a major depressive episode for this to happen.

Sometimes the onset is drug related or the result of other forms of mental illness, but not always. A person with dysthymic depression might have difficulty in usual social, professional, or academic settings."

"What causes it?"

"Well, that's an impossible question to answer. If the disorder can't be linked to a cooperating illness, then there could be a myriad of causes. Perhaps a stressful life event or some sort of very deep fundamental loss based on a false interpretation of events."

"How is it treated?"

He sighed. "What you're dealing with here is a chronically—for lack of a better word—moody person. Due to the length of which the disorder presents itself, people tend to assume it is just the status quo. I assume this is a friend of yours. The most you can do is try to be supportive. Do whatever you can to boost their self-esteem, offer strong support when they need it, teach them reliance, and offer keys to cope with stress. I'm sure your background of practiced theories could help with such tactics. Therapy has also shown promising results. Dysthymia is ultimately a disorder that won't resolve itself unless the person redefines their faulty beliefs that they're responsible for what they can't control and that they deserve nothing more than the unsatisfying life they're living. They struggle with coping and, unless someone shows them how, they aren't likely to possess the tools to change."

"Thanks, Reggie."

He nodded. "No problem. I have some texts I could loan you if you're interested. Try to get your friend to see a specialist. Even a family doctor could offer some antidepressants that might help, but I only recommend that in collaboration with therapy."

Alec nodded, not sure if any of that was likely to happen. "I'll be sure to pass that information along."

He sat for a few more minutes making small talk and when he got to his car he faced a dilemma. To go to her or not to go?

"Shit." He shut his eyes, knowing he couldn't stay away. He did love her. There was no doubt in his mind, but his pride was bruised. She'd let another man kiss her only a week into their relationship. He was smarter than this. He knew people who didn't start relationships on an honest playing field often continued the relationship with worsening acts of deceit.

But she told you right after it happened.

She *was* being honest. But Alec wasn't sure if her honesty was some sort of self-sacrifice, done in hopes that he throw her over, which he'd basically done like a complete twat, or if she was trying to right a wrong.

Jesus, this entire situation was a bloody mess. Her brother should have worked out his shit with his lover by now. And Tristan...*why wasn't anyone protecting Sheilagh?* They were all twisted in this mess and no one seemed content. Now he was involved and equally as torn up over the turn of events.

He didn't know what to do. His main concern was making sure she was all right. He backed out of the parking space and drove to her apartment. When he spotted Wesley's car, he hesitated. Parking a block away, he walked to the building and hoped he didn't run into his son.

The halls were quiet. When he reached her door, directly next to his son's door, he quietly knocked. There was no sound from the inside. Knocking again, he waited.

He didn't want to call her name. If Wes heard him and came to investigate there would be a whole bunch more explaining to do and he simply didn't have the energy at the moment. If he and Sheilagh managed to work things out he would tell her his son was the neighbor she hated and do the same with Wes. One thing at a time.

He pulled out his phone and texted her.

I'M AT YOUR DOOR.

A SECOND LATER HE got a reply.

GO AWAY.

. . .

FROWNING, he texted back.

NOT UNTIL WE TALK.

SHE WAS OBVIOUSLY HOME. Her text came through a moment later.

I HAVE nothing to say to you, nor do I need another lecture. I'm perfectly aware of all the terrible things I've done and I don't need any reminders. Now leave me alone.

HE STUFFED the phone in his pocket and knocked on the door. "Sheilagh, open the door."

"Go away!"

He sighed. "I'm not bloody leaving until we talk. Now let me in before I make a scene."

There was some movement inside and then the door opened. Jesus. He pressed into her apartment and quickly shut the door. It was a disaster. *She* was a disaster.

Her hair was a tangle of knots. Her eyes had dark shadows under them. Her clothes were mismatched and stained. But the worse sight was the tears in her eyes and the red rings behind her lashes that told him she'd been crying for a very long time.

"There. You've seen me. Now leave."

He didn't know what to do. He glanced around at her apartment and searched for some inspiration. Finally, he gripped her hand and dragged her into the bathroom. He turned on the shower and adjusted the water.

"Take off your clothes."

"No."

"Sheilagh, I'm not playing around. You're going to shower and then we'll talk. Now strip." He was really just using the shower to stall.

"Why are you here, Alec? We broke up."

"We didn't break up, we had a disagreement."

"I kissed someone else."

"We'll talk about it after you shower."

"I'm not taking my clothes off in front of you."

"Fine. I'll leave you be. When you're finished we'll talk."

He left her to her own devices and as he thought about what would happen when she finished, he tidied up her place. Dishes went into the sink, clothes into the basket, and books onto the shelf. He frowned when he saw she hadn't even unpacked her bag from last week.

As he carried some papers into her bedroom that was actually her office, he accidentally bumped her laptop and the screen lit up. It was an email yet to be sent.

Dear Dr. Lasik,

I'm still not feeling well. I'll get the notes, but likely won't be in class again this week.
Sincerely,
Sheilagh McCullough

He frowned. She hadn't gone to class last week? No matter how bright a student was, attendance was necessary. There was only so much a professor would excuse before requiring a doctor's note. What was she thinking?

She's not thinking!

He left her office and started on the dishes in the sink. The water shut off in the bathroom and he quickly tossed the cloth he'd been drying with and went to sit on the couch.

She would likely notice he'd cleaned up, which wasn't the issue. Clearing his throat, he eased back and waited.

The door opened a moment later and she came out in nothing but a cloud of steam and a blue towel. "You cleaned."

"I just put some things away."

She had no apparent reaction to this, no lowering of her brow, no show of gratitude. Not that stimulating a reaction was why he did it. It concerned him how monotone her statement had been and how blank her expression remained.

She went to the dresser on the wall and pulled out a shirt. Her damp head popped through the neck and as the shirt covered her hips the towel fell to the floor. He watched as she stepped into a pair of black panties and that was all she apparently intended to wear. She sat on the bed, a look of exhaustion in her eyes and waited for him to speak.

"Can we talk?"

She shrugged and wouldn't meet his gaze. "I'm fine, if that's why you're here."

"Have you talked to your brother?"

"No."

He'd expected her to ask which one. The fact that she didn't need clarification told him she hadn't spoken to *any* of her brothers. "Have you heard from Tristan?"

Her narrow green gaze sliced through him. Good. That was at least some reaction. "No and I don't plan to. He knew the minute he kissed me it was all wrong."

"And how did you feel when he kissed you?"

"Horrible," she said, turning away.

"Why horrible?"

"Because it wasn't you. I didn't want to hurt you or Luke, but that's what I did."

He frowned. When she'd first told him he was drunk. The absolute worst possible scenario played in his head. He saw two young people wrapped in each other's bodies, lost in passion, taking what had been denied for so long.

He was an idiot.

He knew better. His ex-wife was gay. He'd seen her make an open commitment to Claire at a ceremony many years ago. That was when he knew his reality had been a sham. Elizabeth was gay. Tristan was gay. There was a severe difference between affection and actually being *in* love with someone.

"Sheilagh, how long did this kiss last?"

She shrugged again. "I don't know. Thirty seconds, maybe less."

He sighed and rubbed his eyes. "He kissed you, though? You didn't initiate the kiss?"

"No," she said empathetically. "I wouldn't do that."

He nodded. "Your brother's angry right now, but the way I understand this, it's not your fault."

"It's always my fault."

"That's ridiculous."

"You don't know, Alec. I've thrown myself at Tristan a number of times. Not since I found out about him and Luke, but the opportunity was sort of always there. It isn't like I used the word 'no' a lot."

"Do you think you were a whore?"

Her lips tightened and her eyes shimmered with unshed tears under her rapidly fluttering lashes. She didn't answer.

"You *are not* a whore, Sheilagh." When she looked ready to either break or argue he stood and went to the bed. Taking her face in his hands, he forced her to look at him. "People sleep together. It's one of the sure ways to discover if we suit another person. Doing so more than once does not make you a terrible person."

"It does when you know that person isn't the one, when you spend the time wishing he was someone else, and afterwards you're so disgusted with yourself you wish everything would just go away, including yourself."

He dropped his hands. "When we're together, did you ever wish I was someone else?"

She met his gaze and blinked. "No. I always knew it was you. You were who I wanted."

Thank God.

"Good."

"I'm sorry, Alec."

He pulled her into his arms. "I'm sorry too."

She wrapped her arms around him and rested her head on his shoulder. He simply held her for a while, knowing it was probably what she needed most. "Have you eaten?"

"Not since last night."

"Why don't we order some take-out? Or we can go to my house and I'll make something for you."

"You don't like my apartment."

"It's not that... I...I have a confession to make."

She eased back and frowned at him. "What?"

Taking a deep breath and licking his lips, he said, "You know your neighbor?"

"Yeah?"

"He's my son."

She drew back and blinked. "No, he's not. He's not British. His last name's Hill."

"He's British. He just has an American accent and

Hill's his mother's name. Wes was born before I returned to the UK. He sometimes goes by Devereux, because he had it legally changed—hyphenating the two—when he turned eighteen, but for most of his life it was simply Hill."

Her face scrunched up as if this information offended her senses. "But he's an asshole and you're so…diplomatic."

He smiled tightly. "I've asked him not to call you a bitch. Please don't call him an asshole."

Her mouth opened. "He called me a *bitch*?"

"You just called him an asshole. You also threatened to beat him with a bat until he screamed."

"Oh my God, does he know we slept together?" she shouted.

There was suddenly a knock on the wall. His son's muffled voice came through the plaster. "Keep it down."

She glared at the wall then turned on him. "You want to handle this, *Dad*?"

He rolled his eyes. "Sheilagh, it isn't that big of a deal."

"Your son hates me, Alec."

"He doesn't know you."

"This is just wonderful," she said, crossing her arms.

She was angry, but angry was better than morose. "Look, it isn't what anyone expected, but it is what it is. Perhaps—knowing this—will give the two of you the ground to start fresh."

She gaped at him. "Alec, I'm two years older than him.

How do you think he'll feel knowing I'm sleeping with his father?"

"You're talking about a kid with two moms. He's not judgmental."

"I can't believe this."

He stood. "Put on some pants."

"What? Why?"

"Because I'm going to talk to Wes."

"Alec, maybe you shouldn't."

"Sheilagh, he's my son. You're my girlfriend. I have to hide you from enough people. I refuse to treat you like some shameful secret around my family."

"What if he's pissed?"

He tossed her a pair of polka dot pajama bottoms. "We won't know until we find out. And if he is, he'll get over it."

Shaking her head, she shoved her feet into the pants. "I think you're making a mistake."

He went to the door and opened it. Leaning into the hall he knocked on Wesley's door. "Too late now."

He stepped into the hall and his son opened his door, a look of surprise on his face when he saw him standing there. Sheilagh stood on the other side of the wall where Wes couldn't see, worrying her lip.

"Dad, what are you doing here?"

"I have to tell you something."

"Is everything all right? Is Mom—"

"Everything's fine. I need to tell you…" He glanced back at Sheilagh. "I'm in love."

Her eyes widened and his son laughed. "What? Since when?"

"It's recent. I met her in January and we've been a couple for a short time, but I'm certain and I wanted you to know."

"That's great! I'm happy for you. Do you wanna come in and have a drink or something?"

He glanced at Sheilagh. "Aren't you going to ask me who she is?"

"Do I know her?"

"Actually, yes."

"Who is it?"

He reached out a hand and his son's smile fell. Sheilagh took a hesitant step forward and slipped her hand in his.

"You've got to be kidding me," Wes muttered. Then he scowled at the both of them. "This is ridiculous. What could you possibly see in her?"

He felt Sheilagh draw in a sharp breath. She tried to untangle their fingers, but he tightened his grip. Glowering at his son, he hissed, "That's the last time you say something unkind to or about her. Do you understand me?"

Wes gaped at him, then snapped, "She's my age. You'll wind up losing your job. I'll lose my tuition! Are you insane? This is completely selfish!"

After sticking out a marriage for as long as possible to

a gay woman for the sake of family, he found it difficult to believe he was being accused of acting selfishly. Such blame seemed better suited for his son. "No one is losing their job or tuition. Get a grip, Wes."

"You get a grip! What the fuck, Dad? And you…" He shook his head, growled, then slammed the door in their faces.

Alec glanced at Sheilagh. Her head hung and her hair hid her face. He brushed it out of her eyes and frowned when he saw her laughing. "Are you laughing?"

She gave him a look of innocence. "Seems to me he's the one acting like a bitch."

He grunted out a short laugh. "He'll get over it. Come on. Let's go to my place."

Her laughter fell away and she stared at him with so many questions in her eyes. She seemed to have the weight of the world on her shoulders. "Alec, why are we doing this?"

"Doing what?"

She waved her hand between them. "This. Us. There are so many reasons for us not to get involved."

"None of those reasons are good enough for me."

"Your job? Your son? They seem like pretty solid reasons to me."

"Wesley will come around. He's just reacting right now. Give it three days."

"What happens in three days?"

"Nothing. I just believe that's how long it takes to deal

with something clearly, without emotions clouding your judgment."

Rather than getting her things together she sat on the couch. He followed her in and knelt in front of her. "Sheilagh, I know you're hurting. Please. Let me in. Let me help you."

Her lashes blinked rapidly. "I can't."

"Why? I love you."

"Stop saying that."

"It's how I feel. I don't want to stop."

"You don't know me."

"I think I know you better than most."

Her body sagged as she sighed. "Sometimes...I'm so sad and I don't know why."

"We all get sad," he told her softly. "There are ways to deal with it. Then when the sadness comes it doesn't hurt so bad."

"I'm not always like this. Most of the time I can be happy, but then it always comes back and sometimes I don't know why."

He contemplated for a moment and then slowly sat beside her. "Do you remember when I talked to you about Stoic Philosophy?"

"You talk to me about a lot of philosophies."

"This one I think you'll be interested in. Do you want me to tell you about it?"

"Okay."

He leaned back on the couch and pulled her to him.

He'd suffered over the past few days too and needed to hold her. She snuggled into the curve of his arm and he spoke softly as though he were telling her a bedtime story.

"Stoicism comes from Athens around the third century B.C. The Stoics believed that our errors in judgment caused destructive emotions. Over time, their beliefs have become a way of life for many. Stoicism is a choice, founded in the virtue of happiness.

"There are a few points I think—if you really applied yourself—you could gain a great deal from. The first is accepting the limit of our control. We can only influence so much of the world around us. We need to recognize the external things we have no control over and accept what we cannot control. We are only responsible for ourselves, our personal behavior."

"I'm not controlling," she said quietly.

"But you let other people's behavior weigh on you as if you're responsible for it and you own it. Think of your past. Think of the things you've shouldered unnecessary blame for. You need to convince yourself to let those things go. Excuse yourself. You're only human."

"Tell me more."

"Another element is living in the moment. Guilt is a useless emotion. There's no point in reliving sadness simply because it once existed. Let the past go. Notice how when you lose yourself in the moment, with your family, your classes, you forget you're supposed to be sad.

Keep forgetting, Sheilagh, because you aren't supposed to be anything, but alive. Live."

"But sometimes the things I try to lose myself in make me sad anyway."

"Well, you need to make conscious decisions and be aware of who you are. Regardless of your virtue, I don't think you're a woman who can handle casual sex. Sleeping with a stranger might have offered a distraction in the past, but the emotional repercussions were far too great and not worth the cost of a few minutes of escape. So many of the stresses that harass us are superficial and hardly worth stressing over. If you can't change it, let it go. It's only weighing you down in the end."

"What else do the Stoics believe?"

He smiled, glad he'd piqued her interest. "We are what we repeatedly do. If you pretend to be someone by behaving a certain way and continue to repeat that behavior, you eventually become that person. Our habits make us who we are. If a mean person pretends to be nice by doing nice things, they are essentially turning into a nice person. Do you see? I think you're so used to being sad when others aren't looking, you forget how not to be. It takes a conscious effort to change one's self. Maybe they need a phrase as a prompt when they're tempted to go back to the old way of living."

"Like what?"

"Well, it could be something as simple as saying, 'I deserve to be happy.' Reminding yourself of this and choosing opportunities to practice being so, will eventually conclude with happiness."

"There isn't always something to do."

"Being a philosopher is about contemplation. You'll have to take time to know yourself. Keep a journal and compile a list of things you enjoy. Keep adding to it as you grow old."

"I keep a journal."

He squeezed her shoulder, not surprised. "Good, but rather than focusing on the negative, try using it as a tool for the positive. Write down goals and contemplate strategies for happiness rather than dwelling on misfortunate incidences that are over and done with. There's really no need to keep them alive and record such things."

"What else?"

"There's one more point and I think this is a big one."

"What is it?"

He kissed her hair. "Love. Plato believed the root of philosophy was love, learning to love, loving others, loving what is beautiful and good, and loving it passionately. Don't be afraid to love, Sheilagh. It's a wonderful gift. You possess it, but you're afraid to use it."

Brow tight, she sighed. "Why do you love me, Alec?"

That was a hard question. Why did anyone love another? Was there really any definite answer for that?

"I love you because I think you're smart and your mind fascinates me. You discourse with me on an intellectual level I so enjoy. You stimulate me in a way most people don't. I love you for the way you laugh and for the mischievous nature you sometimes possess. I love that you're tenacious and self-assured in certain things. I'd love to see you become that confident in all things. You're a very capable woman. You just let the fear of failure get in your way sometimes.

"I love the way you kiss me. I love that you won't take a bite of salad until you're certain not a single olive is hiding in the lettuce, but you're too polite to ask the waitress to specialize the order. I love that you're messy and I love that your socks never match. I love the moments when I can't tell what you're thinking, but I love it more when you share what's going on in your head."

"There's a whole lot more to me than the way I order my food and being book smart, Alec."

"I know. There are also parts of you I don't care for, but I love you anyway."

She turned and frowned at him. "That's not very nice."

He chuckled. "That's honesty, Sheilagh. Anyone who says they love their partner and like every single thing about them is full of shit. No one's perfect and we all have different tastes. If someone loved me, I'd expect them to love me enough to tell me when I'm wrong or when I doing a disservice to myself or others. Loving someone means helping him or her be a better person. We're all just trying to be the best we can in this short life."

She sat up on her knees facing him. "Alec?"

"Yeah?"

"You're a shitty essay grader, you hog the left lane when you drive and never go more than ten miles over the speed limit. You lose your keys constantly and pronounce 'beer can' like *bacon.* I'm telling you this because I want you to be a better person and because I love you."

He stilled. She loved him? "You love me?"

"Yes. I love you."

He smiled and leaned in and kissed her. The kiss was cut short as he pulled away and said, "Beer can. Beer can. Bollocks, it does sound like bacon."

She giggled. "That's okay. I think it's kind of cute."

"Will you come home with me now? I desperately want to make love to you, but am a wee bit shy knowing my son can hear us."

"Do I need to get dressed?"

"I think you're rather adorable in what you're wearing."

"Excellent. I'll get my purse."

WHEN ALEC PULLED his car in front of the garage, he turned the key and all was quiet. Glancing to his right, his heart stuttered with a touch of worry and his blood pumped with excitement. She was here, where she belonged.

"Are we all right?" he whispered, tracing his finger

over her knee.

Her copper hair caught the fading light as she faced him. He wanted to kiss away every worry line trapping the beauty of her jade eyes. She was fighting a war with a one-man regime and she didn't have to go at it alone.

Slowly, her mouth curved into a smile. "I missed you."

God, he missed her too. "Let's go inside."

They made it into the kitchen and then he couldn't resist another second without touching her. Catching her wrist, he pulled her slowly to him. His lips brushed over hers as he whispered, "You've gotten inside of me the way no one ever has, Sheilagh. When you aren't there I'm hollow in ways I don't enjoy."

Her shimmering eyes blinked up at him as her arms slithered around his waist. "I know that emptiness. It's dark and lonely. You chase away the shadows, Alec. I want *us.* I don't want to run from it because it's scary and unpredictable. I deserve to be happy. *You* make me happy."

He brushed his lips over hers and their fingers laced together. In quiet accord, they ascended the stairs. When they reached his room he kissed her with a slow building passion he worried he wouldn't be able to contain.

Her hands pulled at his neck as he stripped her of her clothing. Once they were both undressed, they fell into bed. Their bodies moved slowly, coming together like dawn over the distance and when they were one, all the darkness disappeared.

He filled her with purpose, needing her body like a

man needs a home. She was his respite, his vessel, his peace. When she came her head tipped back in sheer surrender. His arms banded around her, holding her close as they rocked through the intense ecstasy of their joining. Never had it been so beautiful, so perfect.

Their union left their secrets exposed. Every façade had fallen, brick by brick, broken down with each caressing gaze, every stroking finger. No more boundaries. No more hiding. This was where they each desired to be and they would somehow make it work, because they each seemed to need it more than their next breath.

CHAPTER 10

~~I deserve to be happy. God, I sound like a corny after school special. This is stupid.~~
I deserve to be happy. I will be happy. I will stop using my past as a weapon to beat me down. Alec makes me happy. Last night he braided my hair as we sat by the fire. Such a simple act, yet its value was immeasurable, overflowing my heart with foreign emotions. Those sharp little flutters in my chest are happiness. I love when he tickles me that way.

"Why don't you start by telling me why you're here?"

Sheilagh fidgeted on the small green loveseat. It was cushy, broken in, and the small office was altogether brighter than she'd expected. On the low table sat a bowl of Dove chocolates. She reached forward and grabbed one, not eating it, but gaining comfort from the slight weight in her hand. Her finger flicked at the foil wrapping.

"I cry a lot."

Megan nodded. What kind of therapist went by "Megan"? "What do you cry about?"

"Sometimes my family, sometimes nothing. It hurts, like I'm wringing myself dry, but afterwards I feel lighter."

"When you cry about your family, what sort of thoughts are you having?"

Visions of her brothers and sister flashed through her mind. Her mom dominated the picture, seeming larger than life, radiating love, while her father sat quietly at her side. "I miss them."

"Do you visit home often?"

Her shoulder lifted then dropped. "Every time I visit I have to eventually say goodbye. I don't like leaving them." She didn't mention she'd cried when she'd lived there too.

"Yet you chose to come to Princeton."

Her lips tightened. Chose? Forced? "My brothers said I

was losing myself in a place that never changed. I needed to get out."

"Is Center County a small town?"

"Very. It's your typical redneck township, built around a main street cleverly named Main Street. Everyone knows the mechanic, the butcher, and the taxidermist, and no one's private business is ever really private."

"Does that bother you, the lack of privacy?"

"I've never had privacy. There are nine of us in my immediate family."

"Did you have your own room growing up, a space you could retreat to without disruption?"

These were some of the questions Megan asked over the first four weeks of therapy. It was tedious, but she continued to go to her every week, per Alec's suggestion. In Sheilagh's opinion, she wasn't an interesting case study. No one had ever done anything terrible to her. She wasn't held up at gunpoint, preyed upon by a relative. There was no real trauma to speak of and she imagined her therapist eventually growing bored with her whining, and inability to accept life and happily chug on.

Something was definitely wrong with her.

She returned to class and continued to ace her assignments. It was all very mundane. Her moments with Alec were fleeting and clandestine, but they opened a world of emotion inside of her she was still trying to figure out.

Somehow, he helped her get lost—from herself, the

pain, the darkness. He was a key to her peace and she never passed up an opportunity to see him.

Their time was limited, so one random Tuesday she decided to pop in and catch his lecture. As he rambled on about the great philosophers of the past she shut her eyes and listened. His voice treated her to a symphony of memories playing through her mind. She could listen to him for hours. It was different, not having to take notes. The absence of pressure did something to her, allowed her to simply be in the moment.

As he excused his class she opened her eyes, sensing his approach. "Ms. McCullough. I didn't expect to see you here. Is there something I can do for you?"

Students gathered their belongings and left the lecture hall. She met his gaze and smiled. He was so beautifully cliché in his tweed jacket and white button down. "My afternoon was open and I felt the need for something cerebral."

"Would you like to come to my office?"

She nodded slowly, gathering her belongings. As they walked through the halls of the philosophy building, she kept a keen appraisal of their distance. He held the door to his office and she entered.

The soft click of the door closing flipped a switch inside of her. Her bag dropped to the floor and her body heated with his closeness as he pressed his chest to her back. Hands coasted over her sleeves and she shivered.

"I've missed you," he whispered against her hair.

Tipping her head to the side, her eyes shut as he softly brushed her hair away from her neck and pressed a kiss there. Shivers danced over every patch of skin he touched and she abruptly turned. Her fingers dragged through his hair as she pulled his mouth down to hers. Their breath drew in as they devoured each other.

He backed her up until her ass crashed into his desk, rocking the belongings perched on top. "God, you're sexy."

She lifted and scooted onto the surface. His body filled the space between her thighs as her legs wrapped around his hips. His hands sifted under her shirt and cupped her breast. She arched into his touch and moaned into his mouth.

The sense of outsiders walking by heightened her excitement. "Fuck me, Alec."

He growled into her mouth and suddenly he was gone. The lock on the door clicked and his fingers made quick work of unsnapping her jeans. He hoisted her to her feet and spun her so her belly was flat on his desk. Papers scattered to the floor as his zipper came down. Warm hands cupped her ass and her knees widened as much as her jeans bunched around her legs would allow.

When his fingers found her sex she was wet and ready. "This is very brazen, Sheilagh," he said as his finger thrust deep.

"Do it. I need you inside of me—now."

The soft material of his pants brushed the back of her

thighs as he lined his cock up with her sex. He entered her swiftly, with a hard thrust, burying himself. She went up on her toes and grunted.

"Shh…"

"Hard, Alec. I need it hard."

He withdrew and thrust deep. The wood of his heavy desk dragged over the tile floor with every solid advance. She bit her lip to keep quiet and savored the sound of his ragged breathing.

She wouldn't come, but that was okay. That wasn't what this was about. This was about needing to feel his possession, the potent need he held for her. "Harder."

His speed doubled and she luxuriated in his ownership of her body. The muffled smack of his hips against her ass drove her to places where only he could take her. His body tensed and shivered, swelled deep inside of her, and then he was coming. When he finished, he collapsed on her back, breathing hard.

"I can't believe we just did that here."

She sighed contently. "I love you."

His lips pressed to her ear. "I love you too."

He withdrew and quickly helped her right her clothing. As he tucked in his shirt she picked up the items that had fallen to the floor. He unlocked the door and looked at his watch. "I have another lecture in twenty minutes. Will I see you tonight?"

She nodded. "I have to go to the library for a bit, but I'll be by later."

He approached her and kissed her tenderly, his thumb dragging over the line of her jaw as he stepped away. "I'm sorry. I have to go."

She collected her things and kissed him one last time before easing out of his office. As she shut the door and turned, she stilled. A professor she'd never had, but recognized as a university employee gave her a strange look. Letting her hair fall over her face she quickly walked past him in the direction of the library.

"Tell me about Alec."

Sheilagh leaned back on the green loveseat and sighed. "Alec is…good."

"Why good?" Megan asked.

"He helps me escape."

"What is it you're escaping from?"

She shrugged. "Nothing tangible. It's more an escape from myself."

"Are you intimate?"

She laughed. "Yes."

"Why does that question amuse you?"

"We had sex in his office."

"Is the sex good?"

She grinned. "It's incredible."

"How so?"

"I'm there. He makes sure I'm present."

"And this is different than the relations you've had with other men?"

"Well, yeah. With others it was always a way to blank out, sort of hide. Escape."

"But you said Alec helps you escape."

"It's different. He frees me. The others let me hide." She wasn't sure how, but it was completely contrary to every other sexual encounter she'd ever had. "It doesn't matter if we're going at it like monkeys or making love, he makes me…feel."

"Emotionally?"

"Yes."

"And you like that?"

"Yes."

"Are you in love with him?"

"Yes."

"Does he tell you he loves you?"

"Every day."

"And how does that make you feel?"

She thought about this for a minute. "Normal."

"And is normal good?"

"I think everyone wants to be normal."

"What do you think about being different?"

Sheilagh grabbed a piece of chocolate from the dish. "I just want to be normal."

"Normal is an opinion based on social expectation and not deviating from the rule."

Sheilagh raised a brow, not disagreeing.

Megan continued. "Your relationship with Alec is a secret."

"It has to be. He could lose his job."

"Yet he makes you feel normal, even when no one else sees."

"*I* see."

Megan nodded. "And you like the perception of yourself in his presence?"

"Yes. I guess...*he* sees me as normal." She frowned. "Although..."

"Although?"

She sighed and slouched back on the couch. "If you asked Alec what was normal he'd say normal doesn't exist."

"He's smart."

"He's a know-it-all."

Megan smiled. "Does that bother you?"

"No. He *is* smart. He sees the world differently and I agree with him most of the time."

"How did your relationship start?"

"He gave me a bad grade. I thought I deserved better."

"Do you still believe that?"

"No. I wrote a good paper, but it was evasive and he saw through my tactics."

"What was the topic?"

"Plato's *The Republic*."

"Will you redo the assignment?"

"I dropped the course."

"But the course is a requirement. I must say it's unethical for you to have him as your teacher and I advise against that, but perhaps it would do you good to actually write the paper the way it was intended to be written. You'll eventually have to take the course again."

Sheilagh grinned. "I don't want to give him the satisfaction."

"Why?"

"Because he's right too often and I like having that part of myself he can't get."

"Could it be something else?" she asked.

Misunderstanding, Sheilagh said, "Like what?"

"Maybe just think on it."

She paused. Think on what? There was nothing to think about. Did she think she was *afraid* to write the stupid paper? "I'm not scared to write it."

Megan pressed her lips tight, saying nothing.

"You think I'm using it somehow, like, to keep Alec at a distance?"

"Where did that come from?"

Sheilagh frowned. "That doesn't make sense. It's in my head. I know what I'd write."

"Do you? You have a habit of hiding from things you don't like to face, truths that may be somewhat unpleasant to let surface."

"I'll write it," she said with indifference.

"But will you give your honest appraisal of the story?"

"Why wouldn't I?"

"Will you allow Alec to read it?"

"No."

"Because he'll see through it?"

She ground her teeth. "Do you know him?"

Megan laughed. "No, I don't know him. But I think he knows you. I've read *The Republic*, several times. It's not an easy concept to grasp, but it's an easy enough read."

"You sound like Alec."

"Does that bother you?"

"No. I just don't like feeling forced."

"We're just talking."

Sheilagh sighed. "I know what the story's about. I've read it several times."

"What's it about?"

"The whole dilemma questions if an unjust man is as happy as a just man."

"And?"

"Well… Yes, I think he is."

The therapist's brow lifted. "How do you figure?"

"*The Republic* was written in B.C. Plato had yet to see the modern day tyrant. Some people are completely evil, but also quite satisfied with themselves."

Megan adjusted her posture. "I think we're getting off topic."

"Which is what? Plato? It's a stupid assignment which is no longer required."

"For now."

Sheilagh frowned. Maybe she was missing something.

Everyone seemed to think this ridiculous book had the key to all that ailed her. She didn't want to look that deeply into herself. It was easier to look at others and make assessments.

Megan crossed her legs and waited.

"What?"

"Why are you angry?"

"I'm not angry," Sheilagh snapped.

"You're shouting."

She *was* shouting. Tightening her lips, she mumbled, "Sorry."

A few moments passed and Megan said, "Think about the word *normal.* You've used it a few times today. Once regarding Hitler's ideals in comparison to Plato's and once in defining how Alec makes you feel."

"You're twisting my words."

"I'm only trying to address the fact that "normal" may be something even you strive for, but in your case it's based on *your* perception. What's your definition of right and wrong, Sheilagh?"

"It's the same as everyone else's."

"Which is?"

She shrugged. "I don't know. The Ten Commandments."

"Are you a Christian?"

"I'm Catholic."

"Do you believe you are a just person?"

For some reason she didn't answer. She couldn't. Was

she just? She was sitting there arguing with her therapist over the similarities of Hitler and Plato, which was obviously off tangent to her own crap. She could go on and on about philosophies and analyzing other's mistakes, but when it came to herself, she didn't have a single answer.

The problem with that stupid assignment is that Alec never asked for Plato's thoughts. He'd asked for his student's. Why was it so difficult for her to divulge such information? She knew the text by heart, but couldn't seem to apply it to her life. Every time she tried, part of her pulled back as though shying away from a frightening shadow.

The commandments rolled through her head. She never killed anyone. She sort of went to church. She was as respectful of her parents in her own screwed up McCullough way. She believed in God, but didn't hassle people about their personal beliefs in other Gods—to each his own...

But...

She shared a bed with a man who was not her legal spouse. She'd been with lots of men, dishonored her body, which was meant to be her temple. She didn't want to get wrapped up in all that. It was a catch many Catholics faced and other than her brother Kelly's wife, no one really waited until marriage anymore. Yet, knowing this didn't restore a bit of the dignity that scraped away each time she gave her body to someone she didn't love.

However, Alec was different. She loved him. He loved

her. If he asked her to marry him—*whoa!* She was *not* going there.

"What are you thinking about?"

"Marriage," Sheilagh replied, a little surprised at the course of her thoughts.

"Whose marriage?"

"I guess mine."

"Are you thinking about Alec?"

She shrugged. "We aren't there yet."

"Do you think you're a good person, Sheilagh?"

She nodded, but couldn't vocalize her agreement.

Megan waited for her to look at her as if knowing there were conditions to her assessment of herself.

Sheilagh shrugged. "I coveted my brother's lover."

Megan appeared surprised by this admission. "Could you expand on that?"

Shrinking into the couch a bit more, she said, "His name's Tristan."

"Your brother's gay?"

"Yes. Bi. I don't know. He's been with Tristan for years, but no one knows aside from me."

"And who is Tristan to you?"

"He moved to our town after my brother returned from college. Luke blew out his knee and lost his scholarship. I was just a kid. When I met Tristan I was in love."

"How old were you?"

"Sixteen or seventeen."

"So you were very young. How old is Tristan?"

"He's almost thirty now."

"Are you typically attracted to older men?"

"Not really. I mean, yes, Alec's older, but Tristan always seemed more on my level."

"Emotionally?"

"In a way. More socially, but I guess I sort of hero-worshipped him so maybe that's not true."

"When did you find out about him and Luke?"

"When I was eighteen. I was supposed to be leaving for college soon. I wanted to tell him before I left. I had no idea he was dating anyone, let alone Luke. He never acted gay. I...found them together."

"They were being intimate?"

"Luke was wearing a towel and waiting for Tristan to join him in the shower."

"What was that like for you?"

She scoffed. "To say I was blown away is an understatement."

"And did this discovery affect other parts of your life?"

"No. Maybe. At first. I think I wanted to see what would happen. I couldn't accept what I saw."

"You were in denial."

"Yeah, but as time went on I saw more than their relationship. I saw their love. In a look, a longing glance, a stolen touch. It sometimes seemed so blatant I wondered how no one else saw it. It makes me angry that they keep their relationship a secret."

"Why?"

"Because Tristan deserves more than that."

"What about your brother?"

"Luke and I haven't been the same since. Things are worse now."

"Why?"

"Because last time I was home Tristan kissed me."

"And…"

"Alec was home visiting with me."

"Does Alec know?"

"Yeah. We broke up for a while, but then we calmed down and talked about it. He says Tristan is confused and it isn't right for him to play with my head."

"And what do you think about that?"

"I think he's right, but my instinct always has me jumping to Tristan's defense."

"Why do you think that is?"

"I don't know. Everything having to do with him has gotten so confusing."

"How did the kiss make you feel?"

"Angry."

"Why angry?"

"Because six years ago I would have given anything to have him kiss me, but he waited until I was in love with someone else."

"And how does your love for Alec compare to your love for Tristan?"

"It's different."

"Different how?"

"Alec is… He sees me, not as some little kid or a little sister to his friend. The word McCullough means nothing to him. He sees me as a woman, as his equal."

"How would you describe what you feel for Alec?"

Sheilagh considered this. "Genuine."

"And Tristan?"

"Maybe not so genuine. When he kissed me it changed things. He was always the man I couldn't have, either because I was too young or because of Luke. He removed the obstacle and suddenly I realized I no longer wanted him. It's like I've been walking around in a haze of make believe, using him as an excuse for being miserable all these years. If it's not him, then what is it?"

"That's what we're trying to figure out."

"Maybe it's me."

"You said your relationship with Luke has gotten worse since the kiss. Does he know about the kiss?"

"Yes. He flipped out. I don't blame him. Everything he said was true."

"Do you remember what he said?"

"He said enough is never enough with me, that he was tired of feeling guilty over some childish crush I had on Tristan." She looked down, shame resurfacing. "He said he was done with me."

"Did you fight back?"

"No. I just stood there and took it, like I had it coming."

"I find that people who believe in religions formulated on penance tend to be extra critical of themselves and often unforgiving of their wrongs. As a Catholic, do you follow the practices of confession? And if so, does it bring contentment?"

"I go to confession, but I never really get deep with the priest. I just brush over the basics, missing mass, cursing, pre-marital sex."

"Does the idea of pre-marital sex bother you?"

"Not really."

"And cursing?"

"No. I was raised by a woman whose favorite word is cocksucker. They're just words."

"Then why ask for forgiveness?"

She shrugged. "That's what Catholics are supposed to do."

"And when you're absolved of these so-called sins, do you feel better?"

"Not really." She looked at Megan. "I guess I'm not really a very good Catholic."

"Who says you have to be?"

"God. My parents."

"And what do you say?"

She laughed. "Sometimes I just want to say fuck it."

"Meaning?"

"There are so many rules. I'm tired of them. I'm tired of beating myself up for not being perfect."

"And what is perfect, Sheilagh? Who do you see in your mind when you imagine someone of perfection?"

She thought for a minute. "I guess no one."

"Is that okay?"

Sheilagh shrugged, digesting all of this. For the first time since meeting her therapist she actually felt like she was getting some therapy. "So what do I do?"

"What do you want to do?"

"I want to start over."

Megan nodded. "Is anything stopping you?"

"People. They have this idea of me and if I changed it would all be fake."

"Fake to…"

"Them, but being fake is my reality."

"Does it have to be?"

They were running out of time. Sheilagh didn't want to leave until she had an answer. A hint of what direction was the right one. "People hate change."

"What makes you say that?"

"Experience. They have something in their head and the minute you surprise them they get all nutty."

"Who's they?"

"Everyone. My family."

"So you're saying your family expects you to be a certain way and it might disappoint them if you don't deliver "old Sheilagh"?"

"Yes."

Megan waited.

"If I wanted to test that theory I'd have to go home. I can't do that."

"Why?"

I'm ashamed, scared, all of the above. Her chest tightened. "Because everything's all messed up. My parents are acting different. Luke hates me. Tristan's an issue I don't want to face."

"How are your parents acting different?"

"They've turned the house into their personal love nest. It's gross."

Megan laughed then turned serious again. "Do you honestly believe your brother hates you?"

"Yes." There was no question about it. Luke made his feelings perfectly clear and she couldn't even argue with him.

"Do you hate Luke?"

"No, I love Luke," she stated emphatically.

"And you don't believe he holds the same unconditional affection for you, his sister."

"He didn't try to take the person I love from me."

"You said Tristan kissed *you.*"

"He did."

"Then how is that your fault?"

She frowned. "It's not, I guess, but I let it get to that point."

"How?"

"I don't know. I flirted."

"It takes two people to flirt."

"I propositioned him."

"When?"

"When I was eighteen."

"And nothing since?"

She shrugged weakly. "We danced together. We flirt. We're always making private jokes."

"Sounds like a lot of *we* and not so much you."

"Maybe."

Megan glanced at her watch "We're out of time. I'd like you to do something for me."

"What?"

"I'd like you to write a letter to Luke. It's not to give to him, but I want you to write down everything you feel regarding him and bring it with you next week to our session."

"Okay."

When she left Megan's office she felt heavy as though the things on her mind were truly weighing her down. She returned to her apartment and opened up her notebook intending to write up the lab she had due, but found herself distracted. An hour later she was on the fifth page of a scribbled letter to her brother.

She made a pot of tea as she reread her words. Her eyes prickled with tears as she worked around the kitchen, heating up soup and stirring sugar into her favorite mug. Grabbing a pen from the few wedged in the bun of her hair, she adjusted her wording and scratched out some things that came off harsher than she wanted.

The sun set and her apartment turned dark, forcing her to move to the couch by the lamp. Sometime later there was a knock at her door. As she finished scrawling out her thoughts she frowned. It was after ten.

Holding the sheaf of well over eighteen pages in her hand, she shuffled to the door and opened it.

"Oh, good, you're alive," Alec said, a look of irritation on his face.

"What?"

"I've been calling you for hours."

She frowned. "My phone must still be on silent from this afternoon." She always set her phone to vibrate when she met with Megan.

Alec stepped inside and shut the door. "I was worried, Sheilagh. You usually call me after your sessions."

"Sorry."

He glanced around her apartment. "Is everything okay?"

"Sure."

He frowned. "Did something happen today?"

"Everything's fine, Alec. I lost track of time."

His gaze went to the rumpled papers in her hand. "What are you working on?"

"A letter to Luke."

The magnitude of this registered in his eyes. His expression softened. "Have you been crying?" His fingers caught her chin, turning her face to his.

"A little. It's helping."

"Did Megan suggest you write him?"

"I'm not giving it to him. It's just for me." *And to share*

with Megan so she can make me look at things I really don't
want see.

"Okay."

He was so good like that, always understanding her quirky behaviors and never asking her to be anything other than herself. "Did you eat?"

"I had a cup of soup."

His mouth pursed. "Those dreadful wax noodles that seem the staple of every college student's diet are not food. Why don't we order something? We can pick it up on the way back to my place."

"I want to stay here tonight."

He stilled, but didn't appear disappointed. "Why?"

"I don't know. I just… miss my space."

"I see." He shifted and glanced at the floor.

"You could stay."

"Is that what you want or are you simply being polite?"

He was so cute when his own insecurities showed. She smiled. "Stay. My apartment could use a good cleaning. I know how you love my decorating of dirty laundry and dishes turned science project."

He chuckled and stepped closer. When his arms wrapped around her hips he pinched her ass. "Are you making fun of me?"

"Yes."

He kissed her. "You're a slob."

"And you're arrogant, so I'll let you enlighten me by tidying up my place as I finish this letter and we wait for pizza to arrive. You can show me all the right ways to be tidy. I know you love pointing out how smart you are."

"Brat."

"You love me."

"I do." His lips found hers and they both laughed as they kissed their way to the couch, tripping over shoes and whatever else littered the floor along the way.

CHAPTER 11

Sometimes I wonder if I can't see the future because there isn't one. Maybe I'll die before I'm thirty. Or maybe I just can't stand not knowing what will happen, as if knowing will somehow direct me to do the right thing. I need to stop searching for answers that aren't there and start really considering what it is that I want, what will make me happy. I have no fucking clue what that might be and sometimes I feel like I'm the only person in the world struggling to unearth the obvious. For being a supposedly smart person, when it comes to myself I'm shockingly ignorant.

That night they lay in her cramped bed as the TV flickered shadows across the wall. They'd made love quietly, doing their best not to disturb her prickly neighbor. Alec held her against his long body, his hand still massaging her breast as they whispered to each other in the dark.

"Do you think you'll ever get married again?"

He stilled. "Perhaps."

What kind of answer was that? "Perhaps...what?"

"It depends," he said, his hand no longer playing with her.

She turned and faced him. "What does it depend on, Alec? Give me real answers."

"Why are you asking, Sheilagh?" He didn't look pleased with the topic.

"Jeeze. Forget it." She went to turn away and he gripped her shoulder, halting her escape.

"Tell me why you're asking."

No longer wanting to discuss the subject, she said, "I was just curious."

He let go of her shoulder and she rolled away from him. The room was suddenly too quiet. Where was the remote?

"You're very young." She stilled at his quiet statement. "You're very young and one day you'll want a family."

A cold, heavy feeling filled her stomach. Dread. "Not everyone wants children."

"Do you?"

Yes. No. "I don't know."

"Sheilagh…"

"What, Alec?" she snapped.

"I love you, but I love you enough to want to see you happy."

She blinked at the television, her eyes burning. "And you know what makes me happy? Funny. Even I don't know that. I have fucking professionals working around the clock trying to figure it out."

He kissed the back of her head and whispered, "Don't be angry with me, love. We both know what the reality of our situation is."

She scoffed. "I don't. Why don't you explain it to me, professor, since you seem to have us all figured out and can suddenly predict the future?"

"I don't want to be another person who holds you back."

"You aren't holding me back!"

"I can't give you children. I won't live as long as you—"

"For fuck sake, Alec, stop acting like you're seventy. You're forty fucking years old."

"And you're barely into your twenties!"

She swung her head around and scowled at him. "Does this suddenly bother you?"

"No, but it may someday bother you. I don't ever want to be someone you resent."

"Then stop trying to decide for me. I'm an adult. Have the respect to treat me like one."

"Sheilagh, you're twenty-four. When I was twenty-four I was nothing like I am today."

She stopped thinking. Moments from her session with Megan flitted through her mind, words about change and being the person she really was versus pretending to be something she wasn't to satisfy others. "You make me happy," she said quietly. "You're the only person who's truly done that for me in…a *long* time. Don't take that away from me for stupid reasons, Alec."

His gaze turned scrutinizing. His lips twitched as if he were prepared to tell her what was best for her. After a while he sighed. "I'd marry you, Sheilagh. If that's what you want I'd marry you in a heartbeat, but it isn't something I require."

She stared at him for a minute. Neither of them said a word. Finally, she rolled her eyes and dropped her head to her pillow. "That was the shittiest proposal in the history of mankind. You need to work on your game."

He didn't laugh. She'd turned away and wasn't sure what his expression was. She was too afraid to look. Commercials played silently on the television and she waited for him to say something, but he never did.

When she woke up in the morning, he was gone.

ALEC NODDED toward a colleague as he headed back to his office after his first lecture of the day. As he shuffled his coffee and briefcase he found his door already open and nudged it the rest of the way. "Wes? What are you doing here? Don't you have class?"

His son pivoted in the chair behind the desk and faced him. "We need to talk."

Alec had been waiting for this. He dropped his briefcase on the chair and sipped his coffee as he shut the door for privacy. "I'm listening."

"Are you? I worry about your hearing, because I think you're already blind."

He stiffened at his son's snide tone. "I don't want to argue—"

"I'm not arguing with you, Dad. I'm giving you the facts. You and that girl are going to get caught. She's going to get expelled and you're going to lose your job. That may not mean much to you—I honestly don't get what you see in her, but she's sure got you under some sort of spell—nevertheless, when your life falls apart, so will mine."

"I'm not going to let that happen, Wes."

"What the hell are you gonna do to stop it, Dad? Stop thinking with your dick and use your head—"

"*Hey!*" Grinding down his molars he drew in a slow

breath. "Watch your mouth. If you think I would jeopardize your education—"

"That's exactly what you're doing! When does it end? I heard you last night giggling. You're acting like an irresponsible kid. I don't get what you and that girl have in common. She's awful!"

"Her name is Sheilagh!" he hissed. "And, while I don't expect your blessing, I do expect your respect, for my privacy, my preferences, and my woman."

Wes's face contorted with disbelief. "Your woman?"

"Yes. I love her, Wesley. It may not be who you'd choose for me, but if you can accept your mother loving another woman I'd expect you can get over this."

"And what about my privacy? Do you think it will be easy for me when my father's ethics are drawn into question and his position is up for review."

"My personal life has nothing to do with yours."

"Obviously, but the repercussions could ruin everything. I like Princeton, Dad. I don't want to switch schools. I don't want our family's personal shit to turn into campus gossip. Can't you try to see this from my point of view?"

"And when will you try to see it from mine? Do you have any idea how lonely my life has become? You run off with your friends or back to your Mom's whenever you're bored. I'm left here twiddling my thumbs. Sheilagh makes me happy. For once in my life I'm actually happy. Doesn't that count for anything?"

His son remained quiet. Disappointment seemed to swallow Alec whole.

"No, I guess not." Moving to his desk, he dropped his coffee cup in his wastebasket and grabbed the papers he had to return to his next class. "If you'll excuse me, Wes. I have a class to teach."

The rest of the day passed in a blur. It wasn't that Alec wasn't worried about Wes's role in all of this. He was. He just couldn't see giving up Sheilagh on the *chance* that something could go wrong. They'd just have to be more circumspect and cautious.

If anything jeopardized Wesley's education, he'd never forgive himself. His son worked very hard to be here and he wanted to see him graduate from a university he loved. The same went for Sheilagh.

Oddly, he was least concerned with his own security. He could teach anywhere, but his employment at the university was key to his son's enrollment. This was the last thing he wanted to worry about today. His mind was already twisted over Sheilagh's question last night.

Of course he'd marry her. There was nothing in his life stopping him, aside from his opinions on the institution itself. He had no issue with marriage, but at this stage in his life didn't see it as necessary to have a fundamental relationship. However, if Sheilagh did, he'd gladly vow his life to hers.

It was Sheilagh that had him hesitating to wander down that road. She was young. Her life had barely started. He didn't want her to have regrets years from now. She was still figuring herself out, and divorce, no matter how amicable, was messy.

He loved her. He loved her more than he'd ever loved anyone, including Wes's mother. And loving her so much meant sacrificing his own desires to secure hers.

Where had the topic of marriage even come from? They'd never discussed it before. His mind went to the facts. He hadn't considered having more children until Sheilagh's youth became so apparent, namely, when he saw her in her family home surrounded by so much family.

It was then that he contemplated his inability to father more children and toyed with the possibility of having his vasectomy reversed, a costly procedure that gave no guarantee. It was the most he could offer a woman like herself —and it was barely a promise at that.

He wasn't even sure if he wanted more children. The son he had now wasn't speaking to him. Parenting was difficult and he never had the relationship with his son he'd always hoped for.

And what of when he was older? He didn't want be pushing his babies as he leaned over his walker. Fucking mortality. When Sheilagh would be thirty-five he'd be fifty-one. He'd be seventy and she'd still be in the prime of her life at a mere fifty-four.

He paused. Why was fifty-four the prime of *her* life, yet he had himself already dead and buried at forty? Was there really that big of a difference? He wasn't making sense, even to himself.

AFTER FINISHING his last class of the day Alec headed to town, settling onto a stool at the local pub and ordering beer after beer without keeping count. When he paid his tab he was surprised by how much he'd actually drank.

He left his car and decided to walk home. As he meandered along the dark sidewalks he passed a store window that was lit beautifully. Jewels and trinkets sparkled inside.

Leaning his forehead on the glass he examined the display, his attention catching on a particularly beautiful setting. That ring would look lovely on Sheilagh.

"Lost?"

He turned, his forehead squeaking along the glass. *Speak of the devil.* "Hello."

She laughed. "You're pissed."

"I'm not angry. Ah… you mean drunk. Yes. Quite."

"Where's your car?"

"In a spot, down there somewhere."

She laughed. "Come on. I'll walk you back to it and drive it to your house."

He caught her wrist and she stilled. "Do you want to marry me, Sheilagh?" he whispered and her smile trembled. "I'll give you anything you want, love, but you have to be sure you know what you're asking for."

She pulled her wrist out of his grip and stepped back. "People are looking, Alec. Come on. Let's go home."

He turned and noticed there were still pedestrians on the sidewalk besides them. He didn't care, but he had to— had to for Wes's sake and Sheilagh's. Getting ahold of himself he stood a little straighter. "I'd marry you. If I believed that was what you honestly wanted, I'd marry you in a second. You're brilliant. You make me happy. Our sex is incredible."

"Alec."

"Just let me know when you figure out what you really want," he said, talking over her. "If it's me, you have me. All of me. I'm yours."

"I'm taking you home."

She turned and he followed. They maintained an appropriate distance as they made their way back to his car, which wasn't exactly where he remembered leaving it. He handed her his keys and she adjusted the mirrors as he slouched in the passenger seat admiring her beauty.

"Wes isn't speaking to me," he announced as she pulled onto the road. "He's mostly yelling at me. He's worried about his enrollment and what will happen if we're caught."

"I can understand that," she said, not taking her eyes from the road.

"Does that worry you? Are you afraid you'll get expelled?"

"No."

He laughed. "Who are you, Sheilagh McCullough? You worry about issues of little consequence, because they might change people's opinions of you, but real penalties don't scare you at all."

"What does it matter what school I go to? I could go to any school and get the same degree. There's only one of you."

"I love you."

She smiled. "How much did you drink?"

"Sixty-two dollars' worth."

"What were you drinking?"

"I started with beer and then moved onto whatever tickled my fancy."

She laughed. "I love it when you use manly terms like *tickle my fancy*."

They pulled into his driveway and she turned off the car. "I have a dilemma," he confessed.

"If you're going to puke, open the door."

"I love it when you speak with such feminine eloquence."

"Touché. What's your dilemma?"

"Since you've mentioned marriage I find myself wanting to marry you."

Her smile fell. "What?"

"I not only love you, I like you. I like you more than I

like most people. We're very different from each other, but I like that about us. I like us. I would be honored to say you're my wife. I think you'd show me what it really is to be someone's husband, more so than anyone else ever has."

"Again, with the top notch proposal. You really have to work on your game."

She said the words sarcastically, but there was no laughter in her expression. He laced his fingers in hers. "Do you want to be my wife?"

"Alec." She frowned. "I have no doubt you'd be a wonderful husband, but I'm the farthest thing from the perfect wife."

"I don't want perfect. I want you."

She pulled her hand away. "You're drunk. The other night I was just curious where you stood on the subject. It's a big decision, one neither of us should rush into."

She was right, of course. "I'll ask you another time, perhaps." He was a putz. Even drunk he could see how ridiculous he was acting.

"Perhaps."

When they made it inside she made him a sandwich, which helped sober him up. He was ravenous, because he hadn't eaten all day. She fed him and he adored her for it. Once his belly was full they went to bed.

Sheilagh showered and he fell asleep before she returned. The next morning he woke up with a pounding headache that was his due for being such an ass. He considered what he'd said about marrying her and actually found himself still agreeing with his stance. He *did* want to marry her. It was something he hadn't realized until she suggested it. The problem was, she hadn't really suggested it at all. She merely mentioned it and he clung to the word like a drowning man to a life raft.

Basically, he was fucked.

SHEILAGH AVOIDED Alec for the next few days. He was well aware of what she was doing. He texted her often and called her right out using words like avoidance and communication. If he was going to be so predictably Alec, she decided to be predictably Sheilagh. Her replies were snarky and immature, taking zero accountability and excelling in sarcasm.

She got away with three whole days of hiding until he came to her apartment. Surprisingly, he wasn't angry. "Are you done with your tantrum?" he asked as she opened the door to let him in.

"Maybe. Are you done making a spectacle of yourself?"

"I make a spectacular spectacle, I find."

She rolled her eyes. "You can only come in if you promise not to use the words marriage, wife, marry, spouse, husband, bride, or wedding."

"Fine." She let him in and shut the door. "I would make a rather dashing *groom*, though, don't you think?"

She laughed. "I hate you."

He caught her wrist and pulled her to his chest. "You love me."

"Only on holidays and Tuesdays and days that start with S. The rest of the time it's touch and go."

His lips pressed to hers as he smiled. "I want to touch you."

"Mmm, Dr. Devereux, you haven't touched me in days." His fingers found the hem of her shirt and pulled it over her head, tossing it to the floor. "I'll ask that you not make a mess of my apartment."

He laughed. "You're right. I'll only end up picking it up again. Lord knows you can't clean."

Unhooking her bra, she backed toward the bed. "Oh, really? I'll have you know I am quite an excellent maid."

He stripped off his shirt. "Then why does your apartment always look like a bomb hit it?"

She shucked her pants, balled them up, and threw them at his chest. "Because I think it's sexy when you clean up after me."

He toed off his socks and shoes, stalking her steps slowly. "Lazy little liar."

"Pretentiously pompous neat freak."

He lunged and she squealed as he tackled her to the bed. Laughter belted out of her as he tickled and wrestled with her. "Mercy! *Mercy!*"

He kissed her. "Smart ass brat."

She pressed her breasts to his chest and arched beneath him. "*Your* brat."

Pinning her hands above her head, he lowered his head and nipped at her breast. "Yes. *My* little brat. All mine."

He took his time once he had her. His mouth kissed every exposed inch of flesh and he brought her to climax twice before entering her. When he came, he made sure she went with him. They fell asleep in her cramped little bed, a tangled mess of limbs. Yeah, she'd marry him. He just had to ask the right way.

CHAPTER 12

I read the book *Great Expectations* when I was seven. My favorite parts were the hintingly frightening themes, mostly in the curious characters I didn't know how to judge, but wanted to label evil. In the end, nothing was as it seemed and the wicked were the saviors while the seemingly generous were corrupt and motivated by revenge. What motivates me? Surely I'm not wicked or corrupt when measured against society as a whole. I feel the pressure of such great expectations weighing on me, yet… I'm not quite sure what I expect of myself. The more I think on it the simpler it seems.

I want to laugh every day.

I want to focus on the highs and forget the
lows.

I want to love without restraint or worry.

When the semester ended Sheilagh decided she wasn't going home. It was a snap decision, but one she was sure of.

"But what do you mean you aren't coming home, love? School's over," her mother cried into the phone when she told her.

"There's summer session, Mum. I want to keep going, make up for lost time so I'm not thirty when I graduate."

"Does this have to do with your man?"

Sheilagh grinned into the phone. "Maybe."

"I see. Well, don't you go gettin' yourself all moon eyed and stupid over him unless he's treatin' you the way you deserve."

"He treats me nice, Mum."

She could sense her mother's smile. "I know he does, love. Otherwise he'd be missing a testicle by now. When will we see you next?"

"Probably August, right before the fall semester starts again."

"Well, you make sure you call, you hear?"

"I will. I love you, Mum."

"I love you too, angel."

It had been a long time since her mother had called her angel. It was what she'd called her as a child, before they all started calling her devil.

Once Sheilagh had her schedule she felt like a weight had been lifted. She hadn't realized how much anxiety the thought of returning home had been giving her. That mysterious ball of dread she'd been lugging around seemed to evaporate. Now she just had to tell Alec.

As she locked her apartment the door next to hers opened. Wes came out and stilled. He had a large box in his hands. "Leaving for the summer?" she asked, trying to remain pleasant.

"Yes. And moving to a quieter building."

He turned and called his name, "Wes." He stopped but didn't face her. What the hell did she stop him for? "Um… for what it's worth, I love your dad—"

"That's what you two are missing. At the end of the day your love isn't worth shit. It won't pay my tuition or save his job. Have a nice life." He turned and she grabbed his sleeve.

"Hey, you little shit! Where do you get off being so entitled? From the day I moved in here you've acted like you deserve all this and more. What about what your father deserves? He's happy. Doesn't that mean anything to you?"

He eyed her with such disapproval it hurt, but she took it, refusing to give him the satisfaction of intimidating her.

"My dad thinks he's happy because he's banging a girl half his age. He'll eventually—"

"You selfish dick!" She shoved him and the box he'd been holding fell down, DVDs and books spilling over the steps.

"What the hell is wrong with you?"

"Lots of things! Namely, my neighbor's a spoiled prick who needs his ass kicked!"

"Oh, and you're just the one who's going to do it?" he asked snidely, puffing out his chest.

"You better believe it," she said, bunching up her sleeves.

"I don't believe this." He rolled his eyes.

"I'm counting to three and then you better run, motherfucker."

"What? You're crazy."

"One."

"My father's got to be out of his bloody mind messing with you. You're insane."

"Two."

"This is ridiculous—"

"Three." She shoved him.

"Hey!"

"I said run!"

His eyes widened and he bolted. She chased him down the steps shouting everything she ever wanted to say to him about his tight ass rules and banging on the wall. She called him a disrespectful little shit and other not-so-nice things.

He flung out the front door and she followed until she crashed into him. He screamed like a little bitch as she tackled him, pulling his hair. "Selfish bastard," she ground out, yanking his collar back as he crawled over the sidewalk.

"Get off me you crazy bitch!"

A deep voice suddenly boomed, *"Cease and desist!"*

She stilled, a fist full of her neighbor's hair in her hands. Gazing up into the sun she found Alec towering over them.

"What the bloody hell is going on?"

"She started it—*umph!*"

She smacked him in the ear.

"Sheilagh! Stop hitting my son!"

"He deserves it," she snarled.

"I'm sure, but I must insist you let him go."

"Fine," she grumbled, distributing her weight painfully over her victim as she pushed herself off the ground.

"Ouch! My nipple!" he squealed.

"Baby," she snapped.

"Both of you inside," Alec barked.

She led the way back up the stairs, taking care to step on Wesley's scattered belongings along the way. She sighed when she reached the door to her apartment and found Alec helping his son clean up the mess. He scowled at her and she stuck out her tongue. He rolled his eyes.

"Both of you inside," Alec repeated, pointing to Wes's apartment.

She marched inside and frowned at the nice and neat furniture. Alec precisely stacked the DVDs on the coffee table and drew in a long breath. She snickered when she glanced at Wes. His hair was a disaster, his shirt was stretched out, and his cheeks were flushed. Pussy.

"What. Happened?"

"She's crazy!"

"Hey! No name calling. We are going to discuss this like three mature—and I mean mature—adults." That middle part was definitely directed at her.

Arms crossed, she plopped on the couch. Jesus, it was stiff. Probably so Wesley could make sure that rod up his ass stayed firmly in place when he sat down.

"She attacked me," Wes said.

"He deserved it," was her reply, chin in the air, not a hint of regret in her voice.

"You two are supposed to be neighbors, not enemies. I understand you aren't friends, but this is simply too much. Sheilagh, you *cannot* go around attacking people."

"Ask him what he said…"

"Pardon?"

"Ask *your son* what he said that made me attack him."

Alec turned to Wes. "What did you say?"

"Nothing that wasn't true."

Sheilagh cleared her throat. "He said, and I quote, 'My

dad thinks he's happy because he's banging a girl half his age.'"

Alec's nostrils flared as he slowly turned to face his son. "You said *what?*" She bet he wished she'd kicked his ass a little more now that he knew that.

"Oh, come on, Dad—"

"Come on—*nothing!*" he shouted, slicing his palm through the air. "Enough is enough!"

Whoa, he was really pissed. "Alec—"

"Sheilagh, go back to your apartment."

"Hey! What am I, a child? No."

His face was dark with anger. He turned to his son and in a menacingly low voice, he said, "Understand this, the tuition you receive is given by two bodies, your school and your father. Disrespect me or those I love again, and you will find yourself out on your ass."

Wesley shot to his feet and pointed. "For her?"

"Yes, for her!"

"Alec—"

"Sheilagh, please!"

She scowled at him. He was letting this get out of hand. The kid should have had his spoiled ass kicked years ago, but it was too late for all that. Alec couldn't draw a line like this.

"Go to your mother's, but do not think to come back here if you can't be respectful. This is my life, not yours."

She stepped between them. "Uh… listen. I think everything got a little out of hand. Wes, I'm sorry I beat you up—"

"You didn't beat me up—"

"Yeah, I did. Anyway, I'm sorry."

"You did *not* beat me up."

Whispering out the corner of her mouth, she said, "Had you on the pavement squealing like a little bitch, but whatever. I'm sorry."

Wow. He really didn't look ready to accept her apology. This is why it was good to have brothers. Her family beat the crap out of each other on a regular basis. Problems were solved and laughed away by such means. These people didn't seem to get that, though.

"Alec, tell Wesley he can come back in the fall."

He didn't say a word. They simply stared at each other.

Beyond frustrated, she blew out a breath. "Enough! You're family! He's leaving for England in the morning. You can't let things go like this and spend the entire summer apart." And that was when it hit her.

Crap.

Her shoulders sagged and she stepped back. Retreating toward the door, she said, "Wesley, I love your dad. I'll leave so you don't have to and then there will be nothing your father can get in trouble for. Alec, talk to your son. No fighting. I have to go."

"Where are you going?"

"I have to go."

"Sheilagh—"

"Fix. This. Alec. Please. He's your family."

She shut the door and left. Running into her apartment she grabbed her purse, which was still on the floor by the door and her keys. She ran down the steps and out to her car.

As she backed out of her parking spot Alec came running after her. "Sheilagh!"

She had to go. Now.

She made it as far as Route One before the Beemer cut her off and pulled on the shoulder. "Shit."

Slamming on her breaks, she pulled to the side of the road. Cars zipped by and she climbed out. "Are you insane? You could have killed me, cutting me off like that!"

He didn't give her time to say another word. He ran to her and she was shoved against her SUV, his mouth crashing down over hers. "Don't go," he begged, using his body to hold her in place as his lips remained over hers.

Cars honked at them as they sped by. "Alec, I have to and you should be working things out with Wes—"

"Wes is fine. Don't go. I need you. Please, Sheilagh. Stay."

She frowned at him. "I'll be back in the morning."

His head jerked back. "What?"

"I need to talk to Luke. I have to fix this. It's gone on too long."

"You aren't leaving me?"

"Leaving you? When did I say that?"

His brow lowered. "You said you were leaving. I thought…"

She laughed. "Jesus, Alec. I meant I'd switch schools so we could still be together."

He shut his eyes and she realized how easily her words could have been misinterpreted. She laughed. "You moron."

"What did you bloody expect? I thought you were leaving me. Here I am, making grand gestures of love, going about in a high speed chase, and you're only running off to visit family." He pressed his head to her shoulder and groaned. "I am a moron."

"A sweet moron. No one's ever chased after me like that."

He grinned at her. "You make me crazy, Sheilagh McCullough. I think you may truly be the devil, but you're my devil and I won't let you go. I'll chase you anywhere."

Her body shivered as the adrenaline rush faded. He'd actually chased her down. Who does that? He stood up to his son because he'd disrespected her. With all of her quirks and flaws and craziness, he never stopped loving her. "Ask."

"Pardon."

"Ask me. Ask me again."

"Ask you what?"

She rolled her eyes and bopped her head from side to side. "Assssssskkkk."

"I don't know what you want me to ask."

"Jesus, Alec. Ask me to marry you!"

"What?"

Unbelievable. She dropped her arms. "Forget it."

"You want me to propose on the side of the interstate?"

Holding up her hand, she climbed back into her car. "Moment's over, Alec."

"Where are you going?"

"Back to my apartment. I'll call my brother." He followed her to her door and she rolled down the window. He looked lost. "You *really* need to work on your game. I'll meet you back home." She rolled up the window and he shook his head, slowly walking back to his car and climbing inside.

She signaled and pulled onto the highway once traffic let up. When she returned to her apartment, Alec wasn't behind her. That was okay. She had stuff to deal with anyway.

As she climbed the stairs she faced Wes's door and knocked. It opened and he immediately tried to shut it when he saw her. She wedged her foot in the door and barreled her way inside.

"You're like a bull in a china shop," he snapped.

"Deal with it. Everyone else has to cope with the permanent stick up your ass."

"What do you want, Sheilagh?"

She sat on the couch and folded her hands demurely on her lap. "Ah, first names. Progress."

He didn't sit and didn't comment so she said what needed to be said.

"Look, Wesley. You're father and I are going to be together whether you like it or not. Now, I know when our mommies and daddies make special friends it can sometimes be confusing—"

"Don't patronize me."

"Fine. I love your dad. He loves me. We're together and you need to get over it."

"It won't last."

She arched a brow. "What if I told you your dad already asked me to marry him?"

"No, he didn't."

She stretched and smiled, making herself comfortable. "Did too. Not once. Not twice. But *three* times. *Tres. Trí. Trois. Drei.*—"

"All right. I get it."

"Do you?"

He plopped onto the couch and dragged his hands over his face. "Yes."

"You don't have to like me, but you have to accept this is how it's gonna be whether you like me or not."

He groaned.

She made herself comfortable. "Way I see it, we were raised in a house where the mother ruled the roost. If you promise to give me a chance and stop being such a tight ass dickweed, I promise not to beat you with a wooden spoon. We already established I'm tougher than you."

His face contorted with a look that could only be absolute bewilderment. "Where did you come from?"

She smiled and slapped his knee. In a thick, redneck accent she said, "I'm from a little piece of paradise way out in bumble fuck called Center County. You think I'm nuts, you should meet my brothers."

"There's more of your kind?"

"Oh, there's enough to fill a mountain. We call it McCullough Mountain."

"What the hell does he see in you?" he grumbled.

"Oh, I'm a firecracker in bed—"

His hand flew up, cutting her off. "I don't need to hear that."

She shrugged. "It's true." Standing, she said, "I've decided the next time he asks I'm gonna say yes. Isn't that exciting? You'll have three moms."

He glared at her through his fingers. "There's something seriously wrong with you."

She tousled his hair. "Yup!"

Smiling, she let herself out. She'd traumatized the kid enough. Now she had some serious things to deal with.

Digging through her desk, she found her letter to Luke. She read it twice, making last minute changes and once she was comfortable with everything it said, she folded it into an envelope and addressed it to her brother. After discussing it with Megan ad nauseam and coming to regard it as truth, warts and all, it was time she shared it with Luke. She was glad Alec stopped her from driving home.

Once she'd calmed down, she realized the sense of urgency was fear. Even if she called Luke, they'd likely end up fighting. A letter was best. It would give him time to digest and think before he reacted.

Tristan was a little different. She sat on her bed and held her phone in her lap, collecting her courage. Once she was as ready as she'd ever be, she texted.

Are you alone?

A MINUTE later he replied in the affirmative. She dialed.

"Hello?"

"Tristan?"

"Hey, Sheilagh." He didn't sound right.

"What's wrong?"

"Nothin'. What do you need?"

Wow. Talk about to the point. "I was hoping we could talk."

He sighed and his answer took a while. "Okay."

"I—Tristan, are you okay?"

"No."

"What's wrong?" He never spoke to her in such a clipped tone. Something was definitely wrong.

He huffed. "Where should I begin?"

"How about the beginning?"

"You know the beginning. Texan orphan moves to Center County with surrogate family, falls in love with his best friend's cousin, an ex-athlete who's the farthest thing from gay. Bet you can guess the end."

"Tristan, what's going on? What happened? Did you and Luke have a fight?"

"You could say that. We broke up."

Her heart stopped. "What?"

"It's over, Shei."

"Why?" She was shocked at how upset this news made her. "You love him."

"Yeah, well, it gets a little old loving someone who will always hate loving you back. It's over. We're done. I'm actually looking for a new job and I'm going to be moving out of your aunt's house real soon."

She couldn't breathe. "What? You can't move! You're family."

"That's the thing, Shei, I'm not." He was quiet for a moment and she swore she heard him crying. He proved her correct when he spoke, his voice restricted and so full of anguish it was agony to hear. "I just can't do it any more, the lying, the hiding. I want him, but he'll never love me enough to accept who he is."

Oh my God. Her heart broke for him. "Do you want me to come home?"

"No. There's nothing for you to do here. I'll be fine. I'll

get over it. And one day your brother will have the *normal* life he needs."

"Screw normal, Tristan. This isn't fair!"

"Tell me about it. Look, baby girl, I gotta go."

She panicked. If he left, when would she see him again? He was part of going home. He counted as much as the rest of their family. "Tristan, wait!"

"Yeah?"

Tears blurred her vision. This wasn't at all how this was supposed to happen. "I love you."

"I love you too, baby girl."

She sniffled and wiped her cheeks. "No, I love you like a brother. I get it now. You're my friend. I know what he means to you. I need you to know I forgive you for the kiss and that I'm sorry for all the trouble I caused."

"You were young, Shei. We should have handled things different. We wanted to, but…Luke is just…Luke."

"Promise me you'll call me. I can't lose you, Tristan."

He waited long enough that she knew his agreement would be a lie. "Okay, baby girl."

Emotion choked her as the line went dead. Falling to her pillows she cried. She cried for all the trouble she caused. She cried for Tristan's broken heart. She cried for the friend she was doomed to lose. She cried for her brother's fear of being ostracized.

He'd let others' expectations cripple his ability to move forward in life and find his own version of happy. He was chasing some form of normal that never existed at all.

Then she cried, because she was exactly the same way, always trying to be what others expected, afraid to have a bad day or emotional one.

Luke was so certain his friends and family would be upset that he was gay. No one of that ilk gave a shit what he was. They only wanted him to be happy. It was part of the reason she'd been mad at him for years. Tristan was a good man and didn't deserve to be kept like a dirty secret.

She stared at the letter by the door, waiting to go to the post office. So many of the issues they had over the years were suddenly irrelevant. She wasn't sure if she wanted to forgive him, apologize, or be furious with him for hurting Tristan. She climbed out of bed and ripped it to shreds, sobbing as each hopeless piece of her wretched past fell to the floor.

"WHY DID you feel the need to rip it up?"

Sheilagh shrugged, not wanting to go over this again. The green couch wasn't so soft today and the candies in the jar weren't the chocolate ones.

"Do you plan on talking to your brother? Any other ideas?"

Shrug.

"Can you share how you're feeling about it?"

Shrug.

"Sheilagh, why are you here?"

She looked at Megan. "It's our appointment."

"But I can't help you if you don't talk. Therapy is about talking through the issues."

"I don't know what to say."

"What if we pretend Luke was here now? What would you say to him?"

Selfish. Coward. You don't know what you've done. He's too good for you. How could you? You had everything I wanted and threw it away. We love you. No one cares if you're gay.

"I don't know what I'd say to him. It wouldn't be nice."

"No one said you had to be nice. It's just us here."

Her throat constricted. "He broke his heart. I've never heard Tristan sound so hopeless and alone. He's gonna leave now and it's all Luke's fault."

"It sounds like you don't want Tristan to leave?"

"Because…he's family. He shouldn't have to leave."

"Just family?"

She shook her head. "It's not like that anymore. I don't love him any other way now."

She felt Megan's surprise, that strange way she said nothing so Sheilagh would go on. She didn't. "Is there something else on your mind?"

"I beat up Alec's son."

Megan leaned forward a trifle before collecting herself. *Aha! Shocked the therapist at last!*

"Would you care to elaborate?"

"He was rude. He insulted me. I gave him fair warning. He didn't listen. I kicked his ass. Alec broke it up—"

"Alec was there when this happened?"

"Not at first. We sort of ran into him…on the side-walk…as I chased Wes outside and tackled him."

"You tackled him?"

"I gave him a head start."

"What was going through your head as you did this?"

Sheilagh blinked, still not feeling much like talking. "That this kid didn't get spanked enough as a child."

"Did your parents spank you?"

"Yes, but don't get too excited. I don't have any weird issues from it. Most of the time I deserved it."

"What was one of the causes for getting spanked as a child?"

She shrugged. "There were a lot. I never felt unloved. Most of the time I deserved it. Like this one time, I shaved Kelly's eyebrows off and used a permanent marker to give him a beard."

"How old were you?"

"I was maybe eleven. Kelly was thirteen. It's when he started changing and getting into girls. He needed to be brought down a peg."

"And you thought that was your duty?"

"Not really, but Braydon didn't have the balls. Someone needed to do it."

"I see."

"I think that was the last time I was spanked."

"Do you know if Alec spanked Wesley when he was younger?"

She snorted. "Doubtful. He's the philosopher king. Violence is beneath him."

"Do you see spanking as a violent act?"

She shrugged. "No. Not really. At least I don't blame my parents for disciplining me that way. I was a pretty tough kid. But now-a-days it's different. Parents can't do that anymore."

"Do you plan on having children, Sheilagh?"

She blew out a breath, eyes wide. "Wow, doc, way to slip in a loaded question. I don't know. It depends."

"On?"

"Who I marry."

"How does that affect your decision?"

"Well, Alec can't have children. His boys were snipped."

"He's had vasectomy?"

"I know they can reverse it, but that seems like an awful lot of stress down there. If I'm meant to be with him maybe I'm not meant to have children. My brother just had a son and it was really scary. They used nontraditional methods of conception and sometimes I wonder if they messed with destiny."

"Do you believe in destiny?"

"I don't know."

"You seem to pick and choose your belief systems, Sheilagh, assigning certain absolutes to other people and certain ones to yourself, but never using the same measuring stick universally. Why do you think that is?"

Her expectation for Megan's next words was absolute,

desperate. "You tell me. Seriously, Megan, tell me, because I'm not sure I know." Her voice was practically pleading.

"Okay," she said. "I suspect it's because you don't believe you deserve to be happy."

The banter stopped. Megan just dropped a bomb and Sheilagh's instinct was to bolt. "Yes, I do."

"Good. I wanted to hear you say it."

"You tricked me."

"No, I made a hypothesis and gave you the opportunity to disprove it."

"Whatever. Technicalities."

"Does it frustrate you, admitting you deserve to be happy as much as anyone else?"

"No. I want to be happy."

"So what's stopping you? Tell me what would make you happy."

Getting out of this office. She looked at the clock. Damn it. Twenty minutes left. "Alec makes me happy. Christmas with my family makes me happy. Seeing all my siblings makes me happy. My nieces and nephews make me happy. Should I go on?"

"That's a lot of references to family. Do you think this is why you've turned down Alec's proposal?"

"No. I told you. I said no because each time he asked he was either drunk or panicked. A girl can hope for romance."

"Tell me your definition of romance."

She rolled her eyes. "All the same cheesy shit every girl wants."

"You'd be surprised how varying people's definitions of romance are. Enlighten me."

"He came after me when he thought I was leaving him. That was romantic." She glanced at her hands, recalling how frightened he'd been at the idea of losing her. "You should have seen him. He was beside himself. He grabbed me, right there on the side of the road, and kissed me with such desperation, such passion, barely taking his lips off of mine to beg me not to go." She looked at Megan. "It was a total miscommunication, but you get the gist. *That's* romantic."

"So I'm going to try and paraphrase here. Romance, in your opinion, isn't flowers and candlelight. It's raw desire, seeing a man humbled."

"Yes. In a way it's breaking the law, because nothing else matters but that one person."

"Legislative laws or are you speaking of the laws of nature?"

"All of the above. Kelly ended up in jail because a man hurt his wife. Colin went against his God for Sammy. Finn...Finn would never break the rules, but he went after Mallory when she ran and she runs *a lot.*"

"And what about your parents?"

She smiled. "My dad stole my mum. Ran off with her and eloped. When they came home—married—my granddad shot him."

She laughed at Megan's expression of shock. Once again she'd surprised her therapist.

"I see. Do you have an idea where you want your relationship with Alec to go, Sheilagh?"

She grinned softly, feeling all sorts of warm and fuzzy butterflies and girlie crap in her chest. "I think he'll ask again and I'll probably say yes. He chased me. He stood up to his son for me. He stood up to Tristan and my brothers. We're scary people, so that's sort of a big deal." Her smile tightened. "He loves me. I know he does." Something unfamiliar and confident swelled inside of her.

"But more importantly, I love him. He's shown me what real love is and disproved everything I assumed it was. Everything I ever believed about love was a childish impression of the real thing. There's absolutely nothing fake about our feelings for each other. We see each other's flaws and love each other more for them. Funny, how finally understanding that makes me not so concerned about solving all the other puzzles of life. It's like a pressure's been lifted. He's given me something I know I can depend on. I think the Beatles nailed it. All you need is love."

CHAPTER 13

I've always been better at judging others
than judging myself. When I met
Ashlynn, I thought she was a prude. That
was easier than considering myself slutty.
Luke was devastated after losing his
scholarship. In my mind I judged him as
dramatic, throwing away my own opportunities in spite of his loss. Sammy was
too quiet when she first came around and
calling her that somehow made me feel
less obnoxious. But the more I think
about all of them, the more I realize how
much we're all alike. Colin wanted to be
the man he thought the family would
praise. Finn struggled to take on the
family legacy so not to let down Dad and

the uncles. Kelly never tried to do more than fulfill people's low expectations, surprising them all when he stepped up to an incredible challenge. And then there's Luke. Luke had forsaken the very basis of his happiness in order to fit some mold he'd concocted in his head. Just like me, they were all faking it on some level. I'm not sure why, but realizing this truth about Luke makes my own existence that much more shameful. We're the same and I've punished him for everything I, too, was afraid to face about myself. I'm so tired of pretending I'm someone else when, in reality, no one expects me to be anything other than happy.

*A*s Sheilagh walked out of Megan's office she turned on her phone and frowned. Nothing.

What was happening? Alec never came to her place last night and he hadn't returned any of her calls or texts. Who chases someone down then disappears?

She called him and it went to voicemail. "Hey. It's me. Where are you? I guess you might have taken Wes to the airport, but I don't know because you aren't getting back to me…call me. Let me know you're alive. Love you."

Everyone was packing up to go home for the summer and she really had nothing to do, which made Alec's disappearing act all the more annoying. She went home and sorted through her papers from her freshman year, organizing them and tossing away the things there was no point in keeping.

She routinely checked her phone, but Alec didn't call. At one point she got so lonely, she even knocked on the wall. "Wes?" He was gone.

After she had her stuff packed away she tidied up her apartment. Where was he? She hadn't even told him she was enrolled for the summer and staying. Didn't he care? For all he knew, she was leaving that weekend.

Around three she started getting pissed off. She called his phone and hung up when she got his voicemail again. Then everything started to spiral out of control. Her apartment was clean, her books organized, she'd made a list of everything she'd need for her summer courses starting in two weeks, and she sat.

Staring at the television, she considered putting on a movie, but never moved. She sat for probably close to an hour, staring at her phone in her hand. And then the darkness crept in.

Sucking in a deep breath, she stood and forced herself to move. Slipping on a pair of flip-flops, she grabbed her bag and left. It was ridiculous that a twenty-four year old woman couldn't sit alone for a few hours without having a breakdown. And it was even more ridiculous that a forty-year-old man couldn't answer his damn phone!

She walked into town and stared into store windows. Why wasn't he calling? She texted him.

What's going on? Why aren't you getting back to me? Starting to freak out.

A minute later her phone buzzed and she nearly collapsed with relief when she read *Captain Assclown* on the screen. She swiped her finger over the menu and frowned.

Not now.

Sharp pain cut off her breathing. Not now? What the fuck did that mean? Not now. Scowling at nothing in particular, she turned and marched her way out of town and toward campus. *Not now.*

How about screw you?

When she reached the philosophy building she was shaking with a mixture of rage and fear. Was he done with her? How could that be? She told Megan she was going to marry him.

Oh, God... What if Wes said something to him last

night after she left? Why was she such a basket case? If she hadn't been having a breakdown over her brother's love life maybe she could have protected hers.

Her steps doubled as she went to the fourth floor. From the end of the hall she saw his office light shining from his doorway. What if he had another student in there? What if he was hiding from her?

She reached the door, and being her ever unpredictable self, all her anger tucked tail and hid. There was suddenly a fake smile plastered on her face as she knocked and pushed the door open. "Knock knock."

Her false smile fell when she saw Alec's surprise and—disappointment?—at her presence. "Ms. McCullough."

She frowned. "You could answer your phone."

He swallowed. "Right. As you can see I'm with someone..."

What? She turned. Oh. Crap.

"Dr. Strauss, Dr. Othman, this is Sheilagh McCullough, a psychology major at Princeton."

Both men gave her a stern, unimpressed appraisal. She fidgeted and backed toward the door. She'd seen the one professor before while visiting Alec a few weeks back. "I see you're busy, Dr. Devereux. I'll... come back later. I just wanted to return the notes you gave me."

The men stood and something in Alec's expression scared the hell out of her. Who were they? She backed out of the office and shut the door. There was a bench around the corner so she sat there and waited. Footsteps sounded, fading in the other direction, then her phone buzzed.

YOU CAN COME IN NOW.

SOMETHING frightening and cold settled in her stomach. Standing, she slowly walked back to his office. She quietly shut the door. Alec was standing with his back toward her, shuffling papers into a box on the table behind his desk.

"Alec?"

"I'm sorry I didn't call last night or today. I was in meetings all day and unable to use the phone. I assume your session with Megan went well."

He wasn't looking at her. "Who were those men?"

"Colleagues. One is actually a dear friend."

"Are you mad at me?"

He sighed and braced his palms on the table, still not facing her. "No, Sheilagh, I'm not mad at you. I'm upset with myself."

"Why? Did something happen? With Wes?"

He laughed without humor. "Wes is long gone by now. He'll be fine."

"What about us? Why won't you look at me?"

He turned and when he faced her she took a step back. His expression was cold, distant. "I resigned today."

"What?"

"Turns out, the university's policy is quite clear on student-teacher relationships."

"Someone found out?"

"No, I asked."

"What? Why would you do that?"

"Because I don't like hiding. I thought about everything you've told me about your brother and Tristan. I thought about what my son said and I decided you deserve more than to be kept like some shameful secret."

Those were her words, but she didn't want to hear that right now. If he left where would he go? Where would Wes go? This wasn't how it was supposed to work. "I don't mind being a secret if it means having you." She was a hypocrite. Megan was right. She picked and chose her measuring stick, but it was never absolute. "Alec, tell them it's a lie."

"It's not a lie. I love you."

Her vision blurred and she blinked rapidly, refusing to cry. "Then don't leave."

"I'll find another job, Sheilagh."

"What about Wes?"

"I'll work it out. He can get loans and if he keeps up his grades there's no reason for him to leave."

"What about us?"

He smiled, but the expression was sad. "We're free to be together. No one can stop us."

"But I'll live here and you'll be somewhere else."

"There are other schools not too far from here where I can apply." He was already putting things in boxes.

She stepped close and grabbed the books in his hand, tossing them to the desk. "Stop it!"

With ever-present calm he said, "Sheilagh, what would you have me do? They'll have a new philosophy instructor hired by the end of the month. My summer classes have been reassigned to someone else. There's no reason not to keep moving."

A tear trickled down her cheek. "But I signed up for the summer session. Where will you live? What will happen to your house? It's your home."

"Perhaps I'll rent Wesley's place or live with you for the summer."

"Stop being so damn calm! This is your livelihood, Alec."

He laughed and cupped her cheek. "It's just a job, Sheilagh. You're worth it."

Her lips pressed tight and she stepped back. "No, I'm not."

His expression hardened. "Stop. Do not stand there and act like you aren't worth this. It's a bloody job any professor could do. I'd give up all this and more if it meant having you. I have money and a good resume with an excellent track record. I'll find another job at another college."

"I'll follow you."

He shut his eyes. "No."

"Alec, I don't want this."

His eyes turned wide and he stared at her. "Us?"

"No, I want us. I don't want you to lose your job. I don't want you to move. You never should have said anything."

Smiling softly, he said, "Sheilagh, I do intend to marry you some day, but it's too soon. Until we're married, this is how it has to be. It's the ethical thing to do."

"What would happen if we were married?"

He frowned. "Nothing. But you're too young—"

"I'm not too young! Stop saying that. My sister was married and knocked up by the time she was twenty. What does marriage change?"

He met her gaze and drew in a slow breath. "Everything," he whispered. "You'd be mine. Forever."

"And what does it change about this situation?"

He sighed. "If you were my wife no one could say a word. I would never be your professor again, for obvious reasons, but other than that you would have every right to be here as much as my son. You'd even get free tuition."

So what was the problem? There should be a problem, right? She turned and paced to his door. Normal people would see a problem with that, but she couldn't seem to find one. She loved Alec. He loved her.

She spun and faced him. "We'll get married."

"No."

She sputtered. "What do you mean, no? Why not? It fixes everything."

Shaking his head, he approached her, running his hands down her arms. "Sheilagh, marriage is forever. I'm divorced from a very nice woman, but I've been through a marriage that didn't last. I don't want that for you."

"Who says we won't last?"

"Sweetheart, we met less than a year ago. Who knows what tomorrow will bring?"

"Alec," she said with forced patience. "Remember when you told me that loving someone meant telling them when they were being an idiot?"

"That's not what I said."

"Well, you're being a fucking moron right now. If we got married you could keep your job. Wes could continue his education here and so could I. We could live together. No more sneaking around. Stop worrying about what *might* happen and let's do something for us. Step out of the cave, professor."

He took a step back. "You're rushing things."

"Rushing things? Everyone's always telling me I'm too afraid of disappointing others to try. This is *me trying*. Now strap on a pair and let's go get hitched."

He laughed. He obviously tried not to, but it slipped out anyway. "Sheilagh—"

No more arguing. "If you leave, I'll leave too. I'll follow you to every college you go to. You chase me, I chase you. Stop running. I did it for years. It's no fun."

The side of his mouth kicked up as he glanced at her, a

strange look in his eyes. "What happened with Megan today? You're different."

"I cried. You picked a terrible few hours to disappear. A lot's happened. Luke and Tristan broke up."

He frowned. "You called Luke?"

"No. I called Tristan." He stiffened so she quickly went on. "Don't you see? I don't care about any of that. Right now all I care about is you. I can't let you throw away a job you love on my account."

"I wouldn't be throwing it away. I'd be making it possible for us to be together."

She rolled her eyes. Jeeze he was slow. "I get it, but I'm telling you that doesn't have to happen. I *want* to marry you."

He was quiet for a long while. "What about children, Sheilagh?"

"Do you want kids?" she snapped. "Why does that decision rest on my shoulders?"

"Because I already have a son."

"Okay, so I get a step-son—who *adores* me—and we shelve that topic for now. I may someday want kids, but that day doesn't have to be today."

"How long will you wait? I'm already forty."

"And Charlie Chaplin had kids into his seventies."

"What father wants to be in diapers at the same time as his son?"

"Oh, my God. Knock it off! Fine! We'll have kids now. As soon as I graduate. That gives you three years to reverse whatever you got going on down there and knock me up. You'll be forty-three, a perfectly acceptable age to have children in this day and age. Does that work?"

His smile was slow, but told her something she hadn't known. Alec wanted more children. He caught her wrist and pulled her close, kissing her slowly. "Yes, that works. I'd like to try for a boy and a girl, but I don't think I'd want more than three."

"I'll give you two and raise you a third depending on who they take after. If they're McCulloughs, two may be all you get."

He laughed and kissed her again. "Are you serious about all this?"

"Serious as a monkey on a cupcake."

He drew back and frowned. "That doesn't make sense."

"Try getting between that monkey and cupcake and you'll disagree. That's a serious situation. Now, let's go get your job back."

Two birth certificates, one printed and signed marriage license, two witnesses, and seventy-two required hours later and they were on their way to Lambertville. Alec still seemed to be second-guessing their decision, but Sheilagh was whole-heartedly onboard.

She'd given him the address to a place she knew of and the GPS directed them down a windy road along the

Delaware River. She hoped she didn't make a mistake in trusting the one relative she could always count on.

Alec took her hand as he drove. "You're fidgeting. Having second thoughts?"

"No. I'm just worried we're gonna get there and there will be a million McCulloughs waiting."

"We don't have to do it this way. We could have a traditional wedding."

"No. I want to do it quick. Quick and painless."

He laughed. "Don't romanticize it."

She smiled. He got her. At the end of the day that had to be worth everything. Her mum was a maniac, but Sheilagh's father loved her. "You know my parents eloped."

"I believe you mentioned that a few times."

"My dad's older than my mum by quite a bit of years. He was my Aunt Colleen's friend. The first time he saw my mum he said he never looked at another woman the same. She was it."

"Do you think they'll be angry?" he asked, his thumb rubbing softly over her knuckles.

"I don't know. My granddad shot my dad when they got home."

Alec laughed.

"I'm serious. Right in the leg. He has a scar."

Alec glanced at her nervously.

She smiled. "You'd take a bullet for me, right?"

His grip on her hand tightened. "Perhaps we should

call them."

"No."

"Why are you so adamant about this?"

"Because I know them. They'll swarm in and take over everything. Next thing you know, you'll be thrown in a kilt, sucking back whiskey, and scared shitless."

"I don't scare easily, Sheilagh. I've faced them once, I can face them again."

"Oh, you'll be facing them every holiday and family reunion for the rest of your life. Let's keep this moment for ourselves."

The GPS directed them over a bridge and through a historic town then informed them they'd arrived at their destination. "Does this look like the place?"

Sheilagh unbuckled her seatbelt and looked at the property. As Alec slowly pulled into the driveway lined with pretty pink blooms she read the sign. *Dougherty Bed & Breakfast.*

"This is it." As he rounded the old colonial she spotted her brother's car. "They're here!"

Alec shut off the engine and she climbed out, stretching her legs. The back door of the quaint house opened and a woman stepped out, smiling and looking so much like an older version of her sister-in-law.

"You can't be Sheilagh," the woman said, smiling. "Last I saw you, you were a little girl. What a beautiful woman you've grown into!"

Sheilagh waited for Alec then walked over to greet the

woman. "Hi, Mrs. Dougherty. This is Alec."

Mrs. Dougherty shook his hand and hugged her close. "Well, come along. The kids are watching a movie with their grandfather and Sammy and Colin are making dinner."

Alec carried their bags into the house and Sheilagh drew in a deep breath. He paused at the door. "You ready?"

"Yup."

They followed Samantha's mother into the B&B and a shiver ran through her. No backing out now.

"You can leave your bags there by the step and I'll have Sammy's father carry them to your rooms."

The house was beautiful, built for entertaining and secret getaways. As they reached the dining room the scent of pasta had her stomach growling. They turned the corner and there were Sammy and Colin. Colin grinned and held out his arms. She ran to her brother and hugged him for a solid minute.

Kissing her hair, he said, "You know they're going to kill me for this."

"I know. Thank you for coming."

He gave her shoulders a squeeze and whispered, "Wouldn't miss it for the world."

She turned and hugged Sammy. "Thanks for coming."

"That's what sisters are for. I brought you something."

Sheilagh eased back. "What?"

Samantha smiled. "It's upstairs. Come on."

She glanced at Alec who was talking with Colin as he stirred the sauce. She followed Sammy through the house and up the stairs. "Ready?" Sammy asked, turning the knob to one of the guestrooms.

Sheilagh nodded. Samantha pushed the door open and she gasped. Hanging from a sconce on the wall was her Morai's wedding gown, the same gown Samantha had worn when she married Colin.

"My grandmother's gown," she whispered as her hand traced over the delicate Irish lace.

"I was a bit larger, having just had Tallulah when I wore it, but my mom swears she can take it in by tomorrow. She wants you to try it on before dinner."

Sheilagh smiled, emotion choking her. She grabbed Samantha and pulled her into a rough hug. "I love you. I'm so glad you're my sister."

"I love you too. Want to try it on?"

They shut the door and Sammy helped her dress. The gown was loose around the waist, but as soon as Mrs. Dougherty showed up with a basket full of pins they had it fitting properly. The woman was certain it would only take the work of a slight modesty panel and some extra lacing along the back.

After dinner Alec disappeared with Colin. Sammy giggled and whispered, "He brought a kilt for your man."

"No."

Samantha nodded and grinned. "Oh, yeah. He's a McCullough now."

Sheilagh stilled. "Actually, I'll be a Devereux. Sheilagh Devereux. Does that sound all right?"

"It sounds lovely."

She glanced at the door and back at Samantha. Keeping her voice low, she asked, "Sammy, what's going on with Luke?"

Samantha's expression faltered. "What—what do you mean?"

"Is he okay?"

Something flashed in her eyes and Sheilagh sucked in a breath. "Do you know?"

Sammy's gaze darted away guiltily. "Know what?"

"Don't lie to me, Samantha McCullough."

Samantha's eyes were wide, her mouth grasping for words that weren't there. "Are you talking about Tristan?" she whispered.

She knew. "Yes. What's happening to them and how long have you known?"

Her expression turned guilty. "I've known since I was with Braydon. Does anyone else know?"

This was insane. All this time someone else knew and Sheilagh had no idea. "No. I don't think anyone knows. I thought I was the only one. Does Colin know?"

"I don't think so, at least not from me. I've never told anyone."

"Well, what's happening? I talked to Tristan and he said they broke up," Sheilagh quickly rushed out before the others returned.

"I don't know. Luke's so private. He'd never admit to anything. I know Tristan was missing for a while and now he's back, but neither of them have been hanging around. It isn't like it's my place to ask."

"Tristan said he's moving," she told Sammy.

"What? He can't move. Center County's his home."

The sound of Alec and Colin laughing in the hall had them leaning back in their chairs. This was a mess. While she had the chance, she said, "They need to stop hiding."

Sammy nodded and the men entered the kitchen. "Hi," Sheilagh said as Alec bent to kiss her cheek.

"You're brother seems to think I'll be saying my vows in a dress."

Sheilagh laughed. "It's a kilt, not a dress."

"I think I'll wear the suit I brought."

She shrugged as if it made no difference. "That's fine, but just so you know, kilts are sexy as hell." He raised a brow and she tipped her head. "Sammy?"

Samantha turned and nodded. "Yes, nothing sexier than a man in a kilt."

Sheilagh gave him a cheeky smile. "See?"

Since arriving at the B&B, Alec had calmed a great deal. Colin, although not Sheilagh's parent, seemed okay with what they were doing. The evening had been cordial and nothing was as great as seeing Sheilagh so happy.

The girls returned upstairs for some wedding project they were working on and Colin settled back into the kitchen table and slid him a beer after returning from putting the kids to bed.

"I think we should talk about this," Sheilagh's brother said.

Alec liked Colin. He seemed a hell of a lot more level-headed than the rest. Alec sipped his beer and nodded. "Probably not a bad idea."

"I'm going to assume you love my sister and know what you're doing."

"I love Sheilagh very much. Nothing in my past can compare to the feelings I have for her."

"Good. She's a handful and I think you have to love her so you don't wind up strangling her."

"Sheilagh is…" He thought for a moment. Sheilagh was so many things. She was adventurous, yet hesitant. Brave, yet afraid. Wise, yet inexperienced in certain realms. "She's a beautiful example of being human. I love everything about her, even her flaws."

"She's happy with you," Colin said. "I see it, where most people choose not to. Not the happiness, but the absence of the sadness."

Alec put down his bottle and eyed Colin. He wouldn't betray Sheilagh. "She's been facing a lot of her fears, coping with them, and hopefully, in time, they'll fade away."

"I think going away to school was something she

needed."

"Agreed, although it wasn't always something she wanted. She's stubborn and lets the untried parts of life intimidate her."

Colin watched him for a minute, his eyes scrutinizing. "Why did your last marriage end?"

That was a bold question, but in light of their current circumstances and the fact Colin was there to support his little sister, Alec was persuaded to answer. "My ex-wife is gay."

Colin stilled, lips parted, gaze pegged to Alec's as though measuring the truth of his confession. Finally, he said, "I imagine you and Sheilagh have had some pretty interesting discussions on the subject."

That wasn't necessarily Colin acknowledging the fact his brother was gay and Alec wasn't about to divulge information that wasn't his to give. However, there was another man involved—not a McCullough—and Alec wasn't so inclined to protect him. "Are you referring to Tristan?"

Colin made the slightest nod.

Alec sighed and scooped up his beer, taking a long sip. "I won't pretend I care for the man, but I respect the fact he's an important part of Sheilagh's past. That being said, I don't like their relationship and will continue to dislike it until Tristan learns how to be her friend without the head games."

"Sometimes," Colin stated, his voice full of retrospect,

"we're convinced we should be something, but at the end of the day we're just us. It's a difficult journey, life, and we often get lost along the way.

"I've watched my family over the years and we've all had our crosses to bear. The twins, although different, both feel a need to obtain some nonexistent definition of perfect. Kelly is perhaps the only one that rejected the desire to do what was expected, which was never really expected at all. Finn learned that perfect doesn't fit into a nice neat box wrapped in undisturbed beauty. I learned that being human is sometimes better than being godly. Luke will someday learn the same, which is, no matter what tomorrow brings, happiness is the only thing we expect him to accomplish in this life. Braydon...one day Braydon will see that the imperfections are actually the best part.

"I think you're showing Sheilagh this, showing her that all those expectations don't really exist outside of her own scrutiny, and maybe once she realizes that, she can be content with who she really is."

Colin was a smart man. "I hope."

He took a sip of his beer and stood, placing the empty bottle by the sink. "You do realize my parents will be upset. They'll forgive you eventually, but you may want to proceed with caution."

"For the record, I gave her the option of a traditional wedding. Sheilagh wanted a small private ceremony."

Colin nodded. "And so she would. She may play the life

of the party, but anyone who really knows Sheilagh knows she values solitude. She's a lot more introverted than people assume at first glance, always thinking. It may not seem the case, but she needs that time and quiet to embrace what's actually taking place around her. She savors those still moments of reflection when they don't frighten her. You make her brave, Alec. I admire that."

"Thank you, Colin, for saying that and for doing this."

He nodded and quietly left the kitchen.

The house was set in dim lights. Amber highlighted the countertops and the halls were dark. Alec took a few minutes to reflect and found himself smiling. He recalled the conversation he'd had with his son at the airport before sending him off.

"Do you love her, Dad?"

"With all of my heart, Wes. She reminds me I still have a long life ahead of me and makes me want to live it. She makes me feel alive again."

"She's not the most stable person," Wes said.

Alec laughed. "Are any of us?"

"I want you to be happy, like Mom and Claire. You deserve that."

"I promise nothing I do will affect your future at school, Wes. I'll handle it. I promise."

His son looked down at his shoes and shifted his carry-on. "At the end of the day it's just an establishment. I love my friends, but I'd give it all up to love someone like that. It's not the materials, but the souls that we travel with in this world that give our life value. Maybe you finally found the true counter-part to your soul."

Alec grinned. "Well, aren't you turning into the next Socrates."

Wes gave him a knowing smile. "Plato's boring. I'd rather live and burn in Hades with the interesting people."

It was something he'd been trying to teach his son for years, always lamenting that Wesley followed the rules that weren't always justified in the end. He grinned. "Don't go too crazy."

"You know me. I won't."

Alec hugged him. "Just try not to be too perfect. There's no such thing."

"I love you, Dad."

"I love you too. Send your mother my love when you see her and enjoy your summer."

Alec stretched and carried his bottle to the sink. He walked through the empty bed and breakfast, the halls silent and dim. As he approached his door he paused and glanced back to the room Sheilagh was occupying for the night. Turning, he scratched on the wood of her door.

Muffled footsteps were followed by the turn of the nob. Her face peeked through the crack, small and beautiful. She would become his wife tomorrow. "Hi."

"Hi," she whispered, green eyes creased with pleasantness.

Soft light filtering behind her set her red hair in shades of gold. "I wanted to say goodnight."

She smiled. "I'll see you in the morning."

He looked at her and really tried to see her. This would be the face that greeted him every morning for the rest of his life. Warmth spread in his chest. Never had he expected his life to take such a turn.

Once he'd told his supervisor they'd be married by the end of the month all worries simply disappeared. Sheilagh would live with him in the house that had been his home for the past decade. She'd likely decorate it in books and dirty laundry, but that was okay. She'd never be able to legitimately take his courses, but she'd be his wife and they'd fill their days with intellectual discussions until they were old and senile. That was what he wanted.

Leaning in, he stole a kiss. "I'll be the one in the skirt."

She laughed. "It's a kilt."

"I'm sure my British ancestors will enjoy the show."

"Give them a good one. No knickers underneath."

He smiled. "I love you, Sheilagh. Thank you for wanting to be my wife."

"I love you too, Alec. Thank you for dragging me out of my cave."

He stilled. Before he could say anything else, she whispered goodnight and shut the door.

As he lay in the unfamiliar bed of the B&B, he contemplated the days that would follow. He hadn't been married in a long time and suspected this time around would be nothing like the first. There truly was no other person on this earth like his future wife and he was glad for it. She was his.

There seems a different sort of silence surrounding me tonight. My worries have taken shape in the form of content-ment, seeming to surrender in and of themselves and the quiet isn't so intimi-dating. I'm not sure if I believe in destiny, but I'm tired of waiting around for other people's theories on the subject. I'm grab-bing my destiny by the balls and finally doing something for myself. Something that makes me happy in ways I've never imagined. This sense of independence isn't in a social form. It's an emotional epiphany. I've decided facing my fears and admitting those frightening truths is not as scary as the anticipation of letting others down. But the truth is, this is me. He's helped me discover who I am and every day he helps me find her a little more. He likes me, but more importantly, I like me. It's been a long time since I've thought that. I think I'll keep me exactly as I am. No more faking it to please others. If I can face change, so can they. This year has made me different in ways I never expected, but I'm so grateful I'm finally here, grateful I finally understand what happiness feels like.

The ceremony was perfect. Colin was the impeccable officiant and the Dougherty's the perfect witnesses. After a quiet brunch, Mrs. Dougherty gathered up the children and Sammy and Colin said their goodbyes.

"Will you be coming home soon?" her brother asked.

Sheilagh hugged him. "My classes start back up in nine days. I think I'll enjoy my honeymoon."

"When will you tell Mum and Dad?"

"When I see them and after I hide Dad's guns."

"Good call. I love you, Sheilagh."

"I love you too, Colin. You'll never know how much this meant to me. Thank you for everything."

He nodded and shook Alec's hand. "Welcome to the family."

"Thank you."

As they watched them pull away, Alec stood behind her hugging her tight. "You all right?"

"Mm-hmm. I'm happy."

"It's a beautiful thing."

A throat cleared behind them. They turned and found Mrs. Dougherty. "The guest house is ready."

Sheilagh grinned and slipped her hand into Alec's. They followed their hostess through the yard to the little enchanted cottage in the back. She giggled when Alec scooped her up and carried her over the threshold.

Mrs. Dougherty showed them where snacks were hidden and pointed out several bottles of champagne chilling in the discreet refrigerator tucked inside the closet.

Once they were alone, Alec turned on Sheilagh and gave her a full grin. "You're a Devereux now."

She smiled. "True."

He stepped close and brushed his palms down the sleeves of her gown. "*My* Devereux."

His mouth lowered and her body sung as he kissed her softly, passionately. Nothing else mattered and never before had she felt so right with herself, so accepted and loved.

When their mouths parted, she whispered, "I have a wedding present for you."

His brow lifted. "You do?"

"Yes." She turned and found her bag sitting on the rack at the end of the bed. Sifting through it, she found the carefully wrapped gift. Turning, she held it out to him. "Help me with my dress. I'm going to take a bath while you open your gift."

He took the package and smiled. "I feel like a heel. I didn't get you a gift."

She held up her wedding ring. "I'm pretty sure this doorknob on my finger excuses your oversight." It was a stunning emerald ring that he said reminded him of her eyes. She couldn't have picked better herself.

Presenting him her back, he carefully unlaced her gown. His lips pressed into her shoulders and she sighed. She was married, married to her professor. It was perhaps the boldest thing she'd done yet, but she didn't do it in the face of critics or in hopes of a reaction. She did it for her, because she loved him and he made her happy.

For now, she liked that their marriage was secret. It wouldn't be for long. Eventually they'd tell the rest of the McCulloughs, but for now…she liked that it was only about them.

Stepping out of her grandmother's gown, she carefully draped it over the settee in the corner. She went to the brass tub and turned on the water. As she turned, she caught Alec watching her. "What?"

"You're absolutely stunning. You take my breath away."

Her face heated. "Ditto. Open your gift."

She lowered herself into the tub and watched as Alec took up the empty chair beside the fireplace. His fingers peeled back the ribbon and slowly unwrapped the paper.

IT WAS RATHER DISTRACTING, his bride lowering her lush body into that tub only a few feet away. He was touched she'd given him a gift, but his body wanted to join her under all those bubbles.

Peeling back the paper, he pulled his eyes from her lovely face and the creamy slope of her shoulders and glanced at what he was actually opening. His smile froze as his breath caught in his lungs.

My Interpretation of Plato's Republic
By
Sheilagh McCullough-Devereux

HE OPENED the cover and grinned. She'd done it. She'd written the paper. There was nothing trite or elusive about it. Her words decorated the pages and took shape in thoughts, provoking ideas, reflecting her personal ideals in this world. It was a true depiction of *The Republic* the way Plato had intended the reader apply it to his or her own life. It was beautiful, eloquent, honest, and brilliant. It was an A.

As he turned the last page he was sad to see it end. In all of his career, never had a fellow philosopher captured his intentions so well.

> I've come to realize that philosophy is in fact
> the preparation for death. Our time on this
> earth is fleeting and precious. While Plato
> would have us strip away all the material
> elements that bind the soul to the body for
> the Form of the Good so that we may all
> someday be disembodied beings floating
> about in an afterlife of the purest form of
> beauty, there is no true evidence of such
> celestial guarantees. There is no god
> evident enough to disprove yours or mine
> and so there is only the here and the now.
> Plato believed the true nature of good rested
> not in events, but in generalizations
> based on laws, laws dependent on
> customs, ever changing rules that define
> what is just, but it is one's knowledge that
> will decipher such guidelines, and so we
> must continue to learn and grow and
> question what we are told. We must

venture past the masses and into the light
and never lose the courage to live.

HE CLOSED the essay and looked at her. Her hand dragged a sponge over her leg, extended above the frothy surface of the water. The simple motion was so innocent, so unsuspecting and absolutely, fucking erotic. Her toes were painted a rainbow of colors and chipped at the corners, yet she was magnificent.

This was Sheilagh with her guard down, the Sheilagh so many overlooked and the Sheilagh she had been so afraid to show. She was brave and true and finally ready to face the unpredictable tomorrows that would come. She'd face them with him, her partner.

Alec stood and went to her. Holding out his hand, he said, "Let me make love to you."

She glanced at him, her hair forming tiny ringlets under the heat of the steam. Her hand fit into his palm and she stood, water sluicing down her curves. He picked her up, careless of the dampness seeping through his clothes and carried her to the bed. His mouth found hers and she kissed him back with unbanked affection.

"Did you like your gift?" she whispered, her lips tickling the tender flesh beneath his jaw.

"I loved it. I think your mind is perhaps the sexiest

asset you have and I'm so grateful you shared it with me. I don't want you to ever stop."

She ran her fingers under his shirt and pressed her lips to his chest. "Never."

His mouth found her nipple and he drew upon her tender flesh as she arched beneath him. His eyes closed as she placed kisses over his arms, his shoulders, his heart.

Committing this moment to memory, he recognized that the happiness he'd known before her was merely an illusion of what he was feeling now. She was the light he'd been missing, the truth he was afraid to ask for, and so long as she stayed by his side, never faking, they'd overcome any darkness that came their way.

"How much longer are we supposed to wait here in the dark?" Wes asked.

"Until she comes back. Stop your whining."

"I don't understand this. When you invited me here, I thought we'd be having a nice visit with your in laws. I should have known better. There's no normal when it comes to your wife."

Alec chuckled and took another bite of chips. That was the truth. Sheilagh was a lot of things, but normal didn't really apply to her. Not that he was complaining. He wouldn't have her any other way. "Relax. We're on a stake-out. Drink your coffee. It's going to be a long night."

Wes mumbled something and hunkered down in the seat.

Alec sat up and shoved the snack bag on his son's lap. "Is that her?"

"Where?"

He pointed to her black form running from the woods. What the hell was she holding? She could barley carry whatever those long things were in her arms. It looked like a collection of brooms. He rolled down his window and caught the sound of her snickering as she jogged closer.

"Pop the trunk!" she hissed.

He quickly hit the trunk button and there was a clatter as she unloaded her bounty before the trunk slammed.

Sheilagh opened the back door in a fit of giggles and dove onto the back seat. "Go, go, go!"

He threw the car in reverse and quickly backed out. "What was all that?"

She was breathing fast from running and laughing. Her smile was stunning as she leaned over his seat, her hair hidden under a black wool cap that matched her clothing. "My dad's guns."

Alec chuckled. "Great. I now have a trunk full of marshmallow Peeps and rifles. I expect to hear the banjos from Deliverance any minute now."

Wes shook his head. "What the hell is going on?"

"I just saved your dad's life," Sheilagh said proudly, snatching the chips from his lap. "It's tradition in this family for the father of the bride to shoot a groom that dares to elopes with the youngest daughter. I didn't want to risk it."

"What the hell kind of people are these?" Wes asked.

"My people," Sheilagh informed him with great satisfaction, tousling his son's hair. "Alec, turn left here and slow down. Ashlynn's farm's coming up."

He slowed the car and shut off his high beams. It was three in the morning and the roads were desolate. When the old farmhouse came into view he pulled over to the side of the road.

"Whose house is this?" Wes asked.

"My brother, Kelly's. He's first on the list. Wes, be a good boy and hand me that tote by your feet."

Wes passed her the bag and she counted four rolls of plastic wrap. She quickly tore away the cardboard and stuffed three of the rolls in the pockets of her black camo pants. "Let's go."

Alec slid on his wool hat and stepped out of the car. His son cautiously followed. Sheilagh tiptoed along the property line, stopping at various trees along the way to catch her breath.

He caught up to her and whispered, "Which truck is Kelly's?"

"The older one. You ready?"

Alec nodded and they quietly approached Kelly's truck. Wes was several feet behind them. Sheilagh made some hand signals for him to remain quiet as she rolled the plastic wrap under the truck. Alec lifted the tube off the ground and threw it overhead. His wife's muffled giggle rung out in the night.

"Shh!"

"Sorry," she hissed. "You almost hit me. Who taught you how to throw?"

Again and again they slid the plastic wrap back and forth until the roll was empty, at which point Sheilagh started a new tube. By the end of the forth roll, Kelly's truck was unrecognizable. The entire vehicle was covered in a clear plastic seal that would take hours to cut away without scraping the paint.

When they finished the job they were both smothering their laughter as they raced back to the car. Wes looked speechless. He took off for their next stop and didn't stop laughing the entire drive.

"You two are juvenile," Wes said rolling his eyes.

"Oh, lighten up, Wesley. These bastards deserve everything they're getting."

"Damn right!" Sheilagh shouted. "Oh! I wish I could see their faces in the morning. That'll teach them to mess with my room."

"What did they do to your room?" his son asked.

"In March they painted it the most nauseating shade of pink."

"It's August."

"Exactly. I'm like a silent but deadly fart. You never know when I'll strike, but once I'm out there no one's safe. Eventually I'll get you."

His son turned his gaze on Alec, his expression familiar. "And you married into this willingly?"

Alec laughed. "Abso-freaking-lutely." Marrying

Sheilagh had been the best decision of his life. His love for her grew every day. At first, he'd thought he'd be the one teaching her a thing or two about life, but in the end, they both learned from each other.

Sheilagh hardly ever cried anymore. And when she did, it was usually from laughing. She'd said, once she accepted her place in life, something inside of her seemed to settle. It was an extraordinary thing, watching her come out of her depression and her confidence bloom.

She'd moved into his house the moment they returned from their honeymoon. His home was no longer the tidy house it used to be, but that was fine with him. He loved the way her presence manifested itself in every room.

When she finally told her family she was no longer a McCullough and now a Devereux, the McCulloughs went a little crazy, which was expected. Luckily, Colin took most of the heat for keeping their wedding a secret. It was their first visit back to Center County as husband and wife and Sheilagh insisted on bringing Wes, since he was part of the family. She also insisted on getting even for what her brothers had done to her room.

Wesley and Sheilagh had mended their relationship, but still picked on each other constantly. His son seemed to accept his stepmother was a little wild and even confessed to liking that about her, claiming it made Alec more alive than he'd been in years. He was right of course. Sheilagh brought him to life.

When they reached Finn and Mallory's house Sheilagh

unloaded a large bucket, several water bottles, and an enormous box of Peeps. "I don't understand," Wes said, frowning as Sheilagh filled the bucket with water.

"Watch and learn," she whispered, tearing open the marshmallow chicks.

She dunked a chick into the water and hurled it at Finn's truck. It landed with a splat, slid a few inches, then seemed to glue itself in place.

Recalling the first time he'd met her brothers and how they'd harassed him, Alec shoved up his sleeves. "Give me one."

She handed over a chick and he dunked it in the water and heaved it at the truck. He laughed as they continued to lob the Peeps. Twenty minutes later her brother's truck looked as though the Easter Bunny vomited on it. They even got Wes to join in the fun.

A light flicked on and they stilled. Next the porch light came on and Sheilagh quickly scrambled to gather the evidence.

"Who's out there?" Finn yelled as he opened the front door.

"Run!" Sheilagh screamed and took off for the car.

"Sheilagh? What the fuck did you do to my truck?" Finn roared.

Alec bolted toward their getaway car as Sheilagh skidded on her bottom in the dirt. He went back to help her, but Wes got there first.

"Run, man! Save yourself!"

Wes dragged her out of the dirt, their laughter echoing through the woods. As soon as they were in the car he took off.

His wife hooted with amusement. "Did you see his face? Priceless!"

There would definitely be consequences, but she was right. His expression was priceless. "Where to now?"

"Last stop, the lake."

"What's at the lake?"

"Bray's boat. We're stealing it."

Stealing a boat was fairly easy when one had the keys. Sheilagh proved an excellent captain, prepared with sandwiches and plenty of beer for their maiden voyage.

That night they anchored somewhere in the middle of the lake and drank, delighting over their shenanigans as the sun came up. As Sheilagh fell asleep, her shoulder wedged into his son's, he took a moment to enjoy the view. This was his family.

Never had he expected his life to take such a turn. Thinking back on the year, he smiled. Tomorrow would likely be another adventure, another day to live to the fullest. When they weren't working or studying, they lived and she made every bit of living better than it had ever been before.

The End

If you enjoyed BRITISH PROFESSOR, you will love BROKEN MAN, the next story in the McCullough Mountain Series. Skip ahead for a sneak peek inside

ABOUT THE AUTHOR

Never miss another book release!
Click here to sign up for Lydia Michaels' Newsletter.

Follow Lydia Michaels on Instagram and Facebook!

What to Read Next?
Click here to claim your FREE Book from Lydia Michaels!

Billionaire Romance
Falling In | Sacrifice of the Pawn | Calamity Rayne

Small Town Romance
Wake My Heart | The Best Man | Love Me Nots | Pining
For You | Almost Priest

Emotional Favorites
La Vie en Rose | Simple Man | Wake My Heart | Sacrifice
of the Pawn | Forfeit

Romantic Comedy
Calamity Rayne

Erotic Romance
Breaking Perfect | Protégé | Falling In | Sugar

First Books in Binge Worthy Trilogies and Series
Almost Priest | Falling In | Wake My Heart | Forfeit |
Original Sin

Paranormal Vampire Romance
Original Sin | Dark Exodus | Prodigal Son

LGBTQ+ & Menage Romance
Broken Man (MM) | Breaking Perfect (MMF) | Forfeit
(MMF) | Hurt (Non-Consensual) | Protege

Sexy Nerds & Second Chances
Blind | Untied

Teacher Student, Workplace, and Age-Gap Love Affairs...
Oh my!
British Professor | Pining For You | Breaking Perfect |
Falling In | Sacrifice of the Pawn

Single Dads & Single Moms
Simple Man | Pining For You | First Comes Love |
Controlled Chaos | Intentional Risk

Dark Psychological Thriller & Tortured Hero Romance
(TRIGGER WARNING)

<u>Hurt</u>

Non-Fiction Books for Writers
<u>Write 10K in a Day: Avoid Burnout</u>

About the Author

Lydia Michaels is the award winning and bestselling author of more than forty titles. She is the consecutive winner of the 2018 & 2019 *Author of the Year Award* from *Happenings Media,* as well as the recipient of the 2014 *Best Author Award* from the *Courier Times.* She has been featured in *USA Today, Romantic Times Magazine, Love & Lace,* and more. As the host and founder of the *East Coast Author Convention,* the *Behind the Keys Author Retreat,* and *Read Between the Wines,* she continues to celebrate her growing love for readers and romance novels around the world.

In 2021, Michaels released the groundbreaking, non-fiction series, **Write 10K in a Day,** to commemorate her career in the publishing industry. She looks forward to many more years of exploring both fiction and non-fiction writing, teaching about the craft, and learning from the others in the author community.

Lydia is happily married to her childhood sweetheart. Some of her favorite things include the scent of paperback books, listening to her husband play piano, escaping to her coastal home at the Jersey Shore, cheap wine, *Game of Thrones*, coffee, and kilts. She hopes to meet you soon at one of her many upcoming events.

You can follow Lydia at www.Facebook.com/LydiaMichaels or on Instagram @lydia_michaels_books

Other Titles by Lydia Michaels

Wake My Heart

The Best Man

Love Me Nots

Pining For You

My Funny Valentine

Falling In: Surrender Trilogy 1

Breaking Out: Surrender Trilogy 2

Coming Home: Surrender Trilogy 3

Sacrifice of the Pawn: Billionaire Romance

Queen of the Knight: Billionaire Romance

Original Sin

Dark Exodus

Calamity Rayne: Gets a Life

Calamity Rayne: Back Again

La Vie en Rose

Breaking Perfect

FREE! - Blind

Untied

Almost Priest

Beautiful Distraction

Irish Rogue

British Professor

Broken Man

Controlled Chaos

Hard Fix

Intentional Risk

Hurt

Sugar

Simple Man

Protégé

Forfeit

Lost Together

Atonement

First Comes Love

If I Fall

Something Borrowed

Write 10K in a Day

M*anhunt; Age 17*

TRISTAN'S back pressed into the tree. Pine needles prickled his front as the overgrown evergreen shrub swatted against his chest. It was dark and the scent of sap, sweat, and summer swirled around him like a swarm of gnats. His heart raced as he waited, crouching low in his hiding spot for the others to come.

Texas was dry, boring and hot in August, but manhunt was their favorite pastime. Other than sitting inside his family's dank ranch house, sweating his balls off playing video games, there wasn't much else to do.

The snap of a twig had his breath stilling in his chest. He crouched low, careful not to give away his location. A dry flake of dirt stuck to his lip and he quickly peeled it away.

Another step. His body became so quiet he could hear the on-comer's breathing. "Tristan?" a voice hissed.

He wasn't falling for it. Like a fox in a hole, he waited. Another crunch and then the shrub covering his location twitched. Like a soldier diving into a bunker, Jason shot behind the bush and chuckled. "Found you."

"You suck," Tristan said, unfolding his legs to stand.

Jason yanked on his shirt and Tristan dropped back down. "Wait. No one knows we're here."

Tristan frowned. There was a devious gleam in Jason's hazel eyes. Dirt and dust from a long sweaty day outside cluttered the sprinkling of boyish freckles on his cheeks. Jason was sort of the ringleader of their pack. He called the shots and the rest followed. Maybe the game had changed.

"You're still It, right?"

Jason nodded, but put his fingers to his lips warning Tristan to be silent.

"Who are we hiding from then?" he whispered.

Jason grinned. "Everyone."

His frown tightened, but he waited. "It's hot as hell. After this we should hit the quarry."

"Yeah," Jason whispered, but his eyes told Tristan he was thinking about something else. "Listen… I wanted to show you something."

Tristan's eyes skated over his friend's frayed cutoffs

and settled on his hands. They were empty. The laces of his white Chucks, now faded and stained brown, were undone. "What?"

Jason shifted and their small hidey-hole seemed to shrink around them. "Why didn't you look when Timber showed her boobs?"

"I looked," Tristan lied, intuitively aware he had to do so. Boobs were weird. What was the point?

Jason's head shook meaningfully. "Nah. You didn't. I was watching you."

His gut tightened with the same anxious knot he always got when he thought his friends suspected something. "Yeah, I did. They were hot."

His friend's hazel gaze cut to his, challenging, knowing. Fuck. "No, you didn't, Tristan. You squirmed and sat there, lookin' anywhere else, 'til her shirt came down."

"I saw her tits, Jason. Jesus, why do you care so much?"

They were crouching so close their collective breath mingled. He could still smell cola on Jason's, sweet and syrupy. "I know."

Yeah, everyone knew Timber had the nicest rack in their grade. Tristan was the only guy who didn't—

All thoughts cut off as Jason placed his hand on his shoulder, a somehow gentle, caressing contact. Shit. What was going on? Guys didn't touch guys like that. They punched and shoved and sometimes horsed around wrestling, which was becoming more and more difficult to tolerate in Tristan's pubescent years, but the way his friend was touching him now… that shit didn't happen.

Brush it off. Get pissed.

"What are you—"

"Shh," Jason hissed. "I know. About you."

His breath quickened and his muscles tensed down to the soles of his feet, cramping painfully. Were they all out there, ready to kick his ass? Would this be the end of their crew? Who else knew? Maybe he was misunderstanding something?

Play dumb.

"Wha—" His words cut off as Jason's mouth pressed into his.

His heart beat so fast his ribs became a splintering vise on his lungs. Balance gone, he fell back into the tree, bark scraping his elbow, but none of that mattered. What was happening?

"I know," Jason whispered again, angling his mouth over Tristan's.

He'd never been kissed or kissed anyone else. Mostly because, since he was born, he'd liked boys. Never in a million years had he suspected Jason liked boys too. His instinct, growing up in a conservative, bible beating, redneck town, told him this was a trick and he should bale out right now and crucify his friend for being a homo. But something inside of him melted at the first touch of Jason's tongue.

He didn't know if this was a setup or a genuinely

sincere moment. All he knew was that he didn't want to push Jason away. Something inside of him opened up. A weight that had been on his shoulders since the first hard on he got from watching a man on the beach, noticing every bulge and curve under his wet, clinging suit, suddenly slipped away.

This was right. This was him. This was everything he hoped to someday feel. Then his mind jolted as Jason's palm cupped him. His heart went ballistic. The dizzying effect of his friend's hand there nearly knocked him to his ass. This wasn't a prank.

I don't care.

Emboldened, he grabbed Jason by the back of the neck and deepened the kiss. He tasted of cola. His skin smelled like sweat and fresh air. His tongue was soft, but the kiss was hard. It was the most incredible moment of his life.

Then they heard the others coming and reality ripped them apart. Jason wiped his mouth over the back of his hand, lips parted, eyes wide. "Gotchya!" he yelled and stood.

Tristan barely had a chance to recover as Jason flung the branch out, exposing them to the others. Terror for what might happen next gripped Tristan, crippling his vocabulary in the face of fear.

"It's about fucking time," Tim shouted. "I was holed up in Old Man Hill's tree so long the dang branch started to give. You're It, Tristan."

He stood, still trying to comprehend what was

happening. Glancing at Jason, ambling with the others, the picture of innocence, he caught the quick wink of his hazel eye.

Standing on shaky legs, he quickly turned and dropped to a knee, pretending to tie his shoe so he could buy some time and hide other unsightly situations going on below.

Mom. Grandma's underwear. Baseball. Barbara Bush naked. Jason's lips. Jason's touch. Jason's eyes. Fuck!

He stood and moseyed toward the woods, spit, and shouted. "Two minutes. Go!" The others took off running to their next hiding spot and Tristan caught his hand on the nearest solid object, hoping to find solid ground. Everything had just changed.

DON'T STOP THERE! Download Broken Man now!